THE PAWN

A Medieval Romance
Book One of The King's Cousins Series

By Alexa Aston

DRAGONBLADE
PUBLISHING, INC.

Books from Dragonblade Publishing

Dangerous Lords Series by Maggi Andersen
The Baron's Betrothal
Seducing the Earl
The Viscount's Widowed Lady
Governess to the Duke's Heir

Also from Maggi Andersen
The Marquess Meets His Match

Knights of Honor Series by Alexa Aston
Word of Honor
Marked by Honor
Code of Honor
Journey to Honor
Heart of Honor
Bold in Honor
Love and Honor
Gift of Honor
Path to Honor
Return to Honor

The King's Cousins Series by Alexa Aston
The Pawn

Beastly Lords Series by Sydney Jane Baily
Lord Despair
Lord Anguish

Legends of Love Series by Avril Borthiry
The Wishing Well
Isolated Hearts
Sentinel

The Lost Lords Series by Chasity Bowlin
The Lost Lord of Castle Black
The Vanishing of Lord Vale
The Missing Marquess of Althorn
The Resurrection of Lady Ramsleigh
The Mystery of Miss Mason

By Elizabeth Ellen Carter
Captive of the Corsairs, *Heart of the Corsairs Series*
Revenge of the Corsairs, *Heart of the Corsairs Series*
Shadow of the Corsairs, *Heart of the Corsairs Series*
Dark Heart
Live and Let Spy, *King's Rogues Series*

Knight Everlasting Series by Cassidy Cayman
Endearing
Enchanted
Evermore

Midnight Meetings Series by Gina Conkle
Meet a Rogue at Midnight, book 4

Second Chance Series by Jessica Jefferson
Second Chance Marquess

Imperial Season Series by Mary Lancaster
Vienna Waltz
Vienna Woods
Vienna Dawn

Blackhaven Brides Series by Mary Lancaster
The Wicked Baron
The Wicked Lady
The Wicked Rebel
The Wicked Husband
The Wicked Marquis

The Wicked Governess
The Wicked Spy
The Wicked Gypsy
The Wicked Wife

Unmarriageable Series by Mary Lancaster
The Deserted Heart

Highland Loves Series by Melissa Limoges
My Reckless Love
My Steadfast Love
My Passionate Love

Clash of the Tartans Series by Anna Markland
Kilty Secrets
Kilted at the Altar
Kilty Pleasures

Queen of Thieves Series by Andy Peloquin
Child of the Night Guild
Thief of the Night Guild
Queen of the Night Guild

Dark Gardens Series by Meara Platt
Garden of Shadows
Garden of Light
Garden of Dragons
Garden of Destiny

Rulers of the Sky Series by Paula Quinn
Scorched
Ember
White Hot

Highlands Forever Series by Violetta Rand
Unbreakable
Undeniable

Viking's Fury Series by Violetta Rand
Love's Fury
Desire's Fury
Passion's Fury

Also from Violetta Rand
Viking Hearts

The Sins and Scoundrels Series by Scarlett Scott
Duke of Depravity

The Unconventional Ladies Series by Ellie St. Clair
Lady of Mystery

The Sons of Scotland Series by Victoria Vane
Virtue
Valor

Dry Bayou Brides Series by Lynn Winchester
The Shepherd's Daughter
The Seamstress
The Widow

Men of Blood Series by Rosamund Winchester
The Blood & The Bloom

PROLOGUE

Blackstone Castle, Sussex—1325

L ADY SYBIL DE Blays finished her instructions to the cook regarding tomorrow's meals and then sought out the Blackwell steward. Finding him in conversation with their captain of the guard, she signaled for him to follow her to the records room. She quizzed the man thoroughly regarding the tying and winnowing that had been completed yesterday and was pleased with the answers she received. Thanks to her superb management skills, Blackwell thrived—no thanks to her worthless husband.

Lord Adelard de Blays was a handsome man. That was where his talents ended. As the third son of the Earl of Blackwell, Adelard had not been tutored in estate matters. He had fostered far in the north, near the Scottish border, and had attained his knighthood there. Sybil thought his sword skills merely adequate, though he did sit a horse well and passed along his love of the creatures to their daughter. Her husband spent the bulk of his day in the training yard, watching the men at their exercises, while she ran not only Blackstone Castle but the rest of the estate.

Though she had spent a good portion of her time at the royal court before her marriage seven years ago, Sybil actually had taken to country life. Instead of a countess, she thought of herself as the Queen of Blackwell—and expected everyone to bow before her.

Leaving the records room, she went upstairs to see her children to bed. A servant would already have them dressed in their nightclothes but Sybil liked to spend a little time with Landon and Katelyn before they fell asleep. She would ask about what they had done that day and use small moments to share her vast quantity of knowledge before telling them a bedtime tale. Both children worshipped her and Sybil adored them in return. She looked forward to this time, knowing it would only be the three of them together.

Without The Bastard.

Quill Cardon's presence at Blackstone Castle was like a plague that clung to her, one she picked at and flung away, only to find it returned again and again. The boy was the only thing she had no control over. On that, Adelard stood firm. Her husband had proven to be timid around his domineering father and once the old earl succumbed to apoplexy only a week after she and Adelard wed, her husband had been easily cowed by his new wife.

In a way, that had pleased Sybil. She enjoyed issuing commands and found she had an innate sense of how to run a castle and estate. Thanks to her talents, Blackwell flourished. Adelard stayed out of her way, allowing her to make decisions usually left to men.

Except for anything concerning The Bastard.

Sybil never referred to the child by name. She had done everything to see him gone from Blackstone but her husband refused to budge. Apparently, Adelard had had an unnamed lover who carried his child. When his two older brothers perished within days of one another, he had been called home to Blackwell. Sybil had been betrothed to Bardolf, the eldest, who would become the future earl. When Bardolf succumbed to a raging fever, the second brother had become the new heir. Gunter, who was extremely close to his brother, had remained disgustingly drunk for three days and then fallen from his horse in what everyone graciously deemed an accident. She always thought

Gunter, who idolized Bardolf, was fearful of trying to take his brother's place and deliberately tried to make a jump impossible for a sober horseman, much less an inebriated one.

Having come to the castle to prepare for her wedding and get to know her future husband before the ceremony uniting them in holy wedlock, Sybil watched as the two brothers had been put into the ground next to one another in quick succession. Betrothal contracts had been hastily rewritten and she found herself suddenly wed to Adelard, who seemed to blend into the woodwork in every situation, afraid to draw any attention to himself.

When her father-in-law suddenly passed, Sybil knew she could assume the power that Adelard either didn't want or refused to take. She'd been able to order or manipulate or cajole him into any decision—except ones concerning The Bastard.

Adelard brought the babe home to Blackwell even as Sybil found herself with child. He told her his lover had died in childbirth and it was up to him to raise their son. Sybil demanded that someone else assume care for the child. She didn't want to know his name. For the first year, Adelard would disappear from the training yard and Sybil knew he went to see the boy. Once she gave birth to Landon, she demanded that The Bastard leave Blackwell lands for good.

Her husband refused.

Instead, Sybil eventually discovered that the child was being raised by their blacksmith, Will Cardon, and his wife. As Landon grew older, Adelard started including the two boys in outings together. He taught them to ride. Hunt. Fish. Always together. Nothing Sybil said would change her husband's mind.

And so her hate grew, slow and steady.

Taking a calming breath and thrusting all thoughts of The Bastard from her mind, she entered the bedchamber and saw her beautiful children both sitting in their beds, eagerly awaiting her. Sybil told them a tale about a dragon slayer and then a second one about a knight on a quest for the Holy Grail. When they begged for a third story, she declined, telling them it was time for sleep.

"Mother, I forgot my sword in the great hall. May I get it? Please?"

The toy weapon was Landon's newest obsession. Adelard had two wooden swords crafted, one for each of his boys, and the two constantly engaged one another in battle across the bailey. Landon took the sword with him everywhere, even resting it against his leg while he ate and propped against the wooden tub when he was bathed. He would never get to sleep without it next to him in the bed.

"Aye, you may fetch it. No dawdling, though. Retrieve the sword and then come back straightaway. Do you understand?"

"Aye, Mother." Landon yanked back the bedclothes and scurried from the room.

"When do I get a sword, Mother?" Katelyn asked, annoyance obvious in her tone.

Sybil smiled down upon the girl and stroked her fingers through her daughter's long, silky hair. Katelyn had both her father's raven hair and his emerald green eyes, a combination that proved devastating. Already, Sybil could see glimpses of the great beauty that Katelyn would be someday. Her daughter also had a bold spirit and followed her two brothers across the estate, wanting to partake in whatever they did, even surpassing the two boys at times. She was far more adventurous than Landon and enjoyed riding above all else. While she resembled Adelard physically, with her looks and height, her intelligence definitely came from Sybil. At five years of age, Katelyn already grasped how to read. Sybil would make sure this daughter of hers learned not only how to manage domestic issues within the keep but ways to use her beauty to get whatever she wanted from any man.

"Mother, answer me! When may I have a sword like Landon and Quill?"

She kissed Katelyn's brow. "Sorry, my little princess. My mind wandered a bit."

"Where did it go?"

Sybil smiled, loving how curious this child of hers was. "You may have a sword when you turn six. Not before then so don't think to ask me again. If so, I will change my mind and make it seven before you receive one."

Katelyn nodded solemnly, her eyes as round as the full moon.

Adelard would call Sybil harsh for telling Katelyn this but, as a good mother, she knew how to balance severity with love. Because this was how she raised her children, Sybil knew Katelyn would think about the sword every day but never ask again. Her daughter would learn patience and understand that good things came to those who practiced it.

"Time to sleep, my darling. Close your eyes so you can dream of beautiful things."

Katelyn did as she was told and Sybil looked at her daughter with love. It did bother her somewhat how much both children favored their father. Landon also had hair as black as night and the same mesmerizing green eyes. Like Adelard and Katelyn, Landon was tall, even taller than The Bastard, who was a year older. Sybil resented how, in a year, Landon would leave Blackwell to foster as all seven-year-old boys of the nobility did. That she should be separated from her son and still have to look at The Bastard while she missed her own boy would be punishment enough.

Sybil thought she would have to put an end to the outings the three children went on sometime soon. If she didn't, Katelyn would expect to be in The Bastard's company once Landon left Blackwell. Sybil did not want her daughter near the boy. Once again, hatred for Adelard's oldest child swept through her. She worried if anything happened to Landon, Adelard might petition to have The Bastard inherit Blackwell.

She couldn't allow that to happen. Even if it meant lying with Adelard again, something she hadn't done since before their daughter's birth. Though the thought repulsed her, Sybil would do what needed to be done to insure that a true de Blays became the next earl.

Glancing down, she saw Katelyn had fallen asleep. She picked up her daughter's small hand and held it to her cheek, basking in her love for the girl.

The door opened and her husband entered the room. He came in each night to kiss the children goodnight. As Sybil released Katelyn's hand and watched him cross the room, she knew something was wrong. Before she could ask him, he went to the bed and gazed longingly at Katelyn and then kissed her cheek.

The girl stirred and opened her eyes. "Father?"

Sybil resented how her daughter looked lovingly at this man. She wished Adelard would drop dead as his father had so she would be the only one the children turned to.

Adelard kissed Katelyn again and told her to go back to sleep but Katelyn begged him to go riding tomorrow. He assured her they would and she snuggled back against her pillow, falling asleep as Adelard brought the bedclothes around her.

"Where is Landon?" he asked.

Her husband still had a restless air about him. Something was in the wind, though she doubted he would tell her. They spoke as little as possible.

"He went downstairs to retrieve his sword. He left it in the great hall. You know how he takes it everywhere with him. I could not get him to climb into bed unless I allowed him to fetch it."

A look of pain crossed her husband's face. It gave Sybil a jolt. She could see his body tense even as he gave her a look of pity. The combination frightened Sybil to her core.

"I've done something terrible. At least that's what others will say. You and the children will be the ones to suffer for it, though I'm guilty of no crime."

Sybil wanted to scream at him, fool that he was. What idiotic scheme had he involved himself with, especially one severe enough to impact her and their children? Adelard wasn't political, even though he was a cousin to the king. With the general feeling of mistrust spreading across England, thanks to the Despensers' influence over King Edward, it wasn't wise to claim a kinship with whoever sat on the throne.

"I won't tell you what. The less you know, the better it might go for you. Just know that the king's men are coming for me. They will be here shortly. Do your best to guard the children."

Despite his serious words, Sybil couldn't help but smile. Adelard, fool that he was, must somehow be mixed up with some plot against the king. That would be the only reason that he would warn her that the king's men would soon arrive. Thankfully, she knew nothing. Neither did the children, who were too young to understand politics. This might be the chance she yearned for. Adelard would be gone. She would be in complete control of Blackwell and hold it in trust for Landon. She'd never have to couple with this man again.

And she could send The Bastard away. Far, far away.

Or have him killed.

"Farewell," he said. "I am sorry I was not a better husband to you—but, in fact, I was no husband at all."

At first, Sybil thought he referred to not pleasing her in love play. Then something in his eyes betrayed him. Cold fear gripped her.

"What?" she asked, afraid to hear his response.

"No one except for Walter knows. He witnessed my marriage to Cecily Elyot. Quill is my legal son. Landon and Katelyn are bastards."

Sybil sprang from her chair and slapped him hard. Before he uttered another word, she raked her nails across his cheek. Adelard grabbed both her wrists.

"Enough," he said harshly. "I know you will do what it takes to shield our children. No one need ever know. Keep the secret—from them and the world."

Her eyes blazed at him. "And your . . . other son?"

"Gone. You'll never find him."

With that, Adelard released her and strode from the room.

Sybil collapsed into the chair, breathing hard. She wasn't legally wed. Her two children were bastards. *Bastards!* And all along, the true heir had scampered about the estate, blissfully unaware Blackwell would someday belong to him. He didn't know. He couldn't know. With Adelard sending the boy away, he might never know.

She vowed in that moment that Quill Cardon must never learn of his origins.

Landon still hadn't returned, which worried her. Sybil rose and left the bedchamber. If the king's men were to arrive at any moment, she did not want to be separated from her boy in the confusion. Adelard was right in that he knew she would do whatever it took to protect her children and their position within the nobility.

Cursing her false husband under her breath, Sybil rushed down the silent corridor. What had he done that would bring Edward's men to Blackwell to bear him away? Her heart beat frantically as she reached the top of the staircase. Looking down, she saw Adelard embracing Landon.

"Mother?"

Sybil glanced down and saw Katelyn had awakened and followed her. She swept the girl into her arms as the door to the keep crashed open. Dozens of soldiers poured in. Katelyn's tiny hands gripped Sybil's cotehardie as shouted orders came from below. She saw two knights latch on to Adelard and sweep him from Landon as a man began reading the charges against her husband.

Treason . . .

Quickly, Sybil retreated to the solar, a frightened Katelyn clinging desperately to her. Treason changed everything. The king would take all Blackwell lands and the earldom that accompanied it. Her boy— and his inheritance—were already lost to her.

She entered the solar and sat in a chair next to the fire, willing herself not to weep. Not to show any signs of weakness. Sybil looked at the trembling girl in her arms, knowing she would become a pawn to the crown. Waiting, Sybil heard the thundering of boots coming down the hall. The door was thrown open. Her gut lurched.

Life, as Sybil de Blays had known it, was over.

CHAPTER ONE

Convent of the Charitable Sisters, Colchester, Essex—1338

KATELYN DE BLAYS sat alone as she broke her fast, the only time she would be allowed to eat today. Anger sizzled through her as she tore a piece from the small loaf of bread a postulate placed before her. She chewed without tasting it, finishing the bread and then downing the cup of weak ale. She closed her eyes, knowing she needed to harness the fury. She sensed others watching her and opened her eyes quickly, swiveling to her left. Two oblates stared at her, their eyes wide. As her gaze burned into them, they quickly dropped their eyes to the meal in front of them.

Immediately, her anger cooled. These young girls had done nothing to harm her. If anything, something damaging had been done to them. They were the latest oblates to have arrived at the Convent of the Charitable Sisters, daughters from noble families who gave their children to be raised as nuns. Katelyn never understood the multitude of reasons why any parents would do such a thing.

Of course, her own parents had no say in what had happened to their only daughter. As the child of a traitor, the king had banished Katelyn from the world she knew and sent her to one of silence and never-ending prayers. She vaguely remembered attending mass every morning at Blackstone Castle's chapel, sitting next to her brother, but had some recollections of exploring the family's estate. She'd only been five years of age when the king's men came for her father so much of those childhood memories proved to be hazy. Even her father's image had dimmed with time and she could no longer remember his features. Instead, he was a tall, lean man with a face hidden in shadows. She doubted she would ever recall exactly what he looked like.

But she would never forget how much she loved him.

Her relationship with her mother had been entirely different. Where her father was playful, letting Katelyn ride atop his shoulders and chasing her in games of fun, her mother had been stern. Katelyn knew she must always sit up straight and pay very close attention to whatever Lady Sybil said. Every word spoken to Landon or Katelyn was meant to instruct. Katelyn knew it was important to retain every lesson given.

The only time her mother let down her guard was when they were in private. She would tell grand tales of adventure at bedtime each night and Katelyn looked forward to that time. It was a side of her mother no one ever saw but it was the best part of each day.

Now, that very mother was making her life one of misery.

Katelyn rose and headed for the large hallway that led outside. Each day after Prime, the early morning mass attended by everyone inside the convent, she would break her fast and then care for the chickens, feeding them and gathering the eggs that had been laid before milking the goats. It was the only time she spent outdoors so she treasured it. Much of her early years had been lived outside, playing with Landon and Quill or riding horses with her father. Being locked away inside the nunnery for most of the hours in a day had been unbearable.

That's why she'd run away so often.

She sensed someone following her as she reached the door and whirled around. As she suspected, Sister Martha shadowed her movements.

"If you wish to keep up with me, Sister Martha, you might want to stay closer. I'm sure the abbess has told you after yesterday's incident not to let me from your sight."

The nun hurried toward her, a deep frown on her face. "Mother Acelina is very angry with you, Katelyn."

"Because I made it farther than I ever have before?" she snapped.

"Mother wishes to see you once you've finished with the animals," the nun told her, a sly smile crossing her face. "I'm sure you're to be reprimanded for your behavior yesterday. Even beaten again." Now her smile turned broad. "And I hope I am the one chosen to carry out your punishment."

Katelyn gritted her teeth, keeping the sharp retort from escaping her lips. Turning, she left the confines of the convent and stepped into the warm sunshine of the summer day.

On a regular basis for the last several years, Katelyn had sneaked away from the convent. She had no intention of taking a nun's vows of poverty, chastity, and obedience. The abbess had informed Katelyn she had no plans to force her to become a good sister at the convent, but Katelyn couldn't trust the woman who'd given birth to her.

Lady Sybil de Blays had been taken with her daughter to the same convent all those years ago but mother and child had been separated for a long period of time, one Katelyn could not assess since she'd been so young. What she knew now as postulates were the ones who had cared for her as she'd cried for her family and screamed for hours, wanting to go home to Blackwell. When Katelyn next saw her mother, Lady Sybil wore the garb of a nun, her habit tied around the waist with a cloth belt and her head covered with a wimple and veil attached to a scapula. A heavy cross on a chain hung around her neck. Her mother told her daughter that she had completed her postulancy and novitiate and had taken simple vows. She would now be known as Sister Acelina and would take her solemn vows in four more years.

It was as if a stranger stood before her and Katelyn had never been more frightened seeing what her mother had become.

In the years that had since passed, Sister Acelina had become an integral part of the nuns' community, being elected in a secret vote to serve as their abbess, a position she would hold the remainder of her life. Katelyn grew to understand that, for her mother, being named abbess of the convent was the closest thing Sybil de Blays could come to being a countess again. As Abbess of the Charitable Sisters, Mother Acelina would exercise considerable power and would be the equal to men who were secular or religious leaders. She would gain control over not only the convent but the secular life of the surrounding communities and act as a landlord and manager, even collecting revenue. Lady Sybil might have traded her identity as a member of the nobility to become Mother Acelina, but she now yielded as much power—if not more—as she had in her former life.

For Sybil de Blays, it had always been about power. Katelyn's understanding had grown and as she matured, she realized her mother didn't do what she did for God. Mother Acelina did it for herself. She was like an all-powerful goddess who expected everyone to worship her or suffer the consequences.

Yet, she had never forced Katelyn into the religious life. True, she was required to attend mass twice a day, Prime and Vespers, but she had been excused from the other numerous prayer services throughout the day that the other women attended. After Terce, when prayers were recited about two hours after the women broke their fast each morning, Katelyn spent the rest of her day teaching oblates and postulates to read. She enjoyed the time spent with others since reading required her and her charges to speak. Katelyn would read aloud during these lessons and ask those she tutored to do the same. If she hadn't heard voices during these lessons, she might have gone mad long ago since, beyond prayers, silence was observed the remainder of the day, even at meals.

After gathering the eggs laid by the nunnery's dozen hens, she scattered feed across the yard. Her chickens came rushing toward her, clucking noisily as they attacked their food with gusto. Katelyn leaned against the coop and watched them, smiling. One, her favorite, came and plopped upon her foot. She picked the hen up and cradled it, stroking the soft feathers as she closed her eyes. Once, she had done the same with horses. Memories of her running her hands along a horse's flanks stirred. She could smell the horse as she buried her face in its side. Her fingers itched to stroke a long, velvet nose again. Loving horses had seemed so uncomplicated.

"Remember not to dawdle. You shouldn't keep Mother waiting," Sister Martha reminded her.

Katelyn had almost forgotten the nun had accompanied her to the yard. She placed the hen back on the ground and picked up the two large baskets filled to the brim with eggs.

"I'll take these to the kitchen and then milk the goats. Then I'll go straight to Mother's office," she promised the older woman.

Sister Martha's eyes narrowed. "See that you do." The nun stormed off without a backward glance.

For being a woman wed to Christ, Sister Martha wasn't loving or friendly. In fact, Katelyn thought many of the nuns at the Convent of the Charitable Sisters seemed angry with their lots in life. She wondered how many of them had been forced by their families or some political action to take refuge within the nunnery's walls and decided very few of the women present actually had a calling to serve God and the Living Christ.

Katelyn took the gathered eggs to the kitchen, glad that her duties did not include cooking or washing. She thought those the hardest tasks at the convent and was grateful that she had never been assigned to the kitchen or washroom. Returning outside, she milked the goats and fed them, enjoying watching the younger ones scamper as they hopped and butted heads with one another.

"Can we help?"

She saw the two girls who'd stared at her this morning had arrived.

"Aye. If you'll each carry two buckets, I can go and set up for our reading lesson."

Their eyes lit up.

"'Tis our favorite part of the day," one confessed, a shy smile on her face.

"Mine, too," Katelyn assured them. "Be sure to walk carefully so that no milk spills. I will see you after I have spoken to the abbess."

She watched the little girls move away, carrying the buckets of milk. A wave of sadness hit her. This would be the only life these two ever knew, behind the walls of this convent. It made her all the more determined to try another escape. She loved God but wanted to see what the real world was like. A part of her hoped she might find Landon—and Quill.

Landon had been her brother. They shared the same bedchamber and sat together at meals. Quill, on the other hand, had been a part of their lives. He looked so much like Landon that sometimes it was hard to tell them apart, though Landon had their father's emerald green eyes. Quill's could be green or brown, depending upon his mood. Even at a young age, Katelyn knew Quill was one of them—but not. Her mother refused to hear Quill's name spoken in her presence and she despised any time they spent with Quill.

Katelyn learned from eavesdropping on the servants that Quill was her half-brother and that his mother died. She never understood the hatred that her mother felt for Quill.

If she could find Landon, the two of them could look for Quill.

Katelyn bid her goats farewell and started toward the main building again. Her curiosity grew as she saw one of the nuns leading a knight and his horse. The knight, dressed in full armor, looped the reins of his magnificent horse around a post. Katelyn wondered what business he had at the convent. Sometimes, the nunnery would house travelers for the night, though she was never allowed to converse with them. The only other time someone came to visit was when the local priest arrived to hear confession and say mass or the bishop stopped to speak with Mother Acelina regarding Church business. Even then, they never had as grand a horse as the chestnut one now standing in the courtyard.

The lines of the horse intrigued her. She remembered riding one similar, her father sitting behind her. A flood of memories came rushing back as she clearly recalled his features for the first time in years. She glanced from the horse to the knight, whose stance seemed familiar. He removed his helm and she saw thick, raven hair. Again, so reminiscent of her father's. A physical ache tore through her. Something urged her to speak to this stranger. Katelyn lifted her skirts and ran toward him.

She arrived too late, the man's long strides already taking him inside, so she stopped next to his mount and stared at the animal's physical beauty. It turned to look at her.

"Hello, my beauty. I am Katelyn," she said softly, holding her hand up so the horse could sniff it. It did and snorted.

"I'm sorry I do not have a treat for you but I would love to pet you." She kept her tone low and calm.

Reaching out a hand, she brushed it against the long nose and shivered in pleasure. Gradually, she stroked the horse and then wrapped her arms about its neck, burying her face in its coat.

"You smell divine," she told the steed. "I would do anything to ride you."

Though she longed to stay with the horse, seeing its master became more important to her. Mayhap, she could convince the knight to take her away from the nunnery. Katelyn stroked the horse a final time and rushed inside. It took a moment for her eyes to adjust after being in the bright sunlight for so long. The hall stood empty so she gathered the stranger had business with the abbess and had been taken upstairs.

Quickly, she set off for Mother Acelina's office, seeing no one along the way. Katelyn pushed open the door that led to an anteroom and found it empty. The knight must already be inside, meeting with Mother. Fortunately, the door was slightly ajar and she had never been reluctant to eavesdrop. She tiptoed across the room and stood next to the oak door.

"This makes the ninth nunnery I've visited in search of my sister," a deep voice said. "Both the king and I suspected a convent would be the logical place his father might have sent my sister. King Edward has given me half a dozen men and two months to find her before I must return to Windsor Castle. I beg you, Mother, to share with me if any woman here fits the description I've given you. I would do anything to be reunited with my sister."

Katelyn heard the anguish in the man's tone, even as a chill rippled through her.

Could he be speaking of her?

The knight had hair the color of Landon's. His posture and gait had seemed familiar. A faint ray of hope touched her soul.

"I am surprised you do not recognize me, Landon," her mother said.

Katelyn gasped and then threw a hand against her mouth, hoping the abbess hadn't heard the noise. Her heart began pounding against her ribs as tears filled her eyes yet uncertainty filled her.

Would her mother let her leave the confines of the convent?

"I . . . am not sure how we would have met, Abbess."

Brittle laughter followed. Katelyn thought her mother hadn't laughed since their time at Blackstone Castle.

"Look closely, my son."

A long pause ended when the knight asked, "Mother?"

"Aye, 'tis exactly who I am, Landon." She sighed. "You have matured in the years we've been apart but I would know you anywhere.

You resemble your father a great deal. And here you are, a knight of the realm, Sir Landon de Blays. I suppose it was a good thing they forced the king to renounce his throne. It seems your cousin, the present king, has looked after you."

"King Edward has been nothing but kind to me from the beginning. He also wants to extend that kindness to Katelyn. Please, Mother, I beg you to tell me. Is she here?"

Katelyn couldn't wait any longer. She pushed the door open and rushed into the room. Her brother sprang to his feet, joy breaking out across his face as he recognized her.

"Katelyn!"

She fell into his arms, laughing and crying, tears of happiness spilling down her cheeks.

"I have looked for you, Sister," Landon said. He searched her face and then kissed her brow tenderly.

"I knew you were somewhere out there. I prayed the day would come when we would be reunited," she said fervently. "I have fled several times, wanting to find you. *She* always had me brought back. Starved and beaten for disobedience."

Landon released her and glared at their mother. "You have kept her here against her will? Have you forced her to take the vows of a nun, Mother?"

Mother Acelina gave them a cool look. "Nay. In fact, I now realize that your presence here is not in response to my missive to the king. You actually found your sister all on your own."

"You wrote to the king about me? When? Why?" Katelyn demanded.

"Because you are a pawn, my dear daughter. A person others use to gain something. You've become of age to wed. I thought to use you as leverage. After all, you are a cousin to the king. And there are things I want."

Landon's arm went protectively about her. His presence gave

Katelyn comfort—and the strength to speak out.

"You kept me here all these years, wishing to exploit me for your own personal gain?"

Her mother shrugged. "Exploit is such a harsh word. I would say use the advantage I had. You wondered why I never insisted that you take your holy vows. I was waiting for the right time to barter you to the king. I would return his cousin to him, in return for a favor or two."

Rage filled her. "That's all I am to you, Mother? A puppet in a game of power?"

The abbess sprang to her feet. "I have protected you all these years, Daughter. Kept quiet about where you were. Bided my time. I wanted to let you escape this place. *I* never will."

"You are exactly where you want to be, *Mother* Acelina. As abbess of this convent, you have authority and control, not just of me, but over many lives. To think I once loved you. You love only yourself. You are spiteful and hunger for power. I doubt you ever loved Landon or me, much less Father."

Her mother's eyes narrowed. "Your father was a traitor," she hissed. "His actions changed the course of all of our lives. We were stripped of everything, forced into new, unwanted lives. I did whatever I could to rise to the top again. I regret nothing I've done to attain my current position."

"I am taking Katelyn with me, Abbess." Landon's tone turned cold and formal. "The king wants my sister brought to court and will make a good marriage for her."

Mother Acelina fell back into her chair. "Then go. I have no need of either of you ungrateful children. I have my own flock that adores me. I will continue to minister to them."

Katelyn exited the room, Landon following her.

Once they reached the staircase, he paused and said, "You need to collect your things. We will leave immediately."

"I have no things, Landon. Thought I never took the vows, I have lived in poverty. I possess another faded kirtle but the wool has holes in it and the garment has grown too short. I doubt it's something the king would want to see me in." She placed her hand on his arm. "All I want to do is leave this place and never look back."

Chapter Two

Northmere—Northumberland

NICHOLAS MANDEVILLE RACED across the meadow and into the forest, closely followed by men from Northmere and Ravenwood. It felt good to be hunting game and not fighting with the Scots, though their neighbors to the north had continued to slip across the English border and raid Northumberland of livestock and goods during the past year. King Edward might think he'd conducted his last campaign against Scotland but Nicholas felt in his bones that the English and those miserable Scots would clash until the end of time.

The group had met with the huntsman a short while ago as they broke their fast, listening to where he had seen a hart's tracks. Based upon the broken branches and droppings spotted, the hunting party had a good idea where their quarry would be today. The huntsman had already predicted the path the hart would move along and placed relays of dogs along it. This way, the hounds wouldn't tire before the hart and could aid the men in surrounding the quarry and pinning it down.

Nicholas slowed his horse as the trees thickened and listened carefully. He heard barking dogs to the east and urged Sunset on, knowing they must be close. As he rode and then met up with the first set of dogs, he caught sight of a tan flash ahead. The dogs now bayed madly and continued in pursuit of the deer, with the riders close behind them. The target led them on a merry chase, dashing and darting in long, elegant strides. After more than an hour of weaving in and out of the dense wood in pursuit, a horse sped past Nicholas on his right and he identified the blur as Favian Savill, his closest friend since their earliest days. With their families' estates lying adjacent to one another, the boys had grown up together, first as playmates and then becoming closer than brothers when they fostered with Lord Bayard Stone at Stonegate.

Competitive as always, Nicholas bore down on his friend, determined to pass him and reach the hart first. He scrambled past Favian and a short time later entered a clearing. The tired hart had finally stopped and now faced the hunters, ready to defend itself against the band of humans. Both Nicholas and Favian signaled to the hounds so that they would hold in place and not attack the prey.

The rest of the hunting party arrived as the two men leaped from the backs of their mounts. As custom allowed, the most prominent man should make the kill with his sword or a spear. The dozen horses behind them halted as Nicholas gestured to his friend, words unnecessary between them. Each man fanned out in a different direction and approached the trembling hart. The panting beast looked from side to side and then turned to face one of them and then the other, unsure of what to do. Nicholas could see the deer's heart thumping against its breast and felt a moment of pity for it.

With a nod to Favian, he made his move. The hart whipped around and committed itself, charging toward Nicholas. He quickly dispatched the prey with his sword. Favian had moved in to assist him if Nicholas had needed help. At times, he marveled how the two of them could think as a single being. He felt blessed to be close to this brother of his choosing.

Unlike his relationship with Bryce, his own flesh and blood.

Turning, he faced the group of hunters. "'Tis time for the unmaking. Who will help dissect this hart?"

Three men stepped forward. Nicholas pulled his sword from the deer and cleaned the weapon before sheathing it, reminding the men once they finished to reward the hounds with pieces of the carcass so that they would associate their effort today with this reward.

"I know Sunset could use a good watering," he said to Favian. "Shall we take our horses to the nearby stream?"

They led their mounts to water and watched them lap greedily. Nicholas couldn't imagine a more perfect day, full of sunshine and sport, one spent with a man he respected and adored.

"You look happy, Favian," Nicholas noted.

His friend's smile lit up his entire face. "I am, Nicholas. Catherine has made me so. I might have wed a stranger three months ago but now she is my everything. We are both good friends and lovers. I care for her and depend upon her opinions." Favian leaned in. "In fact, I believe I am in love with her."

A pang of jealousy struck Nicholas. Seeing the joy on Favian's face made him want to share in that kind of happiness. He had been betrothed from a young age but the lady had died of a fever, along with her sister and mother, several years ago. Now that he was five and twenty, Nicholas decided he should approach his father and insist it was time for the heir to Northmere to wed. If his mother had been alive, Nicholas was sure a betrothal and nuptial mass would have already taken place. She would long ago have reminded her husband of this duty. Unfortunately, her untimely death had put his father into a dark state of mind the past few years. Since Lord Cedric had not brought up the idea, Nicholas determined he would do so. He might be as lucky as his friend and find a wife he would cherish.

"Come. We should rejoin the others," he said. "That is, if you can stop thinking about Catherine long enough to mount your horse and return home."

Favian grinned. "Tease all you want, Nicholas. I cannot wait for you to wed and enjoy marital bliss as I do."

Nicholas swung into Sunset's saddle and turned the horse. Without warning, a wild boar crashed from the forest, heading straight for them. Sunset whinnied and jerked to the right, almost unseating Nicholas, leaving Favian as the lone target of the charging boar. Before Nicholas could alert his friend to the danger, the animal reached Favian, who had one foot in the stirrups and his back to the boar. It gored Favian in his upper thigh. As blood spurted, he fell to the ground and the boar trampled him.

Vaulting from his horse, Nicholas drew his sword and arced it overhead. It cut through the air and sliced the head from the boar in one fell swoop. The animal collapsed, Favian under it.

Panic seized Nicholas. He shouted for help, hoping it would arrive quickly. Finding a reserve of strength beyond measure, he tossed aside his weapon and thrust his arms under the boar, scooping the beast from Favian and slinging it away.

Kneeling, he laid a hand on his friend's brow and grasped his broken hand. A glance up and down revealed Favian covered in blood, his chest crushed and his breathing labored. Not even a talented healer would be able to save his life. Nicholas saw the dying light in Favian's eyes. He recognized it from his time on the battlefield and knew the end was imminent.

Favian gave him a weak smile. "Take care . . . of Catherine . . . for me, Nick. She won't forgive me . . . for dying. Promise . . . me."

Nicholas squeezed Favian's hand. "I promise."

"Good," Favian wheezed. He coughed violently and blood bubbled up, pouring from his mouth. Favian took a final, anguished breath and fell silent.

"No!" Nicholas shouted hoarsely.

He was dully aware of others arriving. Moving him away from the now lifeless body. Only moments ago, his friend had been full of life. In love with his new wife.

And now Sir Favian Savill lay dead.

What would he tell Lord Terald? And Catherine?

NICHOLAS DOWNED THE last of his ale and left the great hall. He had promised his sister they would go riding today. Bethany loved animals, especially horses, and so he made time to take her across the estate on horseback once a week. Sometimes they ventured beyond the borders of Northmere and went to the local village. Other times, they rode toward Ravenwood so that they could call upon Lord Terald and Lady Catherine.

Three months had passed since Favian's tragic death in the forest. Nicholas remembered his promise to take care of Catherine and decided that enough time had passed. He would speak to Favian's widow first and determine if she would be willing to wed him. He could think of no better way to protect her. Marrying her would help Nicholas keep a piece of his friend with him always. If she agreed to the match, he would then go to his father and inform Lord Cedric that he had arranged to wed their neighbor. Nicholas would enter this marriage knowing his wife loved another and always would but he determined he would be a good husband to her and remain faithful always.

He climbed the stairs and went to Bethany's chamber. She sat on the floor, playing with a doll that he'd made for her. Glancing at the tray, he saw she'd eaten about half of her midday meal. Dining in the great hall was beyond her. Around large groups of people, she became skittish and tearful. They'd found it was better to allow her to eat in private.

Nicholas wondered what his sister might have been like if the accident hadn't occurred, though his gut told him then and now that it was no accident. As a two-year-old girl, Bethany had been bright and inquisitive. She'd walked and talked earlier than her brothers had. He'd doted on her, enjoying carrying her on his shoulders and bouncing her on his knee, telling her stories.

Bryce had been jealous of Bethany from the beginning. Nicholas could never understand why a boy of eight would feel threatened by a newborn girl but Bryce had never liked his new sister. Nicholas had caught him pinching Bethany when she was only a few months old, making her cry as he laughed about it. He'd thrashed his brother, warning him if he ever harmed Bethany again, Nicholas would not just go to their parents.

He would kill Bryce.

After that, Bryce left Bethany alone. The boys were away a good portion of the year, fostering in different households in Northumberland. When they returned home on infrequent visits, Bryce steered clear of his sister. Until the day he didn't.

He tearfully told his parents that Bethany had been crying inconsolably and that he'd picked her up to comfort her. Knowing his brother to be selfish to the core, Nicholas doubted the story from the beginning. It was what followed that he found even harder to believe. Bryce said he knew Bethany liked horses and he thought to calm her by taking her to visit the stables. They'd entered the stall of Devil, their father's unpredictable mount. Everyone, including Bryce, was frightened of the temperamental beast. Somehow, a wiggling Bethany had supposedly broken free from her brother's arms and scampered behind Devil. The horse had kicked her in the head. Bryce then left Bethany in the stall with the beast and ran for help.

Nicholas still remembered Bryce entering the keep, a sly smile on his face. When he saw his brother, Bryce's smile had turned into a frown. Bryce ran toward him. The story tumbled from him and Nicholas had rushed to the stables. He found Bethany unconscious, lying in a heap. Devil stood in the corner. The fact that Devil hadn't trampled the girl to death was nothing short of a miracle. Nicholas had gently lifted his sister's body and returned her to the keep. He'd prayed every step of the way, begging the Virgin to spare his sister's life, promising he would be responsible for her always.

Bethany lay unmoving for four days and then awakened—but she had never been the same since. She could speak only a few words at a time. Though she grew physically, she never matured in other ways, remaining a simple child even now though she was ten and five. Bryce pretended to be contrite but Nicholas saw through his deception. He'd never been fond of his brother before and this incident increased the animosity between them. Nicholas believed that Bryce had wanted to kill Bethany and failed.

And that Bryce would love to kill his brother, as well.

As the oldest Mandeville, Nicholas would inherit the title and estate. Bryce remained resentful that he was two years younger and never bothered to hide his envy. Though he'd become a knight two years ago and returned to Northmere to live, Bryce proved to be a lazy soldier. Nicholas remained wary at all times, believing that if given an opportunity, Bryce would try to eliminate him so that he would become the heir to the earldom. With the way their father favored Bryce, Lord Cedric would probably turn a blind eye and accept whatever tale Bryce told about Nicholas' death.

Bethany glanced up from her play and beamed at him. She dropped her doll and scrambled to her feet. Nicholas strode toward her and she locked her arms about his waist, burying her face against his chest. A sweet pouring of love rushed through him. Bethany was always happy to see him.

She lifted her head, an eager look on her face. "Go ride?"

"Aye, my lady. Where would you have us go today?"

Bethany frowned. He wondered what thought was like for her.

"Catherine," she said at last. "Cat."

Though most people might have thought she used Cat as a nick-name for Catherine, Nicholas knew his sister wanted to go see the

Ravenwood cat which had given birth to kittens. Catherine Savill had promised one to Bethany once they were weaned. The kittens should be eight weeks old now so they would probably return from Ravenwood today with a ball of fur. He better alert Mary, the servant who cared for Bethany.

"Let's go see the kittens and Catherine," Nicholas said.

Mary entered the chamber then and he told her to be ready for Northmere's newest resident upon their return.

"I think it'll be good for Lady Bethany to have a kitten to care for," Mary proclaimed. "She's very loving with her doll and you know how mad she is for animals. Don't worry, Sir Nicholas. I'll have everything ready when you return."

Nicholas escorted Bethany to the stables. As they passed the training yard, he nodded to his father, who stood on a raised platform observing the soldiers' exercises along with Rafe Mandeville, Northmere's captain of the guard and Nicholas' uncle. Usually, Nicholas spent a good portion of his time working with individual men in the yard but his father supported him in his efforts to carve out time with Bethany each week.

When they reached the stables, Bryce emerged. Instantly, Bethany shrank against Nicholas, gripping him tightly.

"Greetings, little sister," Bryce said, winking at her. "I see you're going to ride with your big brother." He gave Nicholas a cool look and walked away without addressing him.

Nicholas took Bethany into the stables and had her remain outside the stall while he readied Sunset. He always took Bethany up with him. Her mind was too simple to teach her to control a horse. Surprisingly, her accident had left her with no fear of horses. She enjoyed brushing them and feeding them apples. She even liked to be given the reins so she could lead Sunset outside and would walk tall and proud as she did so.

He gave her the reins now and kept close as they ventured back outside. Passing the stall Devil had been housed in always brought a bitterness to him. His father had Devil put down after Bethany's injury. Nicholas had thought it a waste of a good horse. Bryce never should have been in the war horse's stall, much less with a small child. Every now and then, Nicholas had a nightmare where he saw Bryce push Bethany behind Devil and jabbed the horse in the side with a needle so it kicked out. He would awake in a cold sweat, knowing between his dream and Bryce's story lay the truth.

He mounted Sunset and brought Bethany up into the saddle in front of him. Though he navigated where the horse went and held its reins, Nicholas allowed her to clasp a portion of the reins lightly so she would feel as if she steered Sunset on her own. They trotted through the baileys and out the open gates.

"Fast!" Bethany cried. "Now!"

"As you wish, my lady."

Nicholas nudged Sunset with his thighs and the horse responded. They galloped past fields of amber and turned west once they reached the road to Ravenwood. Arriving half an hour later, he acknowledged the gatekeeper as they rode past and went directly to the stables. A young boy took charge of Sunset and told them Lady Catherine was in the far corner of the stables with the mother cat and her kittens.

"I go?" Bethany asked.

"You may."

She took off running. Nicholas stayed close behind to make sure she arrived with no problems. Bethany entered the stall where the kittens were housed and dropped to her knees. He saw the mother cat lying contentedly on the hay, watching her kittens scrambling about the stall.

"Greetings, Bethany. Nicholas." Catherine stood and brushed hay from her cotehardie. "I'll bet you've come to pick out which kitten you want to take home with you."

Bethany nodded enthusiastically.

"Play with each of them," Catherine suggested. "I think you'll know after you do so which one is right for you." She moved from the stall and closed the half-door so no kittens followed her.

"How are you today, Nicholas?" she asked pleasantly.

He studied her, noting she looked paler than usual and had dark circles beneath her blue eyes. "Better yet, how are you?"

She shrugged, her eyes revealing for a moment the constant pain she hid from the world. "Some days are better than others. Having this litter of kittens has helped. I come down here and watch them play and it takes my mind off things for a while."

"Catherine, I want to speak with you," he began.

She laughed. "I thought that's what we were doing, my lord," she teased.

Nicholas liked hearing her laugh. He couldn't remember the last time he'd heard her do so. He took her hand and heard her quick intake of breath. Sudden understanding flickered in her eyes.

"Nicholas, I—"

"Hear me out, Catherine." He swallowed, harnessing his courage. He was usually a man of action, not words. "You know I think the world of you and I know how happy you made Favian. Your welfare was on his mind in those last moments. He loved you very, very much."

Tears welled in her eyes. "As I did him."

"Favian asked me to look after you." Nicholas cleared his throat. "I can think of no better way to offer my protection to you than to have us marry. I have no betrothed. I thought to talk this over with you first. If you agree, then I will speak to my father. We can wed as soon as you wish." He paused. "If you wish to do so."

She closed her eyes a moment and then opened them. "I thank you for such a kind offer, Nicholas, but I don't know if I'll ever choose to marry again."

He squeezed her hand. "I understand that you loved Favian. That he would be the only man you would ever love. But I do think we would suit, Catherine. I would be the best husband I could be to you."

She gave him a gentle smile. "I know you would, Nicholas. And that is why you should wed someone else, a woman who will appreciate all the gifts you have to offer." She hesitated. "Besides, I am not able to consider your proposal at this time."

Her free hand went to her belly, her fingers spreading wide. He understood immediately.

"You are with child. Favian's child. I'm so pleased," he said sincerely. "I promise I would love this babe as much as I did him. 'Twould be an honor to help raise his son. Or daughter."

"If I birth a son, he will be the heir to the Ravensgate earldom," Catherine reminded him. "I owe it to Lord Terald to wait and see if I carry a son. If I do, I would wish to remain at Ravenwood with my boy. If it's a daughter, though?" She smiled wistfully. "I would consider your offer to wed."

"Then we will await the outcome," Nicholas told her. He brought her hand to his lips and kissed her fingers tenderly.

CHAPTER THREE

"**B**ETHANY, YOU NEED to thank Catherine for giving you the kitten," Nicholas urged as his sister danced around, a gray and white fur ball in her arms.

She froze and looked at Catherine. "Thank you. For Kit."

Catherine smoothed the young girl's hair. "Is that what you've decided to name her? Kit?"

Bethany's head bobbed up and down. She brushed her nose against the kitten's head.

"That's a very good name," Nicholas assured his sister. "But 'tis time we were off."

Bethany leaned into Catherine, who gave the girl a brief hug. "Come back whenever you like. Better yet, I may need to come to Northmere soon and see how Kit has settled in," she suggested.

Bethany nodded enthusiastically and looked to Nicholas.

"Catherine and all of the Savills are always welcomed at Northmere," he said. Nicholas gave Catherine a smile. "Thank you for the gift of the kitten. She will be a good companion for Bethany."

He mounted Sunset and gestured for his sister to come closer. Lifting her, he said, "You'd best leave the reins to me on our return home so that you can keep Kit safe."

Bethany settled against him, cradling her new friend. Nicholas waved farewell to Catherine and they rode back to Northmere at a much slower pace so as not to jar the kitten unnecessarily. When they arrived, he dropped Bethany at the keep.

Mary awaited them, sitting at the bottom of the stairs. She rose.

"Lookit what you have, Lady Bethany," she exclaimed. "Why, it's a beautiful little rabbit!"

Bethany shook her head. "Kit. My kitten."

"My, that's a smart name for a kitten, one I won't be soon forgetting. Come along, my lady. We'll get a bowl of warm milk for Kit and I'll show you the little bed I've made for it."

Bethany's lip stuck out stubbornly. "Her. Kit's a her."

"Ah," Mary said wisely, "a little lady for a little lady. Very good. Now, come with me."

Nicholas watched them ascend the stairs to the keep, knowing they were blessed to have a servant as kind and patient as Mary. She'd been the girl's companion the last dozen years and loved her as one of her own.

He trotted to the stables and rubbed Sunset down then brushed the horse's dark golden coat. He'd named him for that time of day where the yellow of the sun went gold, mixed with bits of red and orange since it reminded him of the horse's coat. Where Devil had nipped at anyone who came near, Sunset was by far the friendliest and best-tempered horse he'd ever known.

Nicholas left the stables and headed toward the training yard, hoping to catch his father. Even though Catherine had put the idea of a wedding between them on hold, he believed he should inform his father of where things stood. Arriving at the training yard, only their captain of the guard stood on the platform.

Spying him, Uncle Rafe motioned Nicholas over. He joined the knight on the platform and surveyed the exercises. The knight had their soldiers working with maces at the moment. Bryce was nowhere to be seen.

"I was looking for my father."

"Cedric was called back to the keep not long ago," Rafe said. "A messenger arrived from the king."

Nicholas nodded grimly. King Edward had been in constant contact with Northmere, due to its proximity to the Scottish border. He wondered what the king had to say. More than likely, it would be news of further action against the Scots.

"I think I'll seek him out and discover what the king had to say."

Nicholas excused himself and headed for the keep. He went directly to the solar, knowing his father would want privacy not only to read the missive but to contemplate any reply he sent back to the royal court.

Knocking at the door, he heard his father's gruff voice bid him to enter. Nicholas did and found Lord Cedric seated at the table, a parchment unrolled before him.

"I hear the king has sent word to you."

"Aye. I am needed at Windsor."

"Do you wish me to accompany you?" Nicholas asked, not wanting to go but responding as a dutiful son. He'd only been to Windsor once and never to London, finding the trappings of the royal court not to his liking.

"Thank you, but you are needed here more. I trust you to keep Northmere and its people safe while I am gone."

"Do you know how long you will be away?"

"Hopefully, it will be only for a short while. Mayhap I will take Bryce with me, though. 'Twould be good experience for him," Lord Cedric noted.

"As you wish, Father." Nicholas kept his voice neutral but he was delighted that his brother would be gone from Northmere for any period of time. Not only would his absence bring relief to Nicholas but

THE PAWN

Bethany would enjoy having more freedom. She limited where she went inside the keep and on the castle grounds whenever Bryce was in residence.

He decided not to broach the topic of wedding Lady Catherine Savill at this point. The widow would not give birth for probably another six months. His father would return long before that, giving them plenty of time to discuss a marriage between the two of them. Nicholas also knew that his father's mind was already on his upcoming trip to court. While Edward had proved to be a good ruler and kind to his people, Nicholas had witnessed how mercurial the king's moods could be. Lord Cedric would already be preparing himself for his meeting with the king and wouldn't be happy about other matters drawing his attention away from his upcoming visit to court.

"When will you leave?"

"At daybreak tomorrow. I'll speak to Rafe and choose a guard to accompany me to Windsor. Would you find Bryce and inform him of my decision to have him come along?"

"Of course."

Nicholas left the solar, having no clue where Bryce might be. He hadn't been present in the training yard, though he should have been. Nicholas knocked on the door to his brother's bedchamber, wondering if he might have retired there if unwell.

Through the heavy door, he heard a muffled giggle.

Nicholas rapped again. "Bryce, I must speak with you at once." He didn't bother to disguise his impatience.

Raising his hand to knock a third time, the door suddenly swung open. Bryce stood there, not a stitch on, no shame on his face.

"You have need of me, Brother?" he drawled.

Nicholas brushed past him and said, "Get rid of the wench."

A woman he recognized as one of their groomsmen's wives sat up, her hands covering her bare breasts and her eyes wide.

Reaching for the smock on the floor, he tossed it to her. "Dress

35

and leave." Nicholas turned his back and faced Bryce once again, disgusted by his brother.

The woman scurried by him, scooping up her shoes as she went. She brushed by Bryce without looking at him but he grabbed her arm and jerked her back. He kissed her hard and then shoved her away, patting her rear as she fled the room.

Nicholas contained his anger. He knew Bryce enjoyed seeing him riled and refused to rise to the bait.

His brother strolled to the bed and sat, not bothering to clothe himself. Nicholas gritted his teeth and sat in a chair.

"You need to prepare yourself to leave at dawn. You will accompany Father to Windsor Castle."

Bryce's eyes lit with interest. "Why does Father go to dance attendance upon the king?"

Nicholas wanted to slap his brother for being insolent. "Refrain from speaking in that manner when you are around Father—and especially when you arrive at court. Whether you realize it or not, spies are everywhere. Show that lack of respect and you might find yourself stretched upon the rack in a dank dungeon."

His brother shuddered. "I meant no harm."

"Whether you did or not, take heed, Bryce. We all are at the mercy of the king. Edward has been good to our family and very supportive during these trying times involving the Scots. Do nothing that might make him turn away from us. Watch your speech and actions every minute. Anything you say or do reflects not only on you but on Father and the Mandeville name."

"Will you go with us?"

"Nay. Father asked for you to be his companion."

Bryce leaned back, a cocky grin on his face. "Mayhap I will find a rich bride while we are at Windsor. Or a pretty widow to—"

"Enough!" Nicholas roared. "You are to remain by Father's side at all times. Say nothing. Instead, learn from what goes on around you and stop thinking with your cock." He rose. "'Tis a privilege for you to accompany Father. Take advantage of this opportunity."

Nicholas left his brother's presence. He could only pray that Bryce did nothing foolish to embarrass the Mandeville name or anger the king or one of his advisers. Though a score and three, Bryce acted more like ten and three. Sometimes, Nicholas thought Bethany possessed more sense than his brother.

To calm himself, he went to Bethany's bedchamber and tapped on the door. Mary answered right away and ushered him in.

"She's a happy one, my lord, especially now that Kit's here," Mary confided. "I've never seen Lady Bethany have more fun. 'Twas a smart thing you did, bringing Kit home for her."

Nicholas went and sat on the ground where Bethany played with the kitten. He reached inside his gypon and pulled out a length of yarn that Catherine had given him.

"I brought a present for Kit," he said.

Bethany cocked her head, staring at the yarn. "What?"

"You let Kit chase after it," Nicholas explained. "Like this."

He uncurled the string and dragged it across the floor twice. Kit froze, watching the yarn slide across the floor. Then she pounced on it.

"You pull on it gently," Nicholas said as he tugged it.

Kit placed her paw atop it, only to see it slide from under her. She trapped it with her paw again, only to have Nicholas pull it away. He waved it several times, allowing her to chase it, then raised it in the air and let it tease Kit. The kitten danced under the swaying string, slapping it with her paw, then jumping and biting it.

"I do!" cried Bethany.

He relinquished the yarn to her care and watched as she played with her new pet. He didn't know who showed more delight, his sister or Kit, as they worked the yarn between them. Slowly, the tension that had built within him from his meeting with Bryce dissipated.

Bethany gave the yarn to Kit and scooted close to him. She threw her arms around his neck.

"Love you."

He enfolded her. "I love you, too, Bethany."

"And Kit," his sister added.

Nicholas chuckled. "And Kit," he seconded.

The kitten scampered over, the yarn in her mouth, and dropped it in front of them. They took turns teasing the kitten with it. The fur ball never seemed to tire of the game.

A warm feeling enveloped Nicholas. Someday, Catherine might be here with them, playing with Bethany and Kit.

And their children.

He meant what he'd told Catherine. He would love any babe she birthed because it would give him a bit of Favian back. Nicholas understood now why his friend had been so taken with his wife. Catherine was intelligent and kind, not to mention her tremendous beauty. The oval face, penetrating blue eyes, and golden curls proved very pleasing to his eye. If she agreed to wed him, he looked forward to bedding her. She would make a winsome companion and excellent mother. Northmere needed a woman's touch, especially since his mother had been gone so long.

Nicholas hoped Catherine Savill would be that woman.

Chapter Four

Essex countryside

KATELYN STRETCHED HER aching muscles, walking around the camp as the half-dozen soldiers accompanying Landon busied themselves. Already, two men had collected wood and started a fire while another two hunted for food. The remaining soldiers cared for the horses, watering them at a brook and removing their saddles. She found herself drawn to the horses, inhaling deeply and enjoying the combined scents of leather saddles and horseflesh. The men hobbled the horses, one giving her a brief nod as she passed.

They had traveled all day with only a single stop to relieve themselves and move about. Katelyn knew she would be sore in places tomorrow that she hadn't known existed but any discomfort was worth the price of freedom. No more convent, with its judgmental nuns and oppressive rules. Years ago, she had separated the woman she remembered as her mother from the convent's abbess. In her heart, Katelyn knew she wouldn't miss the tyrannical nun who ruled the Convent of the Charitable Sisters with an iron fist for she had no love for that person. The faint memories of Lady Sybil de Blays had been supplanted by Mother Acelina. The convent's leader meant nothing to her. As far as Katelyn was concerned, from now on Mother Acelina was as dead to her as Lady Sybil.

Especially after learning the woman had planned to barter Katelyn for what she truly wanted.

She circled around a final time and watched Landon for a moment. He studied a map of the area. Her brother had grown tall, his body lean yet muscular. He possessed the same jet black hair and vivid green eyes as she did. Katelyn only knew this from the one time she'd had access to a mirror. One of the oblates had brought it with her. Katelyn helped the young girl unpack her meager belongings and came across it. She'd stared at her image in wonder, seeing herself for the first and only time. It triggered memories of her father's eyes, which she remembered from when he held her on his lap and told her stories. The ever-vigilant Sister Martha had come along and ripped the hand mirror from Katelyn's fingers, throwing it across the room. The fragile glass had hit the stone wall and shattered into pieces. The nun berated Katelyn for her vanity as she collected every fragment and took them away.

Still, it had finally given Katelyn an idea what she looked like to others. And now, seeing Landon, she realized how closely they resembled one another.

They hadn't been able to speak as they rode west toward London. That was the only information Landon imparted before he drew her up into the saddle. She was curious about what had happened to him in the years they'd been apart. Obviously, he had done well. His armor gleamed in the sunlight and fit him well, as if it had been tailored to his body. He possessed an air of confidence. The men seemed relaxed around him yet looked to him attentively as he'd given orders.

Determined to learn more, she marched toward him.

"Do you have time to sit and speak with me, Landon?"

He folded the map and set it aside. Giving her a winning smile, he led her to a fallen log and they sat.

"What would you like to know?"

"Everything. Start with that night the king's men came."

Her brother's rich laugh triggered other memories.

"I can see you holding up a large fish, smiling and laughing as you do now."

Landon nodded. "I recall that day. That was the last time I fished." He frowned. "It seems a long time ago."

"Talk to me. What have you been doing since I last saw you? Is it true that we go to court and the king really wants to see me? That we are related to him? What is his name?"

He stared at her a moment. "You have led a very sheltered life, Katelyn, if you do not even know the king's name." Landon sighed. "The king's troops took Father and me to London. 'Twas King Edward the Second whom Father wished to unseat."

"Our father truly was a traitor?"

He nodded. "Father was charged with treason. I wasn't present at his execution but heard his head was placed upon a pike and displayed outside the palace walls in London."

"What a grisly end," she murmured. "Father always seemed to be such a gentle man."

"I think he was led astray by men who wanted to overthrow the king. King Edward was spellbound by the Despensers, a father and son. Most of the barons resented the hold those two had over the king. The younger Despenser was quite cruel to me. I was treated no better than a homeless dog when I was brought to the palace.

"Fortunately, that changed. Our cousin, Prince Edward, has a kind heart. He took custody of me. Fed me. Dressed me. Taught me. I pledged my loyalty to him. I went to France with him and his mother, Queen Isabella, and returned with them and the queen's lover after a time."

Katelyn gasped. "The queen . . . had a lover? How intriguing."

"She and Mortimer overthrew her husband. They forced him to renounce the throne in favor of Prince Edward, who was only ten and four. The queen became regent for her son. Most likely, Mortimer had the king murdered though it was said the king died while in custody. Four years later, our cousin exacted his revenge. He had Mortimer arrested for murder and treason and hanged at Tyburn. The new King Edward asserted full control and has maintained it ever since."

Katelyn sighed. "To think I have had no knowledge of any of these affairs." She thought a moment. "Is our cousin a good king? And are you still close to him?"

"King Edward is intelligent and fair. He is ten times the ruler his father was. I am still in his personal service. While I have fought against the Scots the last few years, I now serve in the royal guard."

"Though our cousin allowed you to come look for me," Katelyn pointed out. "When did you tell him of me?"

"From the first night we met. I was worried about what had happened to you. The prince promised me then that we would find you and he would take care of you."

She scowled. "Then why did it take so long, Landon? You have no idea of how I suffered in that convent. The good sisters were cruel masters. Mother Acelina was the worst of all."

He grimaced. "I am sorry. Once the Despensers had been executed and the old king was dead, no one seemed to know where you were sent. The queen and Mortimer rid the palace of the men who had served under King Edward. During their four years of controlling England, I had no way of finding you. Remember, I was only a child, as you were."

She took his hand. "I understand."

"Still, once the new King Edward came into power, he did send representatives out looking for you. They had no luck."

Katelyn thought a moment. "If they came to the Convent of the Charitable Sisters, the previous abbess might have lied to them, thinking to protect me. For a time, I went by another name. 'Twas only two years ago that I insisted I be called by my rightful name."

"The king was gracious enough to allow me to search for you on my own. He will be pleased I found you." Landon hesitated. "Do you really believe Mother Acelina recently wrote to make him aware of your whereabouts?"

"It wouldn't surprise me. She is greedy to the bone. Knowing I was a cousin to the current king, she would have used that information to trade me for whatever she wanted. Just think, by the time we arrive in London, the king may have already read her missive and know I am still alive."

Landon shook his head. "We aren't going to London. At least, we won't stay there. We will pass through the city on our way to Windsor Castle."

"Why Windsor?"

"Our cousin was born at Windsor and was known as Edward of Windsor in his early years, before he gained the throne. Though he does spend time at the Palace of Westminster in London and other royal residences, Windsor Castle is by far his and the queen's favorite palace."

"Where is it and how long will it take us to get there?" she asked, curious about this journey they were on.

"We will reach London in two and a half days. It will take most of another day to make it to Windsor, which lies west of London."

"Good," Katelyn declared. "The farther I am from Essex, the better."

Landon squeezed her hand. "You sound angry, Katelyn. Bitter. Was life in the convent that terrible?"

She felt her throat thicken with unshed tears. "It was dreadful. When we first arrived, I was separated from Mother. No one would tell me where she was or what had happened to you and Father. After many months, our mother reappeared as Sister Acelina. She is cunning, Landon. She ingratiated herself with the community of nuns, eventually rising to become the convent's abbess. She wields absolute power."

"And what of your life during these years we've been separated, Katelyn?" he asked softly.

She pulled her hand from his, reluctant to speak the truth but knowing she owed it to her brother, who'd searched so long for her.

"It was lonely. I was set apart from the others, not having a religious calling, though I will say many of the nuns there were filled with more cruelty than charity. I was taught to read and write and passed along that knowledge to others who came to the convent. I did menial tasks in the kitchen and barnyard, working longer hours than any servant. I never had enough to eat and found myself chilled since my clothing was inadequate."

Katelyn lowered her head in shame. "The worst of it? I've never had a friend, not in all of these years, nor even had one comforting touch. Mother Acelina was a great believer in the power of physical punishment and had me beaten and starved for disobedience a countless number of times."

Raising her eyes, she met Landon's gaze, seeing his eyes blaze in anger. She took his hand again. "It's all right. Everything that happened made me stronger, Brother. And now you've come for me. I can leave the nightmare of my old life behind me. Every day, every month, every year I'm away from that convent is my victory to claim. Living a long, happy life will be my best revenge on the abbess."

He raised their joined hands and kissed her knuckles. "I wish I could have located you sooner."

"You did your best," Katelyn reassured him. "But what of your life as a knight? Growing up at court and the excitement of becoming a knight."

"I was much more fortunate than you were," Landon admitted. "I only suffered for a short time before being placed in Prince Edward's household. I trained from then on as all boys of noble birth do. I was taught how to care for horses and learned to ride expertly. I spent many hours in the yard, training to fight with every manner of weapons. I shared a tutor and learned not only Latin and figures but history and battle strategies. I became familiar with the knight's code of honor and gained my knighthood. As a member of the king's royal guard, I am acknowledged as one of the best soldiers in the land."

"I'm very proud of all you've accomplished, Landon," Katelyn praised. "Have you a wife? Children?"

He shook his head. "Nay. I don't foresee either in my future. I have no lands. No title. No way to give a noblewoman the creature comforts she deserves. My life is in service to the crown. I have spent every day since we were thrust from Blackstone Castle trying to prove my loyalty to England and our king."

"Sir Landon?" a soldier asked as he came toward them. "Are you and Lady Katelyn ready to eat? We've skinned a few hares." He gave her an admiring smile. "We also have bread and cheese, my lady, and a skin of wine for you."

No one had ever addressed her as *my lady* at the convent. She dimly remembered hearing that from the servants at Blackstone years ago.

"I would be most happy to partake of this meal," Katelyn told the soldier.

Landon rose and offered her a hand. She took it and allowed him to escort her near the fire, where she received more food than she'd been allowed in an entire day at the convent. Trying to hide her shock, she accepted the meal and returned to sit on the log while she ate. Landon and the other soldiers joined her. The men regaled her with stories of war, each trying to present how bravely he'd fought in various battles. She almost laughed aloud as they vied for attention.

Even dressed in her rags, Katelyn was aware of their interest in her. For the first time, she sensed the power she possessed and knew of her allure. She already embraced her intelligence and perseverance, which had helped her endure all those years at the convent. Recognizing she also was beautiful to others surprised her—but she intended to wield every weapon she had by the time she arrived at Windsor

Castle.

Landon might be devoted to the king but this cousin was a stranger to Katelyn. She would need to keep her wits about her so that the monarch might learn she was a force to be reckoned with. Knowing the royal court would be vastly different from everything she knew, Katelyn would need every advantage she had to survive—and thrive.

LONDON DELIGHTED KATELYN, with its teeming crowds and endless buildings. She enjoyed the meat pie Landon bought her, thinking she'd never sunk her teeth into anything that tasted so delightful. Her brother had the escort party stop at the Palace of Westminster, not only for her to see the royal residence but to find her something to wear.

Part of her wanted to go to the king in what she'd worn every day at the nunnery so he could see what her life had been like. Landon convinced her that the king would prefer to see her clothed better. He explained that Edward might feel guilty for what she had gone through and that it was better to keep him calm.

"Our cousin has quite the temper," Landon confided. "I want you to go to him appropriately dressed so he can see how lovely you are."

"Am I pretty?" she boldly asked.

He gave her a charming smile. "You are more than pretty, Sister. You will captivate the king and every courtier in sight."

With that, she had agreed to change into clothing more suitable in which to meet the king. Fortunately, a few of the queen's ladies-in-waiting had been at the palace and given her some items to wear. They'd bathed her and fussed over her hair while a seamstress had altered the cotehardies. Now, Katelyn had three of them, as well as two smocks and a kirtle.

Approaching Windsor now, she wore a cotehardie of deep blue. Several of the knights in their party had complimented her on her appearance. Their words gave her confidence, which she badly needed since nervousness filled her. She worried what the king would think of her. She doubted she could execute the curtsey one of the ladies-in-waiting had taught her, fearing she'd fall on her face when she attempted it. Still, she wouldn't trade her life now for anything.

As they drew near, she saw both the River Thames and Windsor Forest, the royal hunting preserve that Landon had mentioned. Soon, they came close to the castle itself. Positioned on very high ground, Katelyn realized that any enemy who approached would be seen quickly, making the castle more easily defended.

They entered the massive gates and immediately she was struck by all of the activity inside the castle's walls.

"There's the Lady Chapel," Landon pointed out.

"It's incredibly long," Katelyn said.

"Henry the Third built it. He also repaired the great hall and expanded the kitchens during his reign. He even built a separate, more private ward for his queen and their children, as opposed to the Lower Ward, which is where more public functions occur."

Landon drew his horse to a halt and helped her to the ground, instructing one of the soldiers to take it to the stables.

Offering her his arm, they entered the palace. The opulence overwhelmed Katelyn, especially when contrasted to the austere surroundings she'd lived in for so many years.

"I doubt the king will see us right away. He is the most important man in England and his days are full, conducting business with noblemen and representatives from governments across Europe."

She remained speechless, words impossible to express. They began passing courtiers who nodded to acknowledge them. The men were dressed as richly as the women. Katelyn felt her heart pounding violently and thought she might be sick.

"Sir Landon?"

Turning, she saw a small boy run toward them. He beamed at her brother, who whispered, "Curtsey. 'Tis Prince Edward. Call him *your grace.*"

The boy came to a stop and Landon bowed while Katelyn dipped low, hoping she wouldn't make a mistake.

"Who is this, Sir Landon? Is it your sister? Father said you went in search of her." The prince gazed at her in curiosity.

"Aye, your grace. This is my long-lost sister, Katelyn de Blays."

The boy gave a small bow to her and then took her hand. He kissed it and gave her a winning smile. She decided he would definitely mature to be a handsome man and break a string of hearts along the way.

"You are most beautiful, Lady Katelyn," the prince said solemnly. "I am glad Sir Landon found you. He's one of Father's best knights, you know."

She smiled. "I am happy to hear that, your grace." She was glad Landon had told her how to address the royal, knowing she had so much to learn.

"Have you seen Father?" Prince Edward inquired.

"Nay, your grace," Landon said. "We've only just arrived. I know how busy he is."

The boy's eyes sparkled with both mischief and charm as he said, "He is never too busy to see me, Sir Landon. And if you are with me?" He shrugged. "Then I suppose you, too, will get to visit with him. Come along."

Prince Edward took off and they followed closely behind him.

"He is a fine lad. Very smart and kind to others," Landon said softly.

"I believe he will make a fine king of his own one day," she said.

They walked for almost a quarter of an hour. Katelyn tried to take in everything she saw but realized she should focus more on the meeting ahead. Finally, they arrived at a door guarded by six knights. The men allowed the trio to pass. Katelyn swallowed and sent a prayer to the Virgin to be with her as she met the head of all of England.

Prince Edward pushed open the door and gestured for them to come. Once more, they passed through several rooms and came to another door.

"I left Mother and my sisters with Father. They should all still be here," the boy said.

He threw back the door and stepped inside. Katelyn gripped Landon's arm and he gave her an encouraging smile. As they entered the room, a woman sat with a young girl in her lap. Katelyn saw that she was with child and assumed her to be the queen. Another girl, slightly older, sat in the king's lap, her eyes wide as he spoke to her. Both adults looked up and smiled at their son.

"Mother, Father, I found Sir Landon and Lady Katelyn, his sister, so I brought them to see you."

Katelyn swept into a deep curtsey and remained low until commanded by the king to rise. He assessed her from head to toe and then said, "So, you are Lady Katelyn de Blays. Your mother seems to think you are worth quite a bit."

CHAPTER FIVE

IMMEDIATELY, KATELYN SENSED her cheeks heating. Her eyes flew to Landon, who shook his head imperceptibly. She held her tongue, the sharp retort rattling about in her head. She'd always been quick to speak her mind but knew in the presence of royalty it would be unacceptable.

The queen clucked her tongue and gave Katelyn a sympathetic look. She turned to her husband. "You have embarrassed the poor girl. She's spent her life sequestered from the world in a convent and your first words to your long-lost cousin insult her."

"I did not mean to humiliate her, my love," the king apologized to his wife.

"Make it right," Philippa said boldly.

Awe filled Katelyn for how directly the queen spoke to her husband. Something told her that this was not the case with other men and their wives—much less monarchs and their queens.

Edward eased the girl from his lap and approached Katelyn. She trembled from head to toe under his direct gaze.

He paused in front of her and reached for her hand. He kissed her knuckles, his lips cool and dry against her skin.

"Forgive me, Cousin Katelyn. I was merely taken aback at your mother's missive. It bordered on rudeness."

"I have no mother," Katelyn said solemnly. "Mother Acelina is a Bride of Christ and the nuns serving under her act as her children. She no longer recognizes me as her offspring. I lost the woman I knew as my mother many years ago."

"Hmm." The king's eyes narrowed as he thought over her words. "It saddens me that she would write to me in the manner she did, wishing to exchange you for . . . other things."

"I had no idea she would trade on my relationship to you, sire. For that, I am the one who must apologize," Katelyn said.

King Edward returned to his chair and his daughter climbed back into his lap, looking at Katelyn with wide, curious eyes.

"When I received the abbess' missive several days ago, it startled me. Sir Landon had urged me to look for you for many years and those efforts had proved unsuccessful. I did speak with an elderly courtier who confirmed that Sybil de Blays had been sent to a nunnery with her daughter. He'd heard rumors of the lady becoming the convent's abbess but had dismissed them as idle gossip."

The king turned to Landon. "I was waiting for you to return so you might fetch Lady Katelyn to court."

"I was fortunate to happen upon the right convent, sire. Our mother . . . that is, Mother Acelina, was unhappy that her demands wouldn't be met. I insisted Katelyn leave with me without any kind of compensation being awarded to the Convent of the Charitable Sisters."

Edward chuckled. "Oh, I can see how that would rile the abbess." His gaze returned to Katelyn. "She was right, though. You are a beauty. When wearing the proper clothes, there won't be a man at court who won't dance to the tune you set."

Katelyn kept silent, wishing the king could have seen her in what she normally wore.

He turned to the queen. "My dear, you must take charge of my cousin. See that she has an entire new wardrobe at once. Let no expense be spared."

"Of course." Philippa's eyes gleamed in approval.

The king took his wife's hand and gazed at her tenderly. "I know you need your rest. Why don't you and the girls take Cousin Katelyn with you? I'm sure your head lady-in-waiting can find quarters for her." He pressed a soft kiss to her fingers.

Katelyn watched the exchange between the pair in wonder. By the way the king stared at the queen, she knew they were a love match. A wistful feeling filled her. She'd spent so many years suffering, often beaten, usually alone, no one bestowing any affection upon her. Would she ever have the devotion—much less the love—of a good man?

Edward looked to her. "We will meet again soon, Cousin. I think you will enjoy being at court. I place you in my queen's most capable hands." He smiled. "I see a bright future for you."

Philippa slipped her daughter from her lap and stood. "Come, Joan. Isabella. Your father has business to attend to." She smiled at Katelyn. "If you'll come with me, my lady."

Katelyn gave a last look to Landon, who smiled encouragingly at her, and then followed the queen along a maze of corridors until they reached a set of rooms guarded by soldiers. The queen, who'd held her daughters' hands as they'd skipped beside her, handed them off to a servant and then led Katelyn through several chambers. In one, a group of five women sat, some sewing, as one read aloud to the others.

"Have my seamstress sent to me at once," the queen commanded. "And I wish for some of the pear tarts, as well." She slipped her arm through Katelyn's. "We will go to my private sitting room."

They arrived and the queen indicated for her to take a seat. Philippa did the same, slipping off her shoes and sighing.

"Are you unwell, your grace?" Katelyn asked, hoping that was also the way to address a queen.

"Nay, I am in the best of health. I always am when I carry the king's child." She grinned. "But I do have a fondness for fruit tarts during that time."

A servant arrived bearing several tarts on a tray. The queen had her pour wine for them and then dismissed her.

"Please, my lady, enjoy a tart and some wine," Philippa encouraged.

Katelyn eyed the luxury before her. "I . . . I have never eaten one before," she explained. "The food at the Charitable Sisters was plain. And infrequent."

The queen's laughter filled the room. "Then you must eat two. Enjoy!"

She bit into the delicacy and caught the taste of both sweet and tart at the same time. Holding the food in her mouth a moment, Katelyn savored the richness before chewing and swallowing. She fought the urge to inhale every tart before her.

Instead, she decided she should make conversation. "When will your babe come?"

Philippa rubbed her belly affectionately. "Sometime in late November, so in about four months." She paused. "I hope for a boy this time, though the king says he does not care whether I deliver him a son or daughter."

"Is Prince Edward your only son?"

The queen nodded sadly. "I had another boy. William. He died less than three weeks after his birth last year."

"I am sorry to hear that, your grace."

"It was God's will," the queen assured her. "William is safely in heaven. Still, the king and I look forward to a new addition in our household. My husband is an only child. Because of that, he wishes to fill the royal nursery with many babes."

"The king looks at you with great fondness," Katelyn noted. "As if he loves you."

A brilliant smile broke out on the queen's plain face, making her appear almost pretty. "Aye, we do love one another. I know 'tis almost unheard of. We were strangers brought together when we wed but soon found we were of similar minds. Over the years, our friendship blossomed into love. I hadn't ever seen love before, especially between my father and mother. And poor Edward's parents had a relationship so fractured, it led to his father's downfall. Though my husband had parents who frequently ignored him, he is a most generous, loving man and places his family above all else—even England itself."

"You are blessed to have such rich love in your life," Katelyn said, a bit envious.

The queen's eyes sparkled. "I hope you, too, will find the same someday, my lady."

The seamstress arrived and measured Katelyn, promising the queen that a new wardrobe would be created within the next two weeks.

"See that it is," the queen said. "And make it one week. My husband wants nothing but the best for his cousin." She looked to Katelyn. "Do you have any suggestions for what you might like? Any particular colors you are fond of?"

"The question overwhelms me, your grace," Katelyn revealed. "I know nothing of fashion and usually had but one set of clothes to wear at the nunnery. I will be delighted no matter what I receive."

Philippa studied her. "With those dark tresses and fair skin, you can wear many colors well. I see you in rich tones, deep shades of rust, green, and blue. Definitely all hues of green to bring out those emerald eyes." She looked to the seamstress. "You've always shown good judgment in the past. Do justice to Lady Katelyn."

"Aye, your grace. 'Twill be my pleasure to clothe such a fine lady."

After she left, the queen confided, "I have never been a great beauty. The king says I possess it but I see my features revealed in the mirror and know I lack it. He says the more he gets to know me, the more beautiful I am to him. Still, I know my seamstress is happy to have a lovely young woman of both face and figure to create many new things to wear."

"You are being too hard on yourself, your grace," Katelyn insisted. While she'd thought the queen slightly homely at first, the more they spoke and the more animated the queen became, the prettier she seemed. Katelyn could understand why the king felt as he did about her.

Philippa patted her hand. "You are as kind as you are beautiful. I cannot wait to introduce you at court."

KATELYN WALKED ALONGSIDE other ladies-in-waiting as the queen took a turn around the gardens, which occurred early every morning and also mid-afternoon. She'd overheard some of the noblewomen discussing how most women carrying a babe took to their beds and rarely moved about but the queen seemed to enjoy getting exercise. As usual, the two little princesses tagged along. Joan was chasing a butterfly while Isabella sat moving rocks about.

In her short time at Windsor Castle, Katelyn had learned that most royals rarely saw their children, even sending them to be raised at estates far away, under the direction of trusted noblemen. King Edward and Queen Philippa placed a high value on family and spent a good deal of time around their three children and so bucked tradition. Katelyn thought if she ever became a mother that she would model herself after the queen and enjoy having her children near her. To have children, though, would mean making a marriage.

She'd had eleven offers in the seven days she'd been at court.

Landon had advised her to neither encourage nor discourage any of the noblemen who'd offered for her. He'd made it clear that the king would decide who her future husband would be. Katelyn hoped this wouldn't occur for a long time for she was enjoying her time serving the queen and getting to know the other ladies-in-waiting. At first, they had been wary of her, a convent-bred girl who possessed some odd notions about life, but she had won several of them over and had enjoyed making her first-ever friends.

She only wished she could spend more time with Landon. After years of separation from her brother, she was eager to learn everything she could about him. Unfortunately, he always seemed to be busy attending the king. As a lady-in-waiting, Katelyn was often given a few hours each day to spend however she chose. She'd walked the grounds at Windsor and the many corridors of the castle, becoming familiar with her surroundings faster than she'd thought possible. Having the freedom to go wherever she wanted and to eat as much as she desired made each day a pleasure.

While she'd enjoyed the hustle and bustle of London, being in the fresh country air appealed to her more than being surrounded by the foul smells of the large city. She wished she could return and live at Blackwell but Landon told her the estate had been awarded to a favored nobleman after her father's conviction and execution. Mayhap one day she would once again be allowed onto the grounds so she could see her former home.

Katelyn noticed a page heading toward the queen. One often de-livered messages to her from the king throughout the day. The queen's eyes would light up as she read from the parchment, once again making her appear quite pretty. Katelyn guessed the queen and king to both be around a score and five. Together, they made a handsome couple. She hoped they would continue to live and love for many years to come.

The page bowed to the queen and instead of presenting a rolled up parchment, he spoke to her briefly. Philippa nodded and then pointed toward where her ladies-in-waiting stood. The page quickly headed in their direction and came to stand in front of her.

"Lady Katelyn?" he asked, pushing his dark hair from his eyes.

"Aye?"

"The king would like to see you at once. I am to escort you and the queen to him."

She noticed the queen had followed the page at a more leisurely pace and now came to stand before her.

"Shall we go see my husband, Lady Katelyn?"

"Of course, your grace."

The two women followed the page across the slight, rolling hills and back inside the castle. Instead of going to the private rooms where she'd first spoken with the monarch, they were led to a different wing. Katelyn wondered why Edward requested her presence and tried to calm her growing nerves. They entered a grand hall where dozens of courtiers milled about but she saw no sight of the king.

Passing through the room, they came to a smaller one that was still quite large by her standards. She recognized three members of the royal council and numerous servants. Landon was also present, standing near the front of the room, and he acknowledged her with a brief nod. Two noblemen she hadn't yet met stood to the side on her right. The elder was tall, with a balding head and watchful eyes. Next to him stood a man equally as tall but broad in the shoulders. He had light brown hair and a handsome face. When he caught her looking at him, he gave her a beautiful smile. Katelyn curtly nodded and looked away, though she'd been intrigued by the younger man's air of casual confidence.

The king entered and took a seat in a chair at the front of the room. Everyone present bowed and the queen joined her husband, sitting to his right.

"Cousin Katelyn. Please approach," the king commanded.

She did as he asked, holding her head high, pleased that she was wearing the best of the silk cotehardies that had been sewn for her and delivered only this morning. Dropping into a curtsey, she rose when bidden and waited expectantly.

"I realize you have lived a life in isolation, Cousin, and may not be aware of all of the troubles England has experienced with our Scottish neighbors."

"Landon told me he had fought against the Scots in your name, sire."

Edward smiled. "Aye, he did, indeed. Your brother distinguished himself on the battlefield, earning his knighthood in a particularly bloody battle. He became my youngest knight in the land with his brave efforts that day."

Katelyn heard the respect in the king's voice and replied, "I am very proud of Landon, your majesty. He is the best of brothers."

"It is important for me to show my nobles in the north that I continue to support them. Though we have quelled most of the violence, the Scots occasionally ride across the border and cause some mischief, especially near Berwick-upon-Tweed. The city is less than three miles from the border on the east coast and one of my most important holdings."

It puzzled her why the king shared all of this with her but his next words might reveal why her presence was required.

"The largest estate in Northumberland is Northmere, which lies west of Berwick. Since it is the last English estate before the border, it is one of great importance and strategic position. Because of that, I wish to bind the Mandeville family, the owners of Northmere, to the crown. They have been loyal, faithful servants to me. The best way I can do that is through marriage."

Now, Katelyn understood her role. The handsome stranger standing near the wall must be her intended. She kept her features neutral even as excitement built within her.

"Giving my beloved cousin in marriage is not something I take lightly, Lady Katelyn, but knowing you would become part of such a fine family would truly be a gift to both sides. And the fact that my own cousin would become a Mandeville would let the Scots know how committed I am to keeping a strong border and a peace between us."

"I understand, sire," Katelyn said. "I will be honored to represent your name and join with the Mandeville family."

Edward gave her a benign smile. "You will become a countess, Cousin. The Mandevilles are one of England's oldest and most powerful families. I know the earl will take good care of you."

To be thrust from the small confines of the Convent of the Charitable Sisters to such a large seat of power was hard to comprehend but Katelyn trusted that the king did what was best for both her and England.

"Lord Cedric, step forward."

Katelyn turned and almost gasped aloud when the old, balding man headed her way. Her eyes flew to Landon. His face remained stoic but she caught a glimpse of regret in his eyes.

By now, the earl had come to stand next to her. His smile caused her heart to sink. Up close, she could see pockmarks pitted across his cheeks and the yellowed teeth. A foul smell came from his breath.

The nobleman swept up her hand and kissed it gallantly. Katelyn did her best not to shudder at his touch. She glanced back to the king, careful not to reveal her true feelings regarding the match.

"Lord Cedric has expressed the desire to wed at Northmere so you will leave in the morning for Northumberland, my lady. Tonight, we will hold a feast in your honor to celebrate your upcoming marriage."

With a heavy heart, Katelyn realized that she was nothing more than a pawn to be moved around on the chessboard of politics.

CHAPTER SIX

K ATELYN HAD NEVER been wearier than at this moment. As Landon set her on the ground, she clung to his horse's pommel, afraid her legs might give way.

He swung down beside her. "Tired of being in the saddle?"

She nodded. "I've lost track of the days. They have all blended together."

"It's been fourteen," he replied and then looked at her steadily. "We should arrive at Northmere sometime tomorrow."

She tamped down the apprehension that ran through her. "At least I've gotten to see most of England since we've reunited. I've been from Essex in the east to west of London and now hundreds of miles from south to north. I doubt I will ever travel this much again in my lifetime."

The thought saddened her. After so many years apart from Landon, it looked as if they would face a permanent separation. With him dedicated to service in the king's royal guard, she feared unless war broke out with Scotland, she might never see him this far north again.

Her face must have betrayed her suspicions for he embraced her tightly. "Never fear, Katelyn. I promise that this won't be the last time we see one another."

Quietly, in his ear, she said, "You mean if my husband drops dead, you would be willing to see me back to wherever the royal court is?"

Landon drew back and studied her, his own face solemn. "We'll speak after we eat."

Activity had erupted all around them as men took care of all the tasks necessary to make camp for the night. King Edward had sent an additional seventy soldiers to accompany those who returned her to her new home. It was part of the monarch's efforts to shore up the defense of the north, with fifty men remaining at Northmere and the rest going to a neighboring estate. Her husband-to-be had said very little to her during the journey north beyond mentioning that he was pleased to receive the additional troops from the king. Lord Cedric's son, Bryce Mandeville, had proven far friendlier, engaging her in conversation numerous times. The younger Mandeville was cordial and charming. Katelyn wished that he had been her intended instead of his father. From Bryce, she had learned that Lord Cedric had another son and a daughter and that his wife had died three years ago. Though a man who showed little emotion, Bryce said his father had deeply mourned his wife's passing. His son, Nicholas, was five and twenty, two years older than Bryce, and would inherit Northmere upon his father's death. Katelyn wondered what would happen to her once Lord Cedric passed. She didn't look forward to a time where she would be stranded in the north, pushed aside when the new Earl of Northmere took control of the estate.

After they ate, most of the men bedded down as a few others began their guard duty, positioned at strategic points surrounding the camp. Katelyn and Landon took the tin plates and cups used at the meal and went to wash them in the closest stream. Since it wasn't far from the campsite, no other men accompanied them. Once they finished the task, they sat on the bank, where they spoke freely to one another.

"I have learned that Lord Cedric is two score and ten," Landon shared. "He's been a widower for a few years."

"I wish he weren't so old," Katelyn complained. "And his breath is always foul."

Her brother studied her. "I know you have been sheltered from many things, Katelyn. I think I must speak to you about the marriage bed since I doubt any of the nuns mentioned it to you."

She had put all thoughts of her wedding night from her mind. Lord Cedric's touch made her cringe. Still, it would be better to hear what Landon could tell her so that she could prepare herself.

"I have no idea what it entails," she admitted. "What is it like to couple with another?"

"At least the earl has experience," Landon began. "He should treat you gently since you are a virgin. If you are attracted to your partner, it can be a very pleasant experience."

She bit her lip. "I already know it won't be. I dread it, Landon."

"Well, it has to be better than your life in the nunnery," he pointed out. "You will have to allow him to bed you. A wife has no choice in these matters. He's old, though, so he won't have as much stamina as a younger man."

"That's good?" she asked.

"In this case, it will be," he confirmed. "You will suffer some pain the first time you couple because he must break through your maidenhead. There will be a small amount of blood. Not much and the pain is only the first time." He brightened. "The good thing is that you will be a countess. You will be in charge of the keep and make numerous decisions each day in how it is run. You will belong to a great, powerful family, one respected and admired. When the earl is away defending his property, you will be left in charge of the estate."

"I suppose it's an improvement on the life that I've led up until now. At least no one will beat or starve me."

His eyes reflected pity. "I'm sorry you were treated poorly by the nuns."

"I wasn't docile enough for Mother Acelina's taste. The nuns frequently administered punishment for my imagined sins."

He wrapped an arm about her shoulder and pulled her into him. "Then this will be a wonderful life, sweet sister, one of your own making. You may even birth children, though the earl already has his heir." Landon kissed the top of her head. "You are the best parts of our mother and father. I know you would make a good parent. I hope that comes to pass."

Katelyn smiled. "I would raise them to ride as Father taught us. And I would tell them stories as Mother used to do when it was time for bed. Do you remember her stories, Landon?"

He frowned. "Vaguely. It's been a long time. Sometimes, that life at Blackwell doesn't seem real to me. It's as if it happened but it didn't."

"Do you remember Quill?" she asked softly. Being with Landon had brought back memories of the third child that completed their circle.

"I do. I never asked the king to look for him, though. He has no idea Quill exists."

"Why? If you told the king about me and searched for so long, why would you not do the same for him?"

"Father's last words to me were to look after you—and never tell them about Quill."

"Why? Quill was a part of us."

"Did you know that he was our half-brother? Since he was older than I am, Father must have bedded another woman prior to his marriage. Quill was the result. I did learn years later that Mother was supposed to marry Father's brother, who was the heir to Blackwell. He died and she wed Father instead."

Katelyn chuckled. "No wonder she hated Quill so. He was a constant reminder of Father bedding another woman." She paused. "It surprises me that Quill was even brought to Blackstone Castle."

Landon shrugged. "Mayhap his mother died giving birth to him. Or Father might have wanted his son nearby, even if he was a bastard."

"I wonder where Quill is now," Katelyn mused. "Everything was so chaotic that night. I wonder if he might still be at Blackwell."

"I doubt it. Father would have protected him. I'm sure he sent Quill away. Where, I'm sure we'll never know. Mayhap it's for the best."

"Does thinking of Blackwell make you sad?" she asked. "Those lands should have gone to you. You should have been the Earl of Blackwell, not merely Sir Landon de Blays."

A fierce light came into her brother's eyes. "I have worked my entire life to restore our family's good name," he said vehemently. "'Tis my fondest wish to be rewarded for my service to the king by one day gaining my own title and lands."

"You'll get both," Katelyn assured him. "The king has a great affection for you and respect for your bravery." She took his hand. "When you do acquire your own estate, promise that you will come for me if this husband of mine is dead. By the way he huffs and puffs and is constantly red in the face, I believe that will be sooner rather than later. Please, Landon, swear that you'll take me away from Northmere and let me live with you, wherever you are."

Landon pressed a kiss to her brow. "I swear it, Sister. I will always take care of you."

NICHOLAS OPENED HIS eyes and listened. He heard the soft, even breaths of his sister coming from the bed. Last night, she had come to him, terrified, incapable of words. As always, he explained that she'd merely had a bad dream but Bethany insisted he come back to her chamber. The pattern had been established long ago. After Bethany awoke from a nightmare, Nicholas would sit on the bed beside her, holding her hand, until she fell asleep. Then he would remain throughout the night.

He'd learned his lesson the first time it had happened. Sleeping in the chair next to her bed only left him with a sore back and a crick in his neck. Stretching out on the floor proved far more comfortable. As a soldier, he was used to nights spent slumbering on the ground.

Sitting up, he pushed himself to his feet and went to the bed. He placed a hand on Bethany's shoulder and shook her gently.

"'Tis almost morning. I will see you later."

She mumbled something and rolled over so he felt free to leave. Returning to his own bedchamber, he shed his wrinkled clothes and readied himself for the day. At mass, he wondered how long it would be until his father returned. The trip to Windsor and back usually took a month if the weather was fair and much longer if the roads were clogged by mud and debris. Fortunately, it was still summer, though August would soon be done. Nicholas expected the monarch had sent for Lord Cedric to receive a report on the status of the border. He hoped that his father would return with additional soldiers. King Edward had promised when he last left Scotland that new troops would be sent at some point. Both Northmere and Ravenwood could use them.

Nicholas left the chapel after mass ended and went to break his fast in the great hall. Only he and his aunt sat upon the dais. Ellyn Mandeville was a quiet woman and, after greeting him, she left him to his own thoughts. He'd just finished eating when an unfamiliar soldier ran across the room and came to a halt in front of him. The man wore Ravensgate colors so Nicholas knew he came from their neighboring estate.

"My lord, Lord Terald sent me," the soldier blurted out and then paused to draw a few breaths. "Ravenwood has been attacked by the

Scots. They burned part of the harvest still in the fields and made off with some livestock. Lord Terald wanted to warn you to be watchful of Northmere and asked if you might lead his men in pursuit of the bandits."

Nicholas sprang to his feet. "Sir Rafe!" he called and his uncle came hurrying toward him. As captain of Northmere's guard, Rafe Mandeville preferred eating with their men.

Quickly, Nicholas explained the situation and then said, "I will take ten men with me, Uncle. They will remain to help guard Ravenwood while I lead a party of the Earl of Ravensgate's soldiers. Have my horse saddled and the soldiers readied."

Rafe Mandeville left to do Nicholas' bidding.

Turning to the messenger he said, "Meet me in the stables. You can ride with my men and me back to Ravenwood."

"Aye, my lord."

"Henfrey!" Nicholas shouted.

"Right here, my lord," said his squire, a smart lad of ten and three who watched and listened to all around him. He seemed to anticipate what Nicholas needed before he himself knew.

"Come with me. I need to don my armor."

Within minutes, Henfrey had him suited up and Nicholas mounted Sunset. He pushed aside the bitterness that rose in him. Only a few months ago, if an attack would have occurred on Ravensgate lands, Favian would have led the Savill men against the Scots. Now with his friend dead and Lord Terald ailing, Nicholas knew it was his duty to chase down the Scots who had dared cross the border and disrupt the peace.

He and his men rode quickly to Ravenwood. Lord Terald, looking frail and ill, met them in the inner bailey. Catherine stood at his side, holding his elbow to steady him.

"I will leave my soldiers here to look after your people and bolster your defense," Nicholas informed the nobleman. "They can join your soldiers who remain behind along the wall walk and out on the estate. I will command your men as we hunt down those responsible for damaging Ravenwood."

"Thank you," Lord Terald said, his voice feeble. "I appreciate what good neighbors the Mandevilles are."

"We must all bind together in times of trouble," he said, knowing if he were gone Favian would have done the same for Nicholas' family.

"Godspeed, Nicholas," Catherine said. "I will pray for your safe return."

"Thank you, my lady."

Nicholas turned toward his men. "You know what to do. I will return as soon as I can. Protect Ravenwood and its people to the best of your ability."

Motioning to the Ravensgate soldiers who had arrived, he bid them to follow him. Once they left the castle walls, he set a brisk pace toward the north.

They arrived at the Scottish border without spotting anything else amiss, following the tracks left by the sheep and cattle that had been driven from Ravenwood. He raised a hand and the party came to a halt.

"We cross into Scotland now. Though we possess better weaponry and are better armed, most of you know from experience how wily the Scots can be. Keep alert at all times. We'll recover the missing livestock and find the men responsible for burning the field."

Nicholas explained the formation they would ride in and the soldiers fanned out across the road. He wanted them to have room to maneuver in case they were attacked and yet still be close enough to one another for protection. The band of troops quickly assembled as requested. With a swift prayer to Saint Michael for protection, Nicholas urged his force onward, sending one man to ride ahead as their scout.

Three-quarters of an hour later, the soldier returned. Nicholas rode out to meet him, wishing to hear what the man reported in private.

"I spied the Ravensgate animals ahead, my lord," the scout confirmed. "I counted ten and five men driving them. Eight of those were on horseback. The others are on foot, urging the animals onward."

Gazing at the landscape around them, he decided to send half of his party to the west. They would ride around the Scots and then head south toward them. In the meantime, the remainder of the men would continue to push north. Eventually, the Scots would be pinned between the two groups. Nicholas returned to the soldiers and explained his strategy then divided them into two equal groups. He led the ones riding west, having them ride fast at first and arc around before slowing to a moderate pace as they joined with the road and rode southward.

The confrontation took only minutes. The Scots were ill-equipped as usual but fought fiercely. By the time the encounter ended, every one of the invaders lay dead. It took another hour to round up the frightened animals that had scurried away from the hoarse cries and smell of blood and another three hours until they reached Ravenwood, their pace much slower with the livestock in hand.

As they headed toward the castle, Nicholas heard the cheers from the men stationed on the wall walk. Some of the soldiers veered off to return the sheep and cattle to their pens while he led the rest of them through the castle's gates. The men trotted their horses to the stables as he went straight to the keep to report to Lord Terald.

Catherine met him as he entered the keep, her belly more rounded than the last time he had seen her, making it obvious she was with child.

She threw her arms around him. "Oh, Nicholas, I'm so glad you've returned."

He heard the anguish in her voice and pulled back, searching her face. "What's wrong?"

"Lord Terald collapsed after you left. The healer is very concerned." Tears welled in her eyes.

Though he had planned to return to Northmere immediately, he asked, "Would you like me to stay?"

"Could you? I know your father is away."

"I will remain with you until the morning and then return to Northmere. By then, we might know more of how Lord Terald fares."

"Thank you." She lifted his hands and kissed them.

"Let me tell my men."

"Come to the solar when you are done," she urged.

Nicholas returned to the bailey and found the Northmere soldiers had gathered, waiting for his instructions.

"Go back to Northmere," he ordered. "Lord Terald is gravely ill. I've decided to remain at Ravenwood overnight and will be back home sometime tomorrow."

He watched his men mount their horses and ride away. With a heavy heart, he returned inside the keep. Lord Terald had been more of a father to him than his own, both patient and understanding. Nicholas had enjoyed time spent with Favian and his father throughout the years. Especially with Favian now dead and Catherine with child, Ravensgate needed Lord Terald's leadership more than ever.

Hurrying to the solar, Nicholas entered and went straight to the bedchamber within. He pushed open the door and came to stand at the foot of the bed, Catherine and the healer on each side of the nobleman. One look told him Terald Savill was not long for this world.

CHAPTER SEVEN

THEY ARRIVED AT Northmere just before the noon hour. Lord Cedric seemed to come alive once they entered the gates, showing more enthusiasm than he had since she'd been introduced to him.

The nobleman came and helped her from Landon's mount. "I hope you like what you see, my lady. I am very proud of Northmere."

"It is a most impressive estate, my lord," Katelyn told him.

In truth, Blackwell had been the only English estate she had seen, other than the ones they'd passed by on this journey. She had few memories of her former home but she did understand how large Northmere was. As they'd ridden in, Bryce pointed out the boundaries, which stretched as far as the eye could see. Katelyn now looked up at the immense keep, which rose high in the air. To think she would soon be mistress of all of this dazzled—and frightened—her at the same time.

"We will wed today," Lord Cedric continued.

"Today?" Katelyn squeaked.

His eyes gleamed. "Aye. I am ready to have a wife to once again warm my bed. Come. I will let my sister-in-law know. She can have

Cook plan a modest feast and have the solar prepared for our wedding night."

The nobleman strode off, leaving Katelyn dizzy at the speed of events. By the time Landon escorted her into the great hall, servants bustled about. She saw Lord Cedric in conversation with an older woman.

"Let's meet this woman," she suggested to her brother.

They made their way over and heard the woman say, "But Nicholas is gone, my lord. Surely, you don't wish to wed without your son being present for the ceremony?"

"Is he on border patrol?" Lord Cedric asked.

"Nay," she replied. "Ravenwood was attacked by a band of Scots early this morning. Lord Terald asked for reinforcements to be sent to help him and for Nicholas to lead Ravensgate men in pursuit."

The earl noticed Katelyn and Landon had come to stand nearby and motioned them over. "Lady Katelyn, this is my brother's wife, Lady Ellyn Mandeville. Her husband, Sir Rafe, is my captain of the guard. And this is Sir Landon de Blays, my bride's brother."

Greetings were exchanged and then Lady Ellyn said, "I still think you should wait a day or so for Nicholas to join us."

Lord Cedric dismissed the idea. "It's not as if he's missing his own wedding. Besides, these border skirmishes break out with frequency. He could be gone several days. I prefer going ahead. Find Father Gregory and let him know the nuptial mass will take place in two hours' time."

He strode off, leaving them startled. Finally, Lady Ellyn said, "Let me take you to the solar, my lady. Sir Landon, if you will have a few soldiers bring Lady Katelyn's things upstairs."

"Of course." Landon bowed and left the great hall.

The noblewoman instructed for hot water to be brought in order for Katelyn to enjoy a bath. As she accompanied the older woman up the stairs, she caught Bryce smirking. Instantly, the knight's appeal vanished. It was as if Katelyn saw his true colors for the first time. Any trust she had thought about placing in him fled. She'd thought when Landon left, Bryce might become a friend to her. Now, she wanted nothing to do with him.

Within minutes, hot and cold water appeared, brought by a bevy of servants. Lady Ellyn mixed oil into the water and the scent of vanilla permeated the solar. She washed Katelyn's hair and unpacked her things as Katelyn bathed and then wrapped herself in a large bath sheet.

"Sit here, next to the fire," Lady Ellyn instructed. "I'll comb your hair. Oh, my. 'Tis so long and dark. You have beautiful hair, my dear, and your pale skin and green eyes only add to your beauty."

Katelyn enjoyed the luxury of sitting by the fire, something rarely enjoyed at the convent and certainly not in summer. Still, she'd noticed the chill as they'd entered the keep and felt it now. She would be glad for the fire's warmth come evening. The thought of tonight caused her to shiver.

"Is something wrong?"

"Nay," Katelyn said weakly.

Lady Ellyn gave her a knowing look. "Are you worried about your wedding night? Did your mother explain what the marriage bed involved?"

"My mother is dead," she said flatly. "I lived at the Convent of the Charitable Sisters from the time I was five."

"Oh. I suppose 'tis my place to inform you of what is expected. Shall I share with you what I know?"

Katelyn started to tell the noblewoman that Landon had prepared her but didn't think it would be deemed suitable. She merely nodded, hoping more pieces of the puzzle might fall into place.

"The earl will touch you in . . . intimate places." Lady Ellyn paused. "What he does may shock you but you are his by right and must accept whatever he does because it pleases him."

"Like kissing?" she asked, watching the noblewoman blush a bright pink.

"Aye but . . . there is more to it."

"Where should I touch him?" Katelyn asked.

Shock registered on Lady Ellyn's face. "You . . . d-d-don't," she stammered. "Keep your hands by your sides. Do your duty. If you are lucky, you will get with child soon. Men leave their wives alone then." She paused. "Are your courses regular?"

"Aye." Katelyn wondered what they had to do with the conversation. "They usually last six or seven days. Sometimes, eight."

Lady Ellyn said, "Tell him ten," and gave her a tight smile. "Many men refuse to touch a woman during that time."

Dread filled Katelyn. She decided to switch the conversation to something that was more interesting to her.

"Have you been in charge of the domestic duties, my lady?"

"I have. You will now take over for me," Lady Ellyn said sadly.

Katelyn took the woman's hand, realizing it was a surprise for her to suddenly give up her duties without warning. She did not want Lady Ellyn to resent her.

"I know the earl will tell me all I need to know about the estate, my lady, but I will depend upon you to help guide me as I ease into my role as Countess of Northmere. Your knowledge is vastly superior to mine. I'm eager to learn everything you can share with me." Katelyn smiled. "I look forward to being a member of your family. Might I call you Aunt?"

Lady Ellyn squeezed her hand, a pleased look on her face. "I'd like very much for you to think of me as family. Please, call me Ellyn. Aunt is so formal."

"I would be happy to do so. 'Tis a beautiful name."

The noblewoman finished combing Katelyn's hair and then two servants appeared. They helped her dress for her wedding in a gold and cream silk cotehardie. One of the women braided Katelyn's hair in a complicated manner and then placed a golden circlet atop her head.

"Lord Cedric sent it, my lady," the servant said.

"Then I must thank the earl."

The other servant laid out a nightgown for her to wear for her wedding night. "The earl will certainly like this on you, my lady. I will help you remove your wedding finery after the feast and assist you into this. You will look lovely."

The thought sat like a cold lump inside her belly.

Ellyn led her downstairs, where she found Landon waiting for her. He, too, had changed and looked splendid in green and gold. His emerald eyes shone brightly when he caught sight of her.

He kissed her cheek and offered her his arm. "I am happy to escort you to your wedding, Sister. You make a most beautiful bride."

She placed her hand on his forearm, her fingers gripping it as her heart raced. Landon led her from the keep and to a large stone chapel that sat opposite from the keep's doors. People swarmed the inner bailey. Servants. Farmers. Soldiers. Hundreds had gathered to see their liege lord and his intended speak their vows. As she passed by the sea of faces, Katelyn realized that these were soon to be her people. She promised herself to always look after them and see they were taken care of properly.

A priest, who introduced himself as Father Gregory, awaited them. He began the ceremony. Katelyn repeated the vows after the man of God, trying to look her groom in the eye, but found she lacked the courage. She stared instead at his chest. He chuckled at her timidity and placed a ring upon her third finger, repeating after the priest. Father Gregory then led them inside the chapel and conducted mass. At its end, Katelyn found herself being quickly kissed and then pulled along by the earl so that they exited the chapel.

Once they came out into the late summer afternoon, Lord Cedric said, "I did not know you were so shy, my lady."

"I . . . have never spoken wedding vows before," she said, her voice faint.

"Don't worry," the earl told her. "I have. There's nothing to being wed." He gave her a sly smile. "And you have an experienced groom so our wedding night will last well until dawn."

Katelyn thought she might be sick.

She allowed him to lead her back to the great hall. All the trestle tables had been pulled from the walls and benches places next to them. Lord Cedric took her to the dais situated at the front of the room and seated her as workers and soldiers poured into the enormous room. Soon, course after course came from the kitchen. How the cook had managed to accomplish so much in such a short time astounded her. Many toasts were drunk in their honor and then the earl instructed her to go to the solar and ready herself.

Doing as ordered, Katelyn left the great hall. Before she started up the staircase, Landon called her name. She turned, hoping to keep her tears at bay.

"I am across the hall from the solar," he shared. "If you have need of me." He kissed her brow. "Remember, the act isn't something you'll do frequently. Lord Cedric's age will be a factor. The reward is being countess of everything you see."

"I'll remember," she promised. "If I can endure the convent, I can do anything."

"That's my brave girl."

Katelyn walked woodenly to the solar and found the servant waiting for her. The woman had already drawn the bed curtains aside and pulled the bedclothes back. She undressed Katelyn and helped her slip into the beautiful nightgown, embroidered with tiny roses. The queen's seamstress had done well. Katelyn possessed a fine wardrobe. After what she would go through tonight, she would make sure the earl continued to buy her pretty cloth so she could garb herself as the Countess of Northmere should. Mayhap, he might even give her a jewel or two but she didn't relish what she would have to do to receive one.

Finally, she was alone. Katelyn prayed Lord Cedric would drink so much that he would be unable to perform his husbandly duties and then decided she would rather get it over with. Once tonight's mysteries unfolded, she would understand what marriage was about. Knowledge was power. She would take that knowledge and use it and never be frightened of her husband again.

When he finally arrived, she suspected he was drunk from the way he swayed and how carefully he articulated his words.

Words that caused her to go cold.

After greeting her and downing a cup of wine, he stripped off his clothes. Katelyn stared in horror and fascination, having never seen a man unclothed before.

Once his clothing lay in a heap on the floor, he turned to her.

"Get onto the bed," he commanded, his voice suddenly sharp as steel.

She complied, climbing onto the bed and lying on her back, her hands fisted by her side as she remembered Ellyn's instructions. The naked, hairy earl joined her, yanking her to the middle of the bed. His hands went to the neckline of her nightgown and then he rent it in two. The sound of the material tearing caused the blood to pound in her ears. Katelyn wanted to box him soundly but lay still as fear encircled her.

Lord Cedric began to play with her breasts, kneading them over and over, then pinching her nipples. She gasped but did not cry out. Something in his eyes told her that he wanted her to. That alone made her decide not to utter another sound, no matter what happened this night.

He began kissing her then, slobbering all over her mouth and face. His mouth moved down her neck to her breasts, where he licked them. Disgust rose within her as she gripped the bedclothes in both hands. Then he climbed atop her, hovering a moment before he started pushing against the place between where her legs joined. He moved again and again against her and she sensed his frustration building.

"Touch it!" he cried hoarsely. "I must be firm to enter you."

Katelyn looked at what hung between his legs and closed her eyes as she wrapped her fingers around it. It grew for a moment and then became flaccid again.

"Keep trying," her new husband ordered, gritting his teeth. He placed his hand over hers and moved her hand up and down along the small shaft.

She labored for some time but nothing seemed to occur. His anger grew. Even in the dim candlelight, she could see how red his face became. He threw her hand off and pushed against her repeatedly and then growled in fury. Lord Cedric slapped her once, her face stinging as she willed herself not to strike him back.

Before she could ask what she was doing wrong, he scrunched his face as if in pain. Suddenly he collapsed atop her and didn't move.

Katelyn waited to see what he would do next and found herself struggling to breathe. Not having the strength to push him off her, she rocked back and forth until she was able to roll him onto his side. Slipping from the bed, she lifted the candle and brought it next to his face.

She gasped. His eyes stared blankly at her. He was dead.

What would this mean for her?

She was his wife but they had not consummated their marriage. Something told Katelyn that would leave her in limbo. What if they thought she killed him? What should she do?

Remembering that Landon was across the hall, she decided to seek his advice. Opening the door quietly, she could still hear the sounds of merriment faintly wafting up the stairs and along the corridor. Gathering the ruined nightclothes about her, Katelyn saw no one and decided to chance knocking upon Landon's chamber, hoping he had already retired.

She rapped twice against the door. Her brother flung it open immediately. His eyes quickly glanced up and down her, anger filling them.

"Come quickly," she urged, holding her gown together with one hand and grabbing his wrist with her other.

They crossed to the solar and Katelyn shut and latched the door.

"He's dead."

"Dead?" Landon paused. "Did he hurt you? Were you defending yourself?"

"He slapped me once." She held her palm to her face. "The mark will fade."

"Was he able to complete the marriage act?"

"Nay. No matter what I did, his shaft wouldn't stiffen."

Landon thought a moment. "'Twill be better if we say the marriage was consummated, else the Mandevilles will want to nullify it. I signed the contracts with Lord Cedric before the ceremony began. The king already bestowed gold upon you as part of the bridal price. If for any reason your marriage wasn't consummated, it was to go to me. I am happy to hand it over to you."

Katelyn's heart swelled with love for her brother.

"You also were given land. A part of Northmere. Even with a new earl succeeding, that cannot be taken from you. A manor house resides upon it, Katelyn. You wouldn't have to live in the keep. You could live at the manor and have enough to pay servants. Why, you might even wed a man of your choosing this time."

She tamped down her excitement, thinking practically. "The king has already used me once as a pawn. Don't you think he would do so again?"

Her brother shrugged. "I cannot say. But the wealth and land are yours, of that I'm sure. As long as the marriage act was completed. That makes all the difference."

He strode into the bedchamber. Katelyn quickly followed, clutching the torn gown to hide her nakedness. Landon pulled a dagger from his boot and pushed the sleeve up his arm. He sliced a small line across it and dribbled blood onto the sheets.

"This will protect you," he proclaimed. "Stay in the solar the remainder of the night. Try to sleep if you can. Send for Lord Cedric's brother in the morning." His fingers tightened on her shoulders. "Cry if you can. Looked bewildered. Lost. Say how kind your husband was and how tenderly he treated you but make it clear to Sir Rafe that your maidenhead was breached."

Landon led her from the bedchamber and closed the door. "I will ride for Windsor after the funeral mass and inform the king of the tragic events. I'll tell him how traumatized you are and that you need time to heal emotionally. I know Edward and better yet, his queen. Philippa will make sure you aren't rushed into another marriage anytime soon."

"Thank you," Katelyn said. "Wait a few minutes."

She went back into the bedchamber. Finding another, less elaborate nightgown, she changed into it and then took the ripped one to her brother.

"Find a way to dispose of this," she ordered. "If Lord Cedric was to be my gentle lover, we don't need proof of his viciousness."

Landon took the wad of material and kissed her cheek. "I will see you in the morning," he promised. "Stay strong."

She watched him go, latching the door behind him, and then sank into a chair. She would have to give the performance of a lifetime in the morning in order to convince Sir Rafe and Lady Ellyn that her marriage was real.

Katelyn began planning everything to say and do. In detail.

Her future depended upon it.

CHAPTER EIGHT

K ATELYN AWOKE, HER neck stiff and her feet freezing. She sat in a chair next to a fire that had gone cold. She couldn't stomach sleeping in the same bed beside her dead husband and had remained outside the bedchamber all night. Soon, though, a servant would more than likely bring them bread and ale in order to break their fast. Proof would also be sought of the marriage's consummation. After much consideration last night, she'd decided it would be better to be awakened in the bed with a servant as a witness to the fact that Lord Cedric had died in his sleep and that his new wife hadn't been aware of it.

Quickly, she went to the door and removed the latch so that anyone could enter. Steeling herself, she entered the bedchamber but left the door ajar so she would have a warning when someone approached. She drew the bed curtains on the corpse's side of the bed and then came around and climbed into the other side of the bed, pulling the curtain on this side, as well.

Katelyn faced away from the body next to her, burying herself beneath the bedclothes and hoping her feet would warm up soon. Within minutes, she heard the door to the solar open and relaxed her body. With her eyes closed, she started breathing evenly as if still in sleep. The door squeaked faintly as someone pushed it open all the way.

"Here, put the tray down and you may leave. I will awaken the happy couple."

"Aye, my lady."

Katelyn recognized Ellyn Mandeville's voice as the first one who spoke. She heard footsteps receding and kept her breathing steady. Then the bed curtain on Lord Cedric's side eased open.

"Mother of God!" the noblewoman cried out softly.

Playing her role, Katelyn stirred slightly. A moment passed and soft footsteps came around the foot of the bed, slowly drawing aside the curtain next to her. A warm hand touched her shoulder and gently rocked her back and forth.

"Katelyn? Wake up, dear."

She blinked several times and then yawned. "Oh, good morning, Ellyn." She pushed herself up on one elbow, still facing away from the dead earl. "I am so tired. Lord Cedric kept me up half the night."

"Katelyn, let me help you from the bed."

She allowed Ellyn to assist her and she stood. "I should greet Lord Cedric." Turning, she froze as she stared at the wide-eyed corpse on the bed. "Oh. Oh. Dear God in Heaven above . . ." Her voice trailed off.

Ellyn took her elbow and moved her away from the bed. Katelyn shuffled along a moment and then tore away, running to the side where Lord Cedric lay. She stared at her husband a moment and then collapsed atop him. His cold flesh repelled her but she clung to him wordlessly. Her sister-in-law latched on to her arm and forced her away.

"He's . . . he's . . ."

"He's passed on. I know."

She kissed the white cheek and then threw herself at the noblewoman and began sobbing. The tears were all too real. Katelyn had no idea if Landon's plan would work. She clung to Ellyn in true fear.

The noblewoman led her into the solar. "Sit here, Katelyn. I will fetch my husband."

"And my brother," she quickly added. "I need Landon."

"Of course."

Within minutes, both men entered the solar. Ellyn closed the door and locked it. It was obvious by Sir Rafe's face that he had not been informed of the events and realized Ellyn Mandeville was being extremely discreet.

"Tears, my lady?" Sir Rafe shrugged. "'Tis to be expected. It's well known that my brother can be rough in love play. You will grow accustomed to it. In the meantime, I can bear witness that your virgin blood has been spilled and the marriage is now confirmed."

Katelyn raised her face to him. "My husband . . . is dead."

"Dead?" Shocked filled the nobleman's face, then he chuckled. "At least he died doing what made him happy." He looked to Landon, growing serious. "Come with me to verify, my lord."

The two men left the room and appeared moments later. Rafe Mandeville looked deflated.

"I can attest that the marriage was consummated," he said. "Sir Landon, I will see that the monies owed you are paid accordingly."

"And the manor house on the far edge of Northmere?" Landon inquired. "It was also part of the marriage settlement."

Sir Rafe frowned. "Aye, it will also be awarded to the countess. The dowager countess," he corrected himself. "This is a volatile situation."

"You don't want the Scots to know that Lord Cedric is dead," Katelyn said astutely, wiping away her tears.

"Nay. I had intended to send riders out this morning so they could spread the news that the king had sent additional troops to the border and wed one of his cousins to my brother. Word would reach the

Scots sooner rather than later. 'Tis important for our northern neighbors to understand the king has great faith in the families closest to the border, especially marrying one of his own cousins to a Mandeville."

Sir Rafe collapsed into a chair. "I must think on this."

"Shouldn't we send for Father Gregory?" Ellyn asked anxiously. "He must see to Lord Cedric and offer comfort to Katelyn."

The nobleman sprang to his feet. "That's it!" he cried. "I have an answer that will solve our problems."

Katelyn hoped she would play no role in his solution. She longed to go to this manor house that was now her property and spend some time in solitude. Though she realized that Landon would take word back to the king regarding the Earl of Northmere's sudden death, it would take at least a month for him to return and new word to be sent to the far north. Additional time might be required while King Edward decided what was to become of her. Katelyn would relish any time she had alone at her manor house. She resented being used as a pawn by the monarch.

"Sir Landon, fetch my nephew at once—and not a word about the earl's death. I will return with Father Gregory. Wife, lock the door and admit no one except us. I do not want the servants to know." Sir Rafe looked at Katelyn. "My lady, change into what you wore to your wedding."

"Why—"

"Do as I say," he ordered harshly.

Katelyn fell quiet after exchanging looks with her brother, waiting for the men to leave. Then she said to Ellyn, "I don't think I can go back into that room and see my husband like that." She shuddered. "Please, don't make me," she pleaded.

"I will fetch your clothing." Ellyn pushed her into a chair and smoothed her hair. "Wait here."

Her sister-in-law returned with the requested cotehardie and helped her to dress in it again.

"Why do you think Sir Rafe wants me to put on my wedding finery?" Katelyn asked as Ellyn pulled the nightgown from her.

The noblewoman averted her eyes. "Here, let me rebraid your hair. I'll tell you about the daily routine at Northmere while I do so."

Katelyn determined the woman had a good idea as to the answer to the question but chose to let her husband explain. It didn't matter. Katelyn would absorb any information Ellyn gave her. The more she knew about her surroundings, the better.

A rap at the door startled them both. Ellyn went to answer it, only cracking the door slightly. When she saw who stood waiting entrance, she admitted four men and placed the latch on the door once more. Bryce looked curiously about the room, while Father Gregory appeared solemn.

Quickly, Rafe Mandeville explained the situation to the newcomers. The priest gave her a sympathetic glance. Bryce turned aside, covering his mouth, but Katelyn caught the sneer he tried to hide. Once more, she determined not to have any more to do with him. He had shown one face to her on their journey north. Now, he was quite a different man.

"I've decided on the action we should take," Sir Rafe continued. "The best thing is to stay true to the course that began when the king had Lady Katelyn brought north. King Edward sent his cousin to wed the Earl of Northmere." He paused. "That is what she will do. Again."

"You mean for her to wed the new earl?" Landon asked. "Sir Nicholas?"

"Aye," the nobleman confirmed.

This turn of events surprised her. At least she had the manor house. If she didn't like this new husband, she would retreat to her property. The Earl of Northmere would still be wed to the king's cousin. Hopefully, the Scots would be held at bay with this news.

"I think it best for the riders to bear the news that the Earl of

Northmere has married the king's cousin," Katelyn said. "Let the Scots hear that and assume what they will. When time has passed, it can be made known which earl."

"You speak as if you understand politics, my lady," Bryce said, his eyes assessing her in a new light.

She shrugged. "My husband was the earl for many years. The Scots know him and I'm sure they fear him. I know nothing of his son, the new earl, but think it wise to hold back all the facts until a more appropriate time."

"Oh, Nicholas is a fierce warrior," Sir Rafe assured her. "Some might say he is even more clever by half than his father." He gave her an approving glance. "I do agree with you, though. 'Tis shrewd not to reveal all that we know. Let Nicholas settle into his new role. Then it can be made known he has succeeded his father—and is husband to a member of the king's family."

"Has Sir Nicholas returned?" Katelyn asked. "I overheard Lady Ellyn tell you yesterday that he was called away to help a neighbor with a problem. I noticed several soldiers enter the great hall during the wedding feast and wondered if he might be among them."

"Nay, my nephew stayed behind at Ravenwood," Sir Rafe informed her. "Lord Terald fell ill. Nicholas is close with the baron. One of the soldiers told me that Nicholas would return sometime today." He placed his hands on her shoulders. "I can't guarantee when he will arrive at Northmere and do not wish for a delay. Father Gregory will marry you and Nicholas now, by proxy. Bryce can stand in for his brother."

"That . . . can be done?" she asked, bewildered that she could wed and the groom be missing from the ceremony. "We will truly be wed in the eyes of the Church?"

"Aye," Father Gregory assured her. "It happens often within royal families when a pair finds themselves apart and the situation calls for a quick joining together of bride and groom."

"Let's begin, Father," Sir Rafe urged. "Bryce, come stand next to your future sister-in-law."

Katelyn glanced to Landon, who nodded in approval. If she had to wed again, at least it would be to a man much closer to her age this time. Bryce was quite handsome and she hoped his brother, the new earl, might prove pleasing to her eye. Still, anyone had to be better than Lord Cedric. If Nicholas Mandeville would merely show her kindness and be gentle on their wedding night, she would be relieved.

"Wait," Landon said. "Katelyn, remove your ring and give it to me."

She slipped the silver band from her finger and passed it to her brother. Once more, Katelyn uttered the same vows she had spoken less than a day ago, thinking how odd it was to have married a father and then his son—and to have the other son be the one repeating the vows on his brother's behalf. She wondered how her new husband might feel when he arrived home, only to find out he was now the Earl of Northmere.

And a married man.

NICHOLAS LISTENED TO Lord Terald's labored breathing as dawn approached. He'd sent Catherine to bed hours ago, promising he would send for her if the earl worsened. He decided now was that time. Leaving the bedchamber, he found the Ravenwood priest and a servant sitting in the solar.

"Bring Lady Catherine," he told the servant, who left immediately. To the priest, Nicholas said, "It's time, Father."

Nicholas remained where he was and allowed the priest to go in and hear the earl's final confession. After a short while, Catherine arrived, her golden hair hanging loose about her shoulders, dark circles under her eyes.

"Is he . . . oh, I cannot say the words, Nicholas. To lose Favian and now his father so closely together." She began weeping softly.

He embraced her, enjoying the feel of her against him, though he knew she would not commit to him until after the birth of her child. Nicholas led her to a seat and entwined his fingers with hers, hoping that would be of some comfort to her.

Eventually, the priest returned and motioned for them to enter the bedchamber. They did so, each standing on one side of the bed and taking Lord Terald's hands in theirs. They remained that way until his breathing slowed and then finally stopped. Catherine lifted the old man's hand and kissed his knuckles tenderly. Nicholas did the same. This nobleman had been more a father to him than his own. He would miss the earl a great deal.

"I will delay morning mass for a few hours," the priest said. "I'll send servants up to ready the body and have the people of Ravenwood informed of their liege lord's death. That way, all can gather for the funeral mass."

Once he left, Nicholas raised the bedclothes over the old man's face and led Catherine from the room.

"Why don't you rest for a few hours?"

She frowned. "I don't think I could."

"Then I'll send a servant up with something to break your fast. You need to keep up your strength."

Rubbing her belly, she said, "This babe is even more important now. I pray every day and night for it to be a boy. I had wanted to present a grandson to Lord Terald, one that resembled Favian." A tear cascaded down her cheek. "This child could be the heir to Ravensgate."

"I know. Come, let's return to your chamber."

Nicholas took her back and had her lie down. As he left, he passed three servants in the corridor. They entered the solar and he supposed they were the ones who would prepare Lord Terald for burial. He went to the kitchen and asked the cook to have something sent up to Lady Catherine. The woman wiped tears from her face, apologizing.

"No apologies are needed," he said gently. "Lord Terald was beloved by all his people."

Three hours later, Nicholas entered the chapel, Catherine leaning heavily upon him. The building was filled to the brim with workers, servants, and soldiers. He prayed for all of the people of Ravenwood to find solace despite their sorrow and for Catherine to deliver a healthy son come the new year.

Afterward, he saw her back to the keep.

"I am reluctant to leave you," he began.

"You must, Nicholas," she said. "You successfully led our men yesterday but your own home has need of you, especially with Lord Cedric and Bryce gone."

His kissed her fingers. "I will ride over tomorrow and see how you fare."

"All right. If you insist," she said, her mouth turning up in a small smile.

Nicholas went to the stables and saddled Sunset. It was already past the noon hour. He took a shortcut through the woods and then galloped across the meadow toward the castle. Waving to the gatekeeper, he gained admittance and took his horse to the stables. He preferred rubbing down his mount rather than leaving it for a stable hand to do. He gave Sunset more than his usual amount of oats and left the stall.

As he walked toward the entrance, he paused. A woman stood in front of the stall that housed his father's horse, one he'd never seen before. Her cotehardie was of the finest silk, something that he might have seen worn by a lady at the royal court. She had hair as black as night and a tall, willowy figure that included small, rounded breasts and a tiny waist. Nicholas approached her and she dropped her hand from the horse's neck and turned.

He halted in his tracks. The woman was young, probably under a score, and the most beautiful female he'd laid eyes upon. She had startling green eyes and milky white skin. Her rosebud mouth tempted him more than he cared to admit.

"Are you Sir Nicholas Mandeville?" she asked, curiosity written across her delicate features.

"I am, my lady, but you have me at a disadvantage for I know not who you might be," he replied.

She worried her full, bottom lip a moment and a wave of lust rushed through him. He longed to sink his teeth into it.

The woman sighed. "I must inform you that your father is dead, my lord. You are the new Earl of Northmere.

"And I am your wife."

CHAPTER NINE

N ICHOLAS' JAW DROPPED. He was too stunned to speak.

"I am sorry to break such news to you. I know Lord Cedric's death was unexpected."

"Who *are* you?" he demanded.

She gave him a sympathetic look. "I am sorry for your loss, my lord." She looked around and pointed. "There's an empty stall down the way. I sat in it thinking for a long time just now. It would give us privacy for me to tell you everything that has occurred in recent days." Pausing, she added, "I would rather you hear this from my lips. I am finding that others have their own way of viewing events and interpret them differently than I might. Let me share with you what I know and my role in matters before you speak to your uncle or anyone else."

Whoever this noblewoman was, she was savvy.

"I agree," he told her and started for the vacant stall.

When he realized she didn't follow, Nicholas turned and saw her stroke the nose of his Father's horse. It surprised him since it was common knowledge that Lord Cedric's mounts were known for being disagreeable in general. This stranger must have been around Midnight enough to win him over. That made Nicholas believe that she had met his father at Windsor and they'd traveled north together.

Softly, she said, "I know you will be sad about your master's fate, Midnight, but Lord Nicholas will find a new man to ride you. He will treat you well and you will come to trust him."

The young woman kissed the horse then, a sweet gesture that touched Nicholas' heart. Turning away, she caught up to him and led him to the stall she spoke of. They entered and she bent to sit in the hay. He took her elbow and grasped her hand in order to ease her to the ground.

Something occurred from the moment he touched her. Nicholas could see she, too, was affected by it, a puzzled look in her eyes. He glanced down at their joined hands and sensed it was right in a way he couldn't understand. Warmth filled him, along with a feeling that he wished to protect this woman.

Lowering her to the hay, he sat next to her and waited for her to speak.

"I am Katelyn de Blays, my lord, daughter of Lord Adelard de Blays, former Earl of Blackwell."

Her words confused him. "How could your father be a former earl? Unless . . ." His voice trailed off in understanding.

"Aye. My father was accused of treason though I cannot see how. To me and my brother, Landon, he was always good and kind. He placed me in the saddle in front of him before I could walk and we would ride Blackwell together and visit with our tenants. I was only five when he was seized and executed but my heart tells me the full story will never be known."

Sympathy for Lady Katelyn filled him. A traitor got off easily, quickly losing his life. It was the family which remained behind that usually suffered the consequences.

"What happened to you and your brother?" he asked, observing the noblewoman had a sense of calm about her.

"Landon was six when he was taken to London with my father. He was mistreated by the king and rescued by Prince Edward, who now wears the crown. Landon has been with the king all these years and is a member of his royal guard."

Nicholas nodded. "I have heard of Landon de Blays and how his battlefield heroics earned him his knighthood at a tender age."

"My brother searched for me for years and found me recently at the Convent of the Charitable Sisters."

He found himself dumbfounded. "You were a nun?"

She laughed. "I am as far from a nun as you will find, my lord. I am tolerant and kind to others. I enjoy being with people and think laughter is good for the soul." She grew quiet a moment. "I am grateful my brother rescued me."

"The nuns were unkind to you?" Nicholas asked.

"If you call beating and starving me unkind, then I would agree they were."

His heart ached for this beautiful creature being treated so cruelly.

"Oh, I see pity in your eyes, Lord Nicholas. I don't deserve it. What happened to me only made me stronger."

"Where did your brother take you once he discovered your whereabouts?"

"To Windsor Castle. I was there a week in the queen's household as everyone surrounding me tried their best to turn me into a proper lady."

He heard the humor laced in her voice. "And did they succeed, Lady Katelyn?"

"We'll have to see, won't we, my lord?" she countered.

Nicholas enjoyed the way her eyes sparkled. They practically danced with mischief now. In fact, he was enjoying this unusual encounter more than any other he'd had.

"The king sent me north," she continued. "I was to wed the Earl of Northmere when we arrived. I did so yesterday. After our wedding night, I awoke this morning to find my husband had passed on during the night."

Without thinking, he took her hand. "I am so sorry," he murmured. "But you would not be my wife, Lady Katelyn, merely because I am the new earl. You are now the dowager countess." He thought a moment. "If you would like, you could stay at a manor house at Northmere in order to have time to grieve your loss."

She pulled her hand from his and, for a moment, Nicholas felt bereft.

"That manor house belongs to me, my lord. 'Twas part of the marriage contract. As far as grief? I'd barely spoken to your father. I have no plans to grieve for a stranger."

"I see."

Nicholas wondered why she thought she was now married to him. Obviously, the good sisters hadn't instructed her on social customs if she thought she was still a countess, only now wed to the new earl. He needed to tell this woman that he couldn't marry her but it would be hard to do. Already, he was taken by her beauty and sweet disposition. She also possessed an air that spoke to the inner strength she'd referred to. He couldn't imagine the childhood she'd gone through at the nunnery, losing her family at such a young age and then suffering at the hands of the nuns.

"I am afraid you did not become my wife merely because I am the new earl." He paused. "I cannot marry you, Lady Katelyn, though you seem to possess many good qualities."

She frowned. "You are already betrothed?"

"Nay, my betrothed died several years ago. I do have someone I have offered marriage to, though."

Lady Katelyn gave him a sad look. "Do you love this woman?" she asked softly.

Nicholas shook his head. "We are friends. I like her a great deal. Mayhap when we wed, we might grow to love one another someday."

She crossed her arms, hugging herself tightly. "I am so sorry, my lord. You'll have to tell this sweetheart that you cannot marry her. Your uncle has already made the decision for you. Riders were sent out this morning, spreading the news that the Earl of Northmere had married the king's cousin and that King Edward had sent an influx of new troops to Northmere to bolster the castle's defense against the Scots."

Of course, his uncle would have wanted such word to get out as quickly as possible. Lady Katelyn revealing that she was a cousin to the king would make a firm statement of the king's support of his northern lands.

"While I am glad the king made good on his promise and sent more troops to Northmere, I'm afraid he will have to find you a new husband, my lady." Though Lady Katelyn's beauty tempted him, Nicholas still hoped that Catherine would accept his offer after she gave birth to Favian's child.

The lady studied him. "Hmm. Mayhap you are not quite as shrewd as your uncle thought, my lord."

Nicholas pondered what she might mean. Then he recalled her saying that his uncle had already made the decision. Understanding dawned within him, knowing his uncle had been involved. Rafe Mandeville seized opportunities where none existed and twisted them to suit his own purpose.

"News of your father's death has been withheld from all at Northmere," Lady Katelyn said. "Sir Rafe wanted to wait for your arrival today, then Lord Cedric would be found dead and we would hold his funeral mass tomorrow morning."

She held her hand out to him and Nicholas saw the silver band sitting on one of her slim fingers.

"I wore this wedding ring to show the world that I had married your father. This morning, I took it off so that your brother could place it on my hand again." Lady Katelyn looked at him steadily. "You and I were married by proxy a few hours ago, Lord Nicholas. I am your lady wife."

KATELYN'S ADMIRATION FOR Lord Nicholas Mandeville grew as she watched him contain the rage that rippled through his magnificent body. When she confirmed that he was her new husband a few minutes ago, a sense of pride had enveloped her. This man was a man among men—strong and tall, with a keen intelligence written across his beautiful face. She'd never thought a man beautiful before, even after meeting some of the handsome courtiers at Windsor Castle, but this lord of the north seemed like a golden god. His hair shone like the sun on summer wheat, while his deep brown eyes were soulful and sensitive. If she had to be wed, she was glad it was to a man of such quality.

She saw him harness his fury with a determination that defied reason. Katelyn ached for this new earl. And for the woman he cared for. The one he'd thought to wed. Lord Nicholas was bound to a stranger now, for life, and would have to tell a woman that Katelyn suspected he already loved—whether he knew it or not—that he must withdraw his offer of marriage due to circumstances beyond his control.

If this nobleman hated Katelyn, so be it. She would still be the Countess of Northmere and the one to bear Nicholas Mandeville's children. If he wished to go to this other woman for satisfaction, she must let him. Marriage was a legal arrangement between a couple. She would never keep him from the woman who held his heart.

"If I had known you cared for another, my lord, I would have done everything in my power to prevent your uncle from insisting upon this marriage."

Lord Nicholas laughed harshly. "My uncle did exactly as he chose. He's often thought of himself as a second earl to Northmere. I'll see that does not occur in the future." His features softened as he looked at her. "I regret telling you of my interest in another woman, my lady."

"Nay, my lord. I am grateful that you shared something of yourself. I realize we are strangers and now joined to one another by others. Me, by my cousin. You, by your uncle."

"I would speak to my uncle now. Would you accompany me?"

He rose and offered her his hand. Katelyn reluctantly took it. As before, a bolt of energy seemed to be released between them when they touched. It baffled her. It intrigued her.

And it frightened her.

She wondered if he sensed anything. His features remained stoic so she doubted he did. Lord Nicholas brought her to her feet. They returned to the keep in silence. Katelyn had so many questions she wanted to ask him but recent experience had taught her to remain quiet. He accompanied her first to the great hall, where Ellyn came rushing toward them.

"I'm glad you have returned, Nicholas."

He brushed a quick kiss on his aunt's cheek. "I would see Uncle Rafe in the solar. Now," he said firmly.

"Of course."

They left the great hall, Ellyn heading out the door and Nicholas leading Katelyn to the solar.

When they arrived, Katelyn said, "Your father is in the bedchamber if you wish to see him."

"I don't," he said flatly.

Immediately, she wondered about the relationship between the two men. After all, it was Bryce who had accompanied his father to court, not Nicholas. Katelyn wondered why things might have been strained between father and son and if Lord Cedric had preferred Bryce for some reason, though having now met both sons she couldn't imagine Nicholas not being the favorite.

Sir Rafe entered the solar without knocking, Bryce and Ellyn trailing behind him. Landon had already ridden out this morning for Windsor, deciding not to stay for the funeral. For a moment, Katelyn wished her brother could be here to meet her new husband and give her his impression of him.

"Now that you've returned, we can let the people know of Cedric's death," Rafe began.

"And also of my marriage?" Nicholas asked, his tone colder than a winter's day.

"That, too."

"What gave you the right to marry me off, Uncle?" demanded Nicholas, his voice soft yet dangerous. "Making a decision only the Earl of Northmere should have made."

"It was what your father would have wanted," Rafe insisted. "He was giddy beyond belief when he arrived from Windsor, thrilled that the king had sent his beloved cousin to wed him."

"I wouldn't say beloved," Katelyn interjected. "Though I am King Edward's cousin, I don't know that I mean much to him—other than being used as a pawn."

While Rafe's eyes sparked with anger at her interruption, she saw her new husband hid a smile.

"Nevertheless, the king wanted you to marry a Mandeville. You have now done so," Rafe said.

"Twice," she retorted.

Sir Rafe's mouth twisted. "Lady Katelyn, mayhap you should excuse yourself from this discussion," he suggested.

"I think my new wife should remain," Nicholas said firmly. "Since I am the Earl of Northmere, we will abide by my desire. Lady Katelyn remains."

He took a seat. "I had already planned to wed, Uncle," Nicholas began.

"Who?" Rafe asked, surprise in his voice.

"Catherine."

"Catherine Savill? Why, she already has another man's babe growing inside her, Nephew. That would have been disastrous."

Katelyn wondered who this woman truly was and why Nicholas would have wanted to wed her under such circumstances.

"I think not. Catherine is beautiful and intelligent. I would be happy to call a babe fathered by Favian my own."

Now, Katelyn was aching to ask who Favian Savill might be to Nicholas but she held her tongue. She would find out later, mayhap from Nicholas himself.

"You'll have to tell her you've made other plans," huffed Rafe.

"You mean that *you* made other plans for me, Uncle," replied Nicholas, and Katelyn had to hide her amusement at the older man's obvious discomfort.

"I've already sent out riders to let everyone—especially the Scots— know that the Earl of Northmere has wed a woman who is a member of the royal family," Rafe said. "And think of it, Nicholas. Lady Katelyn might already be with child. We might already have a new heir to Northmere on the way."

"I think not, Uncle." Nicholas steepled his fingers. "If Lady Katelyn conceived a child on her wedding night, as so often happens, it could be a girl. If she gives birth to a son, that child would be my half-brother. As a younger brother to me, he would *not* be heir to Northmere. Nay, I would accept nothing but my own flesh and blood as my heir, not another son of my father's flesh."

Katelyn held her breath for a moment. She could tell them all now that the marriage had not been consummated last night. That would easily solve the problem—but she didn't want to be caught in a lie. With Landon gone, she had no champion in her corner to help defend the choice she'd made.

"I will not couple with Lady Katelyn until at least a month has passed and I know that her womb is empty of my father's seed," proclaimed Lord Nicholas. "I realize that if I asked for an annulment, it would be viewed as a rejection not only of Lady Katelyn—but of the king himself. I am not only the new Earl of Northmere but will be the acknowledged leader of the northern barons. Alienating the king is the last thing I would do. I will treat him—and his cousin, my wife—with the utmost respect."

Nicholas stood and came toward her. Taking her hands, he said, "My lady, you are most lovely and charming beyond words."

Katelyn sensed her cheeks heating at his compliment—and at his nearness.

"Because of that," he continued, "I do not want to be tempted by your presence. I will escort you to the manor house you own. You are to remain there for the next few weeks. Only then, if you are not with child, will I choose to couple with you and make this a true marriage."

CHAPTER TEN

NICHOLAS RELEASED HIS wife's hands and turned to his uncle. "Spread the word that my father has passed. I want the people of Northmere to gather for the funeral mass tomorrow morning. Send Father Gregory to the great hall. I'd like a word with him." He paused. "And Uncle, I am not ready yet to announce my own marriage."

Rafe Mandeville left the solar, a grim expression on his face.

"Aunt, Lady Katelyn will need servants to pack her things. I'll arrange for them to be carried to the manor house after mass tomorrow."

"Should I select a few servants to accompany her, my lord?" Ellyn asked.

"Aye. She'll need one to cook for her and another to clean." Nicholas thought a moment. "A third to help her dress and care for her hair."

Katelyn snorted. "My lord, I've been dressing myself for years now and think I know how to comb and braid my own hair. I doubt I would need a servant strictly for that." She looked to Ellyn. "I don't want to inconvenience you. I really don't wish to take any servants away from the keep where they are needed. I assure you that I will be fine on my own."

"You are the Countess of Northmere," Nicholas stated. "You must begin to think like one."

Katelyn sighed. "It's difficult to change my thinking overnight, my lord. I have always been no one of account. I may possess a grand title now—but I still feel that way."

Nicholas heard the hurt in her voice that she tried to hide and thought of all the lonely years she must have spent in the convent with no family and no one to comfort her. He couldn't imagine a small child ripped away from everyone and everything she'd known and placed in a cold, forbidding place. Once more, a surge of protectiveness toward her overwhelmed him. He wanted to keep Katelyn safe and let her know she was somebody.

To him.

Instead, he dismissed his feelings and brusquely said to his aunt, "Choose two servants for Lady Katelyn's sojourn at the manor house. They will remain with her throughout the month. Have any necessary supplies sent over, including food for five. I will stop in the training yard and select two knights who will exclusively live with and guard her during this time."

"Of course, my lord," Ellyn said, lowering her eyes in deference to him. "I will have the servants pack and take Katelyn's things to another chamber, as well as have yours placed in the solar."

"Nay," Nicholas said. "That can wait." Looking to Katelyn, he added, "I would not want to displace you tonight, my lady. Remain here. I can move into the solar tomorrow once you are gone. For now, I have things to do but I will return in time for the evening meal."

Nicholas left the solar and went straight to the great hall, where Father Gregory awaited him. They spoke briefly about Lord Cedric's death and he told the priest not to reveal that he'd performed a marriage ceremony between Nicholas and Katelyn until given permission to do so. Nicholas left and stopped at the yard where Northmere's soldiers were exercising. He spied the two soldiers he had in mind, Sir Albert and Sir Gerald. They sparred with one another. Once they came to a halt, he signaled them to join him.

When they arrived, he said, "You are two men that I trust implicitly. I have a mission for you. Lady Katelyn will be residing in the manor house on the edge of Northmere for the next month. You will be my eyes and ears, as well as my sword and shield. You are to guard the lady with your lives and see no harm comes to her."

"Aye, my lord," the knights responded in unison.

"She will travel there after mass tomorrow so I wish for you to accompany her then. I will visit each day to see how she fares." Though he hadn't planned to do so, the words had come spontaneously to him. Nevertheless, the idea pleased him. It would be an interesting way to get to know his new wife, away from the prying eyes of others, especially his uncle.

"You do us a great honor, my lord," Sir Albert said.

"Will Lord Cedric accompany her?" asked Sir Gerald.

Nicholas remembered that word about Lord Cedric's death was just now reaching those on the estate and said, "My father has passed. Lady Katelyn will go into seclusion for a month in order to grieve his death."

"We are sorry for your loss," Sir Gerald said. "Albert and I will make sure Lady Katelyn stays safe as she mourns."

"Thank you. You may return to your training."

Nicholas spoke to no one else before he reached the stables. He saddled Sunset, eager to be away from the castle's residents before others knew about Cedric Mandeville's death. He didn't want to deal with people telling them how sorry they were.

Nicholas wasn't sorry at all.

All his life, his father had treated his elder son with disdain. No matter what Nicholas did, it never was good enough for Cedric. At the same time, his father lavished praise upon a lazy, worthless Bryce. Nicholas could never understand the favoritism shown to the younger son, one who seemed lacking in so many ways. It was true that Nicholas was much more serious than Bryce and demanded excellence from others. Nicholas expected much from himself and the same from those around him. If his father didn't like that, it didn't matter any longer. Cedric Mandeville was dead.

Nicholas would now run Northmere as he saw fit.

With his wife.

As he rode toward Ravenwood, conflict churned within him. While he felt the pull of responsibility to Catherine, he was torn by the sudden yearnings he experienced for Katelyn. He supposed it was good that he desired her. His uncle could have wed him to an ugly woman. Thank the Heavens that Katelyn was not only beautiful but intelligent. She had not been a part of the nobility for long but Nicholas could see that she would make a good countess. He saw in her both curiosity and kindness, an interesting mix. He hoped they might create a true partnership and complement each other as they ran different aspects of Northmere together. As friends. And lovers.

Arriving at Ravenwood, he handed Sunset off to a stable hand and strode toward the keep. He found Catherine sitting near the fire in the great hall.

A smile broke out on her beautiful face. "Nicholas! What are you doing back so soon? You've only been gone a few hours. Come, sit with me. I'll have wine brought."

"Nay, Catherine. We must talk."

He took the seat next to her. "Much has happened since I left you. When I arrived home, I discovered that my father had returned from the south."

"I hope he had a pleasant journey and that the king provided the promised soldiers to him."

"King Edward did just that—and sent him home with a bride, as well. They wed yesterday afternoon upon their arrival."

Surprise lit her eyes. "My goodness. I didn't think about your father ever marrying again."

"The king sent his own cousin, Lady Katelyn de Blays, to be joined in wedlock to a Mandeville as a statement to the Scots," Nicholas explained.

Catherine nodded. "That is a clever move on the king's part. Uniting the Mandevilles with the crown shows his strong support for Northumberland. Do you like this new stepmother?" she teased.

"The tale grows stranger," he said, reluctant to share the rest. "My father died sometime during the night."

"Oh, Nicholas!" She placed her hand on his arm and squeezed gently. "I am so sorry to hear that. I know you weren't close to Lord Cedric but it still must have been a shock for you—and his bride."

"The shock came when I found out that my uncle wed me to Lady Katelyn by proxy once he learned Father died." Nicholas swallowed. "That means we cannot marry, Catherine. I'm sorry."

He saw both regret and relief cross her face and a wistfulness filled him for what never would be.

"My promise to you will not be broken, though. I pledge to take care of you now and in the future."

"How, Nicholas?" she asked. "I finally received word from my father after you left today. He said if my babe is a girl, I'm to return to my family with her. He will then arrange a new marriage for me." Her lips pursed in distaste. "If I birth a son, I will remain at Ravenwood to raise the heir. Even then, I'm sure the king will name a man for me to wed to hold Ravensgate in trust for my son."

He knew her words to be true. Since he was no longer free to wed Catherine, a new husband would be found for her. King Edward could not leave an estate so near the Scottish border without a liege lord for long.

"Come home with me now, Catherine. I would like to have you present at Father's funeral mass, which will be tomorrow morning."

She hesitated. "Are you sure this new wife of yours won't mind?"

He chuckled. "I believe you'll actually like her," Nicholas shared.

"That sounds intriguing. All right. I will come to Northmere with you. Let me pack a few things."

"I'll see that Sunset is saddled to a cart since you can't ride in your condition. I'll be waiting for you outside the keep."

Half an hour later, Catherine sat beside him. He'd promised to return her to Ravenwood the next day. As they set out, though, a part of Nicholas felt guilty.

As if he betrayed Katelyn by bringing Catherine to Northmere.

KATELYN DECIDED TO keep to her chair in the corner of the solar as a flurry of activity ensued. First, four male and three female servants arrived. All seven entered the solar. Minutes later, the men came out, bearing the earl's body, wrapped in linen. The women appeared soon after, carrying the bedclothes away. Katelyn was glad she would not have to sleep on them tonight, knowing Lord Cedric had died while lying in them.

New servants arrived with fresh bedclothes. Others came and carted away the dead nobleman's clothing, their arms piled high with clothing and boots. A few soldiers had been dispatched and took his armor and weapons. She wondered where all of these items would go. She guessed the trunks were left behind so that Nicholas would have a place to store his possessions.

Lady Ellyn had supervised the proceedings. As things calmed down, she brought two women to Katelyn. She recognized them from helping her yesterday before her wedding to Lord Cedric.

"This is Dorinda, my lady. She helped dressed your hair yesterday and will perform personal tasks for you, as well as help keep the manor house clean."

Katelyn smiled at the dark-haired woman, who looked to be a

score and ten, and then Ellyn indicated the second servant, slightly built and with light brown hair. "Lucy will also help with the cleaning and is a good cook. They will make your stay go smoothly."

"Thank you. Would you be able to pack my things?" Katelyn asked. "Please leave out a nightdress for sleep tonight and something appropriate for me to wear to Lord Cedric's funeral mass tomorrow."

"We will take care of it, my lady," Dorinda said. "Both Lucy and I are pleased to accompany you during your mourning period."

Katelyn bit her tongue to keep from laughing. Grieving was the last thing on her mind. Moving to the manor house meant freedom to her. She would indulge in long walks. Sit under a tree and soak up the sunshine. Sing. Laugh. Eat. Sleep. This respite from the castle meant everything to her.

"I appreciate you coming to stay with me," Katelyn said solemnly.

"We'll start filling your trunks now, my lady," Lucy said.

Ellyn excused herself, while the servants went into the bedchamber. Katelyn sat contentedly, breathing easily. Then something caught her eye. She looked to the door Ellyn had neglected to shut and, for a brief moment, saw a girl. Before Katelyn could speak, the girl whirled and was gone. Quickly, she rose and hurried to the hallway, where she saw the girl lingering at a doorway. Then she ducked inside a chamber. Katelyn heard the door shut.

"You must be Bethany," she murmured to herself, thinking she was more young woman than girl.

Katelyn had forgotten that Bryce told her Lord Cedric had a daughter, the youngest of his three children. Why hadn't the girl come to the wedding and feast? Brimming with curiosity, Katelyn went to the door Bethany had scampered through and knocked.

A servant she hadn't seen before answered, a wary look on her face.

"May I visit with Bethany? I am Lady Katelyn Mandeville."

The servant looked shocked then regained her composure. Quietly, she said, "You know . . . that she's . . . touched in the head?"

That explained the daughter of the household's absence from the proceedings.

"I am eager to make her acquaintance," Katelyn said. "Do you care for her?"

The servant smiled. "I do. I'm Mary, my lady. Please, come in. You'll find Lady Bethany simple but very sweet."

Katelyn entered the large bedchamber and saw Bethany on the floor. A doll sat beside her, while a kitten rested in her lap. Katelyn made her way to Bethany and crouched next to her.

"I never had a doll. Or a kitten." She gave the girl a warm smile. "I wish I'd had both. You are very lucky."

Bethany gazed up silently at her. The girl appeared about ten and five and had the same golden hair her two brothers possessed. Her eyes were blue, though, where both sons' were brown.

"No doll?"

"No doll," Katelyn repeated, thinking Bethany's language must be limited. She would speak to her with fewer words than she usually used in conversation and hope that Bethany would understand. "No playthings."

"Ever?"

"Ever," she confirmed. "I had chickens."

"Chickens? Cluck. Cluck, cluck, cluck."

"They do cluck," Katelyn encouraged. "I named my chickens."

Bethany giggled.

"I named my goats, too."

Bethany laughed heartily. "You milk?"

"I did milk them," Katelyn confirmed. "I'll show you how if you'd like."

The girl nodded and stroked her kitten.

"Who is that?" she asked.

"Kit."

"Greetings, Kit." Katelyn brushed her finger against the top of the kitten's head. Immediately, purring began.

"Good. Soft. Be nice."

"I will," Katelyn promised.

Bethany stared at her. "Who?"

"I am your brother's new wife. Katelyn."

"Kate-lyn," Bethany tried out.

"Aye. Katelyn."

Bethany thought a moment. "Nicholas?" she asked eagerly.

Katelyn nodded. "I did wed Nicholas." She saw no reason to mention she had also wed their father. It might confuse the girl.

"Nicholas nice." Bethany frowned. "Bryce. Not nice." Her bottom lip stuck out in a pout.

Her words affirmed what Katelyn thought. Even this simple girl knew Bryce wasn't what he portrayed to the world. She wondered if Bethany had been born this way or if something had caused her speech to become limited.

"Father dead," Bethany proclaimed.

"Aye. Nicholas is now the earl."

"I . . . go solar?" Bethany asked hopefully.

"Of course," Katelyn reassured her. "Were you looking for your brother earlier?"

The girl nodded. "Not go before." She brightened. "Go now."

"Your brother will be happy for you to come visit him. Families gather in the solar. You are family, Bethany." Katelyn pointed to herself and back to Bethany. "*We* are now family."

Bethany's eyes widened. She reached out and touched Katelyn's cotehardie. "Pretty."

"Would you like to wear something like this?"

The girl beamed. "Aye! Aye! Aye!"

"Then we'll make that happen."

Katelyn remained with Bethany several hours, drawing her out as they played with Kit and the doll. Mary watched them, smiling with approval. Katelyn didn't know how much time had passed until a servant appeared with a tray of food.

"'Tis time for the evening meal, Lady Katelyn. This is for Lady Bethany."

Katelyn touched Bethany's hair and stroked it a moment. "I must leave now. We'll play again soon."

Bethany threw her arms around Katelyn and hugged her tightly. Katelyn wrapped her arms around the girl, happiness filling her. She released her and allowed Mary to assist her to her feet.

"Does she never come to the great hall?"

"Nay, my lady. It upsets her too much to be around so many people. We do go out and about, though. Walk around the keep and the grounds. Lady Bethany enjoys being outside, no matter what the weather." The servant paused. "Pardon me for saying so, but you're quite good with her, my lady. She's taken to you."

"I don't know when I've enjoyed myself more," Katelyn replied. "I will be staying at the manor house for a few weeks. Could you bring her to visit me?"

"She'd like that but it's very far away. Too far for us to walk. If she's to come, Lord Nicholas would need to bring her. Lady Bethany enjoys riding with him."

"I'll ask the earl to bring her. Thank you, Mary."

Katelyn left, wishing she could do as Bethany did and eat from a tray in the solar. Still, her husband had made a point of telling her he'd return for the evening meal. She didn't want him to come looking for her. She knew in a great household, as Northmere was, that appearances were important.

Making her way down the long, stone staircase, she could hear noise coming from the great hall. She entered and saw the trestle tables had been removed from the walls and benches placed next to them as people began seating themselves. Katelyn headed toward the dais, a brave smile on her face to show Lord Nicholas how confident she was in front of so many. Her smile faded as she approached.

Nicholas sat in the center of the dais, conversing with a beautiful, blond woman seated to his right. Instinct told her who this woman was.

Katelyn went and stood in front of the couple. "Greetings. You must be Lady Catherine. I am Katelyn Mandeville."

Chapter Eleven

KATELYN WATCHED LADY Catherine carefully and saw no guile in the noblewoman's eyes. Instead, she beamed at Katelyn and reached out to her. Katelyn took her hand.

"Oh, it is lovely to meet you, Lady Katelyn." Her words seemed as genuine as the smile that lit her glowing face.

"I, too, am pleased to meet our closest neighbor." Katelyn squeezed Lady Catherine's hand briefly and released it.

Nicholas rose and helped her to the dais. Before he could seat her on his left, Lady Catherine stopped him.

"You can't sit between us, Nicholas. You'll spend the entire meal leaning back so that Lady Katelyn and I can visit with one another. I'm afraid you might starve because we'll keep you from your food." Catherine Savill held out a hand. "Won't you take Nicholas' seat, my lady?"

"Thank you." Katelyn sat, wondering what her husband had said about her to this woman as a servant placed a trencher before them and filled it with meat and vegetables.

"If you're going to ignore me during the meal, I might as well eat with my men." He inclined his head and retreated to the left side of the room, where tables filled with soldiers had begun to dine.

"I hope you don't mind me chasing your husband away," Lady Catherine said in hushed tones. "He told me of your marriage and that, for now, it is not public knowledge."

"Lord Nicholas may do whatever he likes," Katelyn said stiffly, wanting to warm to this friendly woman and yet holding back for some reason.

The noblewoman studied her a moment. "You are most beautiful. I've never seen eyes so vivid. They are remarkable with your raven hair." She cocked her head. "I do believe you must be very intelligent. Nicholas told me I would like you and he knows I don't suffer fools. I hear you came from court before your marriage. You have come a long way, only to marry twice in two days."

Katelyn found Lady Catherine's openness refreshing and began to relax in her presence. Catherine Savill radiated good will and amiability.

"I was barely at court a week," she confided. "My father lost his head in a plot against the monarchy when I was a small child. I grew up in a convent where the silence was deafening. All I wanted to do was laugh and play but the good sisters had other ideas."

Lady Catherine's eyes widened. "That sounds horrible," she said bluntly.

"It was." Katelyn shrugged. "I made the best of it."

Catherine placed a hand over Katelyn's. "I'm sure you did. You must be resourceful and resilient. You will definitely be an asset to Nicholas and Northmere."

Katelyn felt their conversation could not progress until she asked about what stood between them. "Are you sorry I came to Northumberland? That you have lost Nicholas to me?"

"I suppose that's a fair question. I know he must have told you that he'd offered marriage to me. Nay, I'm not unhappy at all. In fact, I wish to become your friend." Catherine looked at her hopefully. "I have four sisters and have been lonely without the company of females ever since I came to Ravenwood, since Favian's mother passed on many years ago."

"Favian?"

Catherine's features softened, making her even more radiant. "Oh, Favian was my husband. He and Nicholas were closer than brothers. They fostered and fought together. Favian asked Nicholas to watch over me before he died. I think Nicholas offering to marry me was his way of keeping that promise to his best friend."

"So, you do not love Nicholas?"

Catherine shook her head. "I love him as my friend. As I would a brother. But, he is not the one for me. No one could ever replace Favian in my heart." She rubbed her slightly rounded belly. "Unless this one does. I have a feeling, boy or girl, that my happiness will revolve around raising Favian's child." She grew serious. "I am no threat to you, Lady Katelyn. As I said, I am open to friendship with you. I fervently hope you will bring happiness to Nicholas."

The statement surprised Katelyn. "Is he unhappy? He projects confidence and strength."

"Nicholas is perfect in everything he does. He is the best swordsman and rider in all of the north. He is loyal and dedicated and full of vitality." Catherine sighed. "For some reason, though, Lord Cedric never praised or encouraged him. Never gave him a crumb of respect. Belittled him. Doubted him. The more he spoke against Nicholas, the harder Nicholas drove himself. The earl always preferred Bryce for some reason. It drove a wedge between the brothers that remains to this day."

Her words startled Katelyn. "Didn't Nicholas go to war with his father and the other men of Northmere?"

"He did," Catherine confirmed. "From all accounts, both what I heard from our Ravenwood men and Favian, Nicholas distinguished himself daily on the battlefield. He is a superb soldier."

"And yet his father never appreciated him."

"Lord Cedric was . . . a difficult man," Catherine shared. "In many ways. I believe Nicholas will be a better earl for the people of North-mere and an even stronger leader in Northumberland. He will command respect."

Katelyn only wished she could tell Catherine just how difficult Cedric Mandeville had been behind closed doors. Katelyn had offered numerous prayers of thanksgiving to the Virgin for the earl's timely death. If she'd had to submit to him on a nightly basis, her life would have become a nightmare, far worse than anything she'd suffered at the convent. By his words and actions, she believed her new husband to be nothing like his father and hoped that when they finally coupled, he would be considerate.

The two women chatted amiably throughout the entire meal and decided to continue their conversation upstairs. Nicholas offered to escort them to the solar but Katelyn waved him away. After hours of talk and a few cups of wine, Katelyn knew more about Northmere than she'd dreamed possible and found she enjoyed Catherine Savill's company quite a bit.

Dorinda knocked and entered the solar. "May I help you undress for bed, my lady?"

"Oh, it's grown late," Catherine said. "I should go to my bed-chamber."

"Must you, Catherine?" Katelyn asked. They had quickly begun using their Christian names in a show of friendship. "I am . . . reluctant to sleep alone . . . in there." The thought of climbing into the bed where Lord Cedric had died bothered her more than she would have thought.

"Would you like me to stay?" Catherine asked.

"Aye."

When Catherine nodded in agreement, Katelyn asked Dorinda to bring Lady Catherine's things to the solar. The servant helped both women undress and even in bed, they talked until Katelyn found herself growing hoarse.

"You need your rest, Catherine. Go to sleep," she ordered.

It comforted her when, as they lay there, Catherine reached out and took her hand. Katelyn fell asleep, happy she had made a new friend.

Her first ever.

NICHOLAS WANTED TO head to the training yard. Instead, he went to the records room where Lewis, his bailiff, awaited him. Numbers had never been Nicholas' strong suit and he dreaded the encounter. He'd spent several hours with the Ravenwood bailiff yesterday after he'd escorted Catherine home from Northmere directly after the funeral mass. With Lord Terald and Favian now gone, Nicholas believed he should take a more active role in helping manage the affairs of Ravenwood. Once Catherine's babe came, the status would change. For now, Nicholas wanted to do as much as he could to help keep his neighbor's estate thriving. He owed that much to Favian and Lord Terald.

Still, he wondered how much time he would be able to devote to Ravenwood now that he was earl of the largest estate in Northumberland. His life had turned upside down the moment he learned of his father's death and his marriage to Lady Katelyn.

He smiled as he thought of her. She had certainly charmed Catherine, who'd sung Katelyn's praises the entire way back to Ravenwood. Already, the two women seemed fast friends. He supposed it was good for them both. Catherine had been lonely at Ravenwood, with no female companionship, and even lonelier since Favian's untimely death. Katelyn, he suspected, had never had a friend. Nicholas thought Catherine would be a good influence on his new wife.

Wondering how she fared at the manor house, he decided he would ride out after his meeting with Lewis and check on her. He had mentioned visiting her daily, though Katelyn knew nothing about that. Nicholas would use the visit to her as an excuse if things proved too excruciating with Lewis and he wished to cut their meeting short.

The bailiff greeted him warmly. "It will be a pleasure to work with you, my lord. You remind me of your beloved mother so much. She took an active role in studying my ledgers and offering advice. I am sure you will manage the estate superbly."

Nicholas laughed. "Only with your heavy involvement, Lewis. I have much to learn about the management of Northmere. I've trained to be a soldier my entire life and that is all I know. Mayhap, you should start slowly. Save the numbers for later. Simply tell me about my estate."

With that, Lewis led him through what activities occurred throughout the year and why those tasks happened when they did. The various plantings and harvests he understood because of their relationship to the weather and different seasons, but Nicholas became more interested when talk turned to livestock. Lewis also discussed various jobs held by men and women across Northmere. It surprised him how many people lived and worked here beyond the tenants, soldiers, and servants. The estate had carpenters. Blacksmiths. Ditchers. A cordwainer. And that didn't include the men he was familiar with who worked on behalf of Northmere's soldiers, such as the atilliator and armorer. He pledged to himself to get to know everyone on his property, no matter how long it took.

"You are a fount of knowledge, Lewis. Our talk has been fascinating."

The steward smiled. "You father never seemed very interested in estate matters. He was all about war. That's why I was pleased your mother took such an interest. Mayhap your own wife, when you marry, will follow in her footsteps."

Nicholas could see Katelyn becoming captivated with how an estate ran. Her natural inquisitiveness would come in handy. He would enjoy pooling their knowledge at the end of the day in order to make Northmere flourish. While he knew the estate's workers to be competent, Nicholas wanted more than that. He wanted his people to enjoy what they did.

"I think this is enough for me to take in for today. I am counting on you, Lewis, to guide me as I grow to learn all I can about my property."

Nicholas excused himself and found they'd spoken so long, the noon meal was already in progress. He thought it might be a good idea to go upstairs and eat with Bethany. The last few days had been busy ones and he didn't want to neglect her. Passing through the kitchen, he grabbed a small round of cheese and used his baselard to slice a few pieces. He tore off a hunk of bread and ate both as he made his way upstairs. It would hold him for now. Reaching Bethany's chamber, he entered quietly so as not to disturb her. Sudden noise often distracted or frightened her so he was always careful not to surprise her.

Her eyes lit up when she saw him. "Nicholas! You came!" She set aside her apple and ran to him, hugging him tightly.

"How have you been?" he asked. "Has Kit been behaving?"

"Kit is good. A good cat. I love Kit."

He grinned. "That's very good, Bethany. You said a lot of words."

"I should . . . talk more. I try. Hard."

"You are doing very well." He kissed the top of her head.

She smiled. "Thank you. I go play now. With Kit."

Bethany returned to the kitten and picked up a length of yarn. She wiggled it in the air and the kitten danced around, her paws slapping at it.

Nicholas came to stand next to Mary. "She normally doesn't put so many words together. I am pleased to hear not only that she's speaking more but that she's aware she is. That's good progress,

Mary."

"It's all thanks to Lady Katelyn," the servant replied.

"Lady Katelyn knows Bethany?" Nicholas wondered when they had met.

"Aye. She spent hours with Lady Bethany. They played and talked. The countess drew her out unlike anyone ever has. Even you, my lord. After her visit, Lady Bethany has spoken more and strung more words together."

It pleased him beyond measure that Katelyn had spent time with Bethany. His sister was precious to him.

"The countess told me she was going to stay at the manor house and asked if I could bring Lady Bethany to visit her. I told her it was too far for us to walk but that I would see if you might take your sister along with you."

"I can do that, Mary. Not today. Though I am on my way to visit Lady Katelyn, I'd like to make sure she's settled in before I bring Bethany along."

"Of course, my lord. Please give her my best. The countess has a kind heart."

"I will."

Nicholas left the keep, his heart light. He saddled Sunset and walked the horse from the stables, encountering Bryce as he emerged into the sunshine.

"Off to visit your pretty new wife?" his brother asked.

He glanced around and saw no one within hearing distance. "Remember, I'm not ready to claim the marriage yet."

Bryce snorted. "At least you had the good sense to send her away so none of the men would be sniffing around her. You should have seen how she drew them to her at court. Like flies to honey. Katelyn de Blays is quite the beauty. You are a fortunate man, Brother."

"She is now Katelyn Mandeville," Nicholas said evenly, containing his temper. Bryce always baited him. Too often, Nicholas allowed his brother to get under his skin.

"Of course. Please send her my best. Nay, on second thought? I think I will also visit her soon."

"That isn't necessary," he quickly said. "Katelyn wants to spend some time in solitude. She's had many changes in her life these past few days."

Bryce smirked at him. "You mean you don't want me to spend time with her. She preferred me to Father. She probably still prefers me—even to you."

He clenched his hands but Nicholas didn't raise one as he wished to. He wished Bryce would leave Northmere. It was in his power to exile him, now that he was the earl, but he refused to be petty.

But if his brother tried to pursue Katelyn in any way, Nicholas would make no promise as to what he might do to him, regardless of their shared blood.

"Good day, Bryce," he said curtly.

He mounted Sunset and rode across the bailey, seething inside, though he kept his thoughts from his face. With a wave to the gatekeeper, Nicholas rode out, passing the workers harvesting the summer wheat. He would make sure to spend some time observing the winnowing and tying next month, having never seen the process before. After listening to Lewis, Nicholas knew he had much to learn in order to be the kind of earl he wanted to be for his people.

As he drew close to the manor house, he came across Albert on horseback and stopped.

"Just riding the perimeter, my lord. Gerald and I decided to alternate doing so on horse and on foot. Best to never fall into any kind of pattern."

"Good. Did the move yesterday occur smoothly?"

"Aye. One wagon brought Lady Katelyn's trunks, while another two brought provisions for the larder and some cleaning supplies. The manor hasn't been used in many years and was dusty beyond belief."

"All seems well on your patrols?"

Albert nodded. "Everything's fine, my lord."

"I'll see you later."

Nicholas rode on and arrived at the manor. He greeted Gerald, who stood watch outside.

"Good to see you, my lord," the knight greeted. "Thank you again for tasking Albert and me with guarding the countess. She is most delightful."

He nodded, thinking that Katelyn seemed to be bewitching everyone from servants to soldiers to his family.

And him.

Nicholas entered the open door of the manor and inhaled the clean scent that permeated the air. Obviously, the servants his aunt sent had been hard at work. He turned to his right and entered what he thought of as the little great hall. It held half a dozen oak tables, each seating ten people. A woman near him hummed as she scrubbed the floor, down on her hands and knees. He walked toward her to ask where the countess might be. As he reached her, she righted herself and brushed an arm against her forehead.

It was Katelyn.

Chapter Twelve

"**M**Y LADY, WHAT on earth are you doing?" he admonished.

She gave him a stunning smile that made him grow weak in the knees. "I am almost finished cleaning the floors of my great hall, my lord. I cannot wait to spread the rushes across and sprinkle them with herbs."

He latched on to her elbow and pulled her to her feet. "You are a countess, my lady. Not a servant."

Her brow wrinkled in confusion. "I don't understand. You seem put out with me. What have I done to displease you?"

"You are not meant to labor this way." Without thinking, he rubbed his thumb against a smudge of dirt on her cheek.

Her small intake of breath and wide eyes caused him to freeze. Then his palm cupped her face. "You have servants for this kind of back-breaking work. I don't mind you weaving tapestries or making candles but you aren't meant—"

"I'll do as I please, my lord." She stepped back, throwing off his arm. "Is this not my house?" she demanded.

He saw anger sparking in her eyes. "It is."

"Then I may do whatever I want in it. If I choose to clean my great hall or burn it down while I dance naked in it, it is my right to do so," she said stubbornly, fisted hands going to her waist.

Nicholas' mouth went dry at the thought of her twirling in the midst of the burning flames, fire warming her bare skin as shadows played along her curves. His eyes must have betrayed his thoughts because she crossed her arms protectively in front of her and looked at him warily.

Pushing aside the erotic image in his head, he told her, "You are right, my lady. The manor house is yours, though I do hope your servants are working as hard as you."

"They are," she said grudgingly and then began to relax. "I think I will be most happy here."

"Happier than when you return to the keep as my wife?" he asked, testing her.

"That is something we need to discuss, my lord."

"Nicholas," he urged. "We are wed, you know. You have my permission to call me by my Christian name."

She swallowed. "Nicholas. About our marriage." She hesitated.

"What about it?"

"I feel we should annul it."

Her words gutted him as if someone had plunged a dagger deep into his belly. "Why?"

Katelyn began wringing her hands nervously. "I know you had no choice in the matter. Your Uncle Rafe seized the last moments of power he would have and tied you to me. You don't have to live with what he did, Nicholas. You are now a powerful earl and can undo your uncle's actions. We have not consummated our marriage. You can petition the bishop for an annulment and choose the wife you want by your side."

"Do you still think I wish to wed Catherine?" he asked softly.

"I don't know. But I do believe you are a strong man with a mind of his own. You shouldn't be forced into a lifetime commitment by an inferior relative."

"Do you not want a lifetime with me, Katelyn?"

Tears welled in her eyes. "In truth, I do. You seem very kind and are well respected by your people. Catherine thinks the world of you and I already trust her opinion beyond measure. I simply believe you shouldn't accept being forced into a marriage not of your own making." She gave him a wistful smile. "You could have any woman in England, Nicholas. One far more suited to be your countess than I ever could be. You don't even know me."

Nicholas placed his hands on her shoulders and felt her trembling. "I am beginning to learn something about you. Your kindness toward Bethany would be enough for me to know what a good person you are. The fact that you want to give me a way out of our marriage shows you are selfless."

"You are being noble, Nicholas."

"Well, I am a titled nobleman now," he teased. "Why don't we compromise?"

Katelyn sniffed. "How? We're either wed or we're not. There is no in-between."

"Give us a month. The month I'd asked for to see if you carry my father's child. We can get to know one another in the weeks ahead. If at the end of the month, you still want to seek an annulment, I will grant you one."

"Will you seek one if I am already with child?" she asked, an odd look in her eyes.

"Nay. I would welcome the child and treat him or her well." He tightened his fingers on her, afraid she was about to flee and be forever lost to him. "I would still stay wed to you, Katelyn. I have already made my decision. The choice now lies with you."

She licked her lips nervously, causing him to want to do the same.

"You want us to get to know one another."

"Aye."

"And if I don't like you—or you change your mind and don't like me—we can end the marriage with no hard feelings."

"Aye."

"All right. I agree."

"Then I promise to visit you each day so we can spend time together," Nicholas said. "We can walk. Ride. Play chess."

"I like to walk."

"So do I."

"I don't have a horse," she pointed out.

"Then I'll get you one. Or you can ride with me." The thought of wrapping his arms about Katelyn made his heart race.

"I don't know how to play chess."

"I can teach you."

"You have an answer for everything, Nicholas."

"See, I would make you an excellent husband. You could come to me for anything and I would solve your problems."

She smiled playfully. "What if I wished to solve yours?"

He laughed. "I would let you."

Katelyn expelled a long breath. "Then I will grant you this month so we can become better acquainted."

"I know one way we can get to know each other." He began to lower his mouth to hers, tired of fighting the urge to kiss her.

"Nay!" she cried and he backed away, still clutching her shoulders.

"You do not wish to kiss me?"

"I don't wish for you to remain wed to me merely because you lust after me," she said, sadness filling her eyes. "I have discovered that others think I am beautiful. I've only seen myself once in a hand mirror, many years ago. I know I have changed since then. Several men at court paid me attention, though. They all had the same look in their eyes as you do now. I don't want to stay wed to you because of desire. I want more than that."

"Love?" he asked.

"Nay. I don't believe in love," Katelyn said firmly. "I want you to want to be with me because of *me*. Who I am. And I need your respect."

"I already like what I know of you," Nicholas said truthfully, "but physical desire is also part of a good, strong marriage. Wouldn't you like to see if we are compatible?"

He realized that she had been a very innocent young woman on her wedding night. Knowing his father's reputation, their coupling had been not only painful but distasteful as her virgin blood was spilled. It would explain her reluctance.

"You are thinking about your wedding night. Did my father kiss you?"

She shuddered. "He slobbered all over me. He . . . did other things, none of them pleasurable."

"Let me try to change your mind about kissing, Katelyn," he said huskily.

Nicholas skimmed his fingers up her long, elegant neck until he cupped her face. "I promise. No slobbering."

She bit back a smile. "All right. One kiss. To become more familiar with each other."

He lowered his mouth and pressed his lips against hers.

Katelyn tamped down the fear that rippled through her, though she craved his touch. The tender way he cradled her face made her yearn for things she had never known and yet now understood she'd always longed for. His lips brushed against hers, feather light, causing her scalp to tingle deliciously. Feeling her knees about to buckle, she gripped his broad shoulders, her nails digging in, suddenly aware of a possessiveness she felt toward him as she marked him.

Slowly, his tongue began outlining the shape of her mouth, making the tingles intensify and an odd sensation burn in her belly. Then his tongue lingered at the corner of her mouth before it slid along the seam between her lips, urging her to open to him.

She did.

Leisurely, Nicholas explored her mouth, his hands releasing her face only to hold her close in an embrace. A thousand thoughts flew through Katelyn's head and yet she couldn't have put words to any of them. She suddenly wanted to please him and allowed her tongue to glide along his playfully. He shuddered, a low groan escaping, and yanked her roughly against him as their tongues began to mate feverishly. Katelyn found her breasts now pressed against his rock-hard chest. They grew heavy, the nipples aching for his touch. She remembered Lord Cedric licking her breasts. Though she had wished to push him away, more than anything she wanted Nicholas to do the same to her, knowing the experience would prove vastly different from before.

Her body burned as time stood still. She hoped to remain lost in his embrace forever. Then Nicholas broke the kiss, his brow resting against hers as his lips hovered just above her own.

"My sweet, sweet Kate," he murmured. He kissed the tip of her nose and worked his lips up it to her brow. Pressing a fervent kiss upon it, he lifted his mouth away and released her.

"Has anyone ever called you Kate?" he asked, his voice rough and low.

"No one," she assured him. "Though I was only called Katelyn again two years ago. I'd been known as Judith."

"Judith? You look nothing like a Judith."

"I felt nothing like a Judith," she agreed. "I knew my name had been Katelyn before I came to the convent. Mother insisted the nuns call me Judith, probably to keep my identity a secret in case anyone came looking for me. I finally demanded two years ago that Mother and everyone at the nunnery call me Katelyn."

"I didn't know your mother was taken to the convent with you. You introduced yourself to me as the daughter of Lord Adelard de Blays. I assumed your mother was dead."

Her mouth grew hard. "My mother is dead. 'Twas the abbess of the Convent of the Charitable Sisters that I referred to."

"You were brave to stand up to her. I've heard an abbess can be fiercer than England's finest warriors."

"I'm not sure about brave. Mother called me stubborn."

Nicholas laughed. "That, too." He studied her a moment. "Do you think we are more familiar with one another after our kiss, Kate?"

"Aye. Mayhap we can have another one sometime," she suggested.

"I think we should share a kiss once a day to further our acquaintance."

"You would come each day to kiss me?" she asked, thinking she would go to the ends of the earth to share a single kiss with him.

"I pledge to you that I will visit each day," Nicholas said solemnly. "And I will never break my word to you, Kate. Never." He entwined his fingers with hers and lifted their joined hands so he could brush a kiss against her knuckles.

They stared at one another for a long moment, their fingers still locked together. Katelyn fought the urge to fling herself into his arms again, hoping he would kiss her senseless.

Nicholas broke the silence. "Would you give me a tour of the manor house? 'Tis been many years since I was here."

"Of course."

He tucked her hand into the crook of his arm and she led him across the great hall to a staircase on the right.

As they climbed the stairs, she said, "Dorinda and Lucy are working on making these two bedchambers inhabitable."

They greeted the two servants and then descended the stairs after seeing both rooms. Katelyn took him to the opposite staircase.

"This side of the manor has another bedchamber and the solar. Unlike Northmere's solar, it is one long room instead of separating the family area from the bedchamber."

"You're sorely lacking in furniture. I will send some tomorrow, as well as more servants to help finish cleaning the entire house."

They returned to the great hall and she showed him the kitchen.

"Walk out with me," he urged.

She saw his horse tied to a post outside. "What a beautiful coat!" she cried out as she hurried toward it and stroked the animal lovingly.

"His name is Sunset. He is named for the colors in his coat and my favorite time of day—though bedtime might soon prove to be my new favorite," he added, a devilish smile playing about his lips.

His suggestive words caused her cheeks to heat and she stared at Sunset, afraid to meet his eyes.

As he mounted the horse, Nicholas said, "I want to walk with you at sunset sometime." He lifted her hand from where she still petted the horse and kissed her fingers. "Until tomorrow, Kate."

Katelyn watched him ride away and thought Nicholas might be as lonely as she was. His mother was dead. His relationship with his father had been fractured. He'd lost his closest friend. His brother was no brother to him. She wondered if fate had brought them together so that they might find a way out from their loneliness.

And become one.

Chapter Thirteen

Katelyn had just finished dressing in a simple smock and kirtle, leaving off her luxurious cotehardie. She had no reason to dirty it while she continued cleaning today. Though Nicholas had said he would send someone else to help, it had to be a low priority when he had so much else to deal with. Hoping with Dorinda and Lucy's help to have the manor house to her liking, Katelyn had set a goal of three more days to complete all the tasks that revolved around making the manor livable again.

An urgent knock sounded and Lucy threw open the door before Katelyn could bid her to enter.

"My lady, wagons approach!" the servant said breathlessly. "Sir Gerald saw them and rode back from his patrol to let us know."

"Who is it?" Katelyn asked, wondering who might be arriving when the sun had barely broken over the horizon.

"They are from the castle." Lucy glanced at her. "Quick. Let me help you into one of your cotehardies."

"But—"

"No buts, my lady. I will help you dress now as befits a countess of Northmere," Lucy insisted.

With the servant's help, Katelyn donned a cotehardie of deep green and came downstairs to await the arrival of those from the castle. She counted eleven carts total. The first three contained servants. The next two looked like supplies, both for cleaning and cooking and some things to help restock the larder. She was glad for that. Feeding so many would have diminished their food supplies substantially. The remaining carts housed furniture and several men, most likely to carry in the heavy objects that rose from the beds.

The wagons came to a halt in front of the manor and a youth of ten and three or possibly four leaped from his horse, which had led the group. He came toward her, eyes bright, brimming with energy.

"Good day to you, my lady," he said as he bowed. "I am Henfrey, squire to Lord Nicholas. He sent me to assist you in any way I can. As you see, I've brought enough servants from the castle to ensure that your manor house will be in order before the end of the day. Address the women first so they may begin their cleaning tasks and then you can view the furniture we brought and instruct the men where it might go. If none of the pieces please you or you have something else in mind, I've brought a carpenter along, as well. Simply tell him what you'd like and he will build it for you."

Katelyn smiled at the boy's self-assurance and eager manner. "Have the women gather so I may speak with them."

By now, both Lucy and Dorinda had come outside and Katelyn motioned to them as the castle servants made their way over. They stood in a semi-circle. She was glad she'd taken Lucy's advice and dressed according to her position. Her clothes from the king fit her well and gave her confidence as she spoke.

"Thank you for coming to right the manor house. Some of the cleaning has already begun. I will divide you into two groups. Dorinda and Lucy will be in charge since they know exactly what I wish to be done."

Katelyn divided them equally, sending the first group with Dorinda to work upstairs in the solar and bedchamber across from it. Lucy's group would finish cleaning the kitchen and then organize the items brought to stock it. She'd glimpsed pots and cups and hoped that the carts contained new bedclothes and bath linens, as well as herbs and spices.

After dismissing the women, she walked with Henfrey to the first wagon of large goods. It was so crowded with furniture that she couldn't see what the pieces looked like, even if she'd climbed into the bed.

"Mayhap the men could unload the wagon?" Katelyn suggested. "It will give me a better idea of what has been sent."

"You heard the countess," Henfrey said to the men nearest them. "Unload it." He raised his voice and shouted to the others, "Unload all the wagons."

After the beds had been emptied, she walked among the contents, pointing out pieces and having them separated from the group. The carpenter introduced himself to her and joined her and Henfrey as she walked them through the various rooms of the manor house. Both men made suggestions as to what could be removed and replaced. Soon, men carried older, less stable pieces from the manor and exchanged them for sturdier ones brought from Northmere.

Her favorite discovery was an enormous tapestry that had taken up most of the final cart. It took eight men to bring in the unwieldy roll. She had them place it on the north wall of the great hall, knowing it would not only brighten the room but help keep the hall warmer come the cold winds of winter as they blew down from Scotland.

Katelyn walked through the chambers again, having some of the new furniture rearranged to her liking. She especially liked the grouping of chairs placed near the fireplace in the great hall. The carpenter suggested crafting a dais since the room had none. He also looked over all of the benches and trestle tables, telling her he would sand some to smooth out the rough spots and construct a few new additions to substitute for ones he felt didn't hold to a high enough standard.

The hours flew by as she supervised the large group from the castle. They stopped for a noon meal and worked another two hours. Henfrey reported that everything seemed in good order so Katelyn went through the entire manor for a final inspection.

"Have everyone come to the great hall," she instructed Henfrey after she made her rounds.

When all arrived, she told them, "You have accomplished so much in such a short amount of time. I cannot thank you enough for your efforts nor convey how pleased I am with the results." She grinned. "What I can do is open some of the casks sent by Lord Nicholas so we can lift a drink to all your hard work."

The men and women cheered loudly. Within minutes, everyone had a cup of wine in hand. Katelyn knew it would probably exhaust what had been sent but she doubted she would be doing any entertaining. She would rather the wine be drunk and enjoyed by those who had endeavored to make the manor house a home for her.

"I see you are liberal with dispensing my wine," a low voice said next to her.

She turned and found Nicholas at her elbow. Finding her mouth had gone suddenly dry, she took a sip from her cup and then offered it to him. He took it and drank down the rest.

"I cannot thank you enough, my lord. My manor house has been transformed in but a few hours' time."

"Nicholas," he reminded her, drawing her hand through his arm. "Why don't you show me what you've accomplished?" He handed the cup to Lucy, who hovered anxiously nearby.

"I can't say I was the one who accomplished anything," she replied as they moved toward a staircase and ascended it. "I merely managed what went on. Your people did all of the work."

"Our people, Kate." He gave her an affectionate smile. "That is, if you wish to have them belong to you."

They reached the top of the stairs and she showed him the two bedchambers. She did the same for the other side of the manor, watching as he assessed each room.

"I like it. I hope you do," he said.

"Oh, I do. Very much."

"Good."

His steady gaze had her grow warm and she began to fan herself with a hand.

"Are you hot? You've been rushing from here to there all day. Mayhap, you'd like to walk outside with me? Or better yet, why don't I take you for a ride and show you some of Northmere?"

He placed his hand atop hers, which still rested on his arm. His nearness caused her heart to pound fiercely. A very masculine scent came from him, something that appealed to her—the mix of leather and horse. She thought what it would be like to be caught up in his arms, atop Sunset, and decided a ride would be far better than a walk.

"I would enjoy riding. You know I am fond of horses."

"Aye." His eyes glowed at her. "I know I said I would bring you one but I haven't had time to find the proper mount for you just yet. Besides a horse, is there any else you might require?"

"Could I have parchment and ink?" she asked.

"You read and write?" She saw his surprise as he added, "You wish to write to your brother?"

"I do read and write," she told him. "In fact, I was tasked to teach both to the oblates at the convent."

Nicholas' nose crinkled. "Oblates? What are oblates?"

"They are young girls, usually six or seven years of age, who are sent away from their families to become nuns."

"That young? Do they ever see their families again?"

"Nay. They are given up to God—and Mother. The abbess and nuns become their family." Katelyn held back the grimace that thought brought. She was far away from Mother Acelina now and would never have to look upon her face again.

"So you taught them to read and write. How else did you spend your time at the convent?"

"I tended the chickens and goats. In fact, I've told Bethany I would teach her how to milk a goat. She seemed most interested in learning."

He smiled. "She did?"

"I think she is intelligent. The fact that she shies away from others may have held her back some but I think she could learn to do many things if given time and patience."

"When I've spoken to her this week, it's been more like a true conversation. She's tried to speak in groups of words. I know that is thanks to you."

"I hope you will bring her to visit me."

"I will. And I can certainly bring you parchment and ink to write to Landon."

Katelyn shook her head. "I don't wish to write to him yet. He is a long way from Northumberland. As it is, it will take him weeks to reach Windsor—or even London—if the king has ventured there."

"You will write him when you decide about our marriage?" Nicholas pressed.

She nodded. "I will. He would need to know of my decision and inform the king as to whether I will remain your wife or let you find one of your own choosing."

Guilt still hung heavily over her, knowing Nicholas had been compelled to accept her as his wife, his uncle pulling the strings. The more she knew of her husband, the more she respected him.

And wanted him to find a wife better suited to being a countess than she could ever be.

"Despite the fact that I told you I want to remain in this marriage, you still resist, Kate."

She loved hearing him call her that. No one had ever shortened her name. Somehow, she felt more a Kate than a Katelyn—when she was with Nicholas. Her background deemed her unsuitable to be the wife of a powerful nobleman, even though she was the king's cousin. Growing up in a convent hadn't prepared her for life outside it. Nicholas would need a much different kind of woman than Katelyn de Blays to share his life and Northmere. When the month ended, she would request the annulment. Until then, she would enjoy his company.

And those promised kisses.

"Remember, I have a month to make up my mind," she said lightly, trying to put him off. "And we are to learn something about each other every day."

"And share a daily kiss," Nicholas reminded her, a glint of desire surfacing in those deep brown eyes.

"That, too," she said dismissively, not wanting him to guess how badly she longed for it. "Come. Show me a little of Northmere. I am eager to see it."

They returned downstairs. Those from the castle were loading up the unused or unwanted furniture and climbing into the wagons in order to return, Henfrey making sure everyone had a place to ride.

Nicholas signaled the squire over. "Henfrey, I hope you did a good job today for Lady Katelyn."

She said, "I could not have accomplished all I did if not for Henfrey's wonderful help."

The squire beamed. "I would do anything for you, my lady."

Katelyn hid a smile, seeing the young man was taken with her.

"I want you to stay at the manor house for now, Henfrey," Nicholas told his squire. "Albert and Gerald are guarding the outside but I have no one inside to protect the countess and her servants. I trust you to defend them."

Henfrey couldn't contain his delight. "Oh, thank you, my lord. Thank you. I will be happy to guard Lady Katelyn from harm."

"She will be in residence for a little less than a month then you may return to the castle grounds. For now, you can bring Sunset here once everyone has departed for the castle. I wish for the countess to see some of Northmere."

"Aye, my lord." Henfrey look to her. "You'll only be able to see a bit of the estate, my lady. It would take you riding through the night and well into tomorrow before you could take in all the land."

The squire scurried off to where the last of the wagons was being loaded.

"He is certainly enthusiastic," she pointed out.

"Henfrey has been at Northmere since he was seven. He's now ten and three and has recently become my squire."

"You won't miss him?"

"He'll be of more use to you than me. Let him move a few things about for you so he can feel manly," Nicholas suggested.

Katelyn laughed.

Nicholas took her hand and brought it to his lips. He kissed it. "I love hearing your laugh, Kate. It makes it seem as if everything is right in my world."

"Here you go, my lord," called Henfrey.

Nicholas released her hand and swung into Sunset's saddle. She stood near and allowed him to lift her in front of him. His left arm came about her waist, drawing her into him. Her fingers locked on to his strong forearm to secure herself and he turned the horse away from the manor, instantly breaking into a gallop. Katelyn gripped him tightly, enjoying the feel of the wind against her face and the possessive arm holding her against him.

They slowed a few times in order for him to point out various things to her and then he brought Sunset to a halt.

"There's a stream nearby," Nicholas said. "I want to water him."

He dismounted from the horse and then clasped her about the waist, bringing her back to the earth. His hands remained on her waist, his eyes searching her face. Katelyn thought he might kiss her but he merely rubbed his thumbs back and forth several times, grazing her ribs, causing her pulse to jump. Nicholas released her and took up Sunset's reins in one hand.

And wrapped his other hand around hers.

He led them into a wooded area and she heard running water. They reached a brook and Sunset lapped up water until his master tugged him away and looped the reins around a low bush. Nicholas hadn't released her hand the entire time and a glow had spread through her.

Now, he backed her against a tree trunk and captured her other hand in his free one.

"I think it's time for our kiss," he suggested.

"All right," she said, her breathing growing shallow in anticipation.

Nicholas stepped toward her until their bodies grazed one another, pinning her loosely against the bark.

"I have thought of nothing else but this kiss," he revealed. "Ever since the last one ended."

When she remained silent, he cocked his head and studied her. "And what about you, Kate? Have you thought about kissing me?"

Her face flamed as he flirted with her. Her nipples began to ache. Her tongued darted out and nervously licked her lips.

"Ah, just what I wanted to do. You are full of good ideas, Kate."

Nicholas' mouth moved toward hers. As he reached it, his tongue touched the center of her bottom lip. Without meaning to, Katelyn moaned.

He whispered, "I want to taste you, Kate."

His tongue glided agonizingly slow along her lower lip, causing her knees to buckle. Nicholas pressed closer to her as his tongue swished back and forth, driving her mad, then moving and doing the same to her upper lip.

"Nicholas," she gasped.

He took her parted lips as an invitation and plunged his tongue inside, kissing her deeply. His hands tightened on hers, almost crushing her bones, and yet Katelyn welcomed the pain mixed with pleasure. He kissed her again and again, her sighs urging him on. He broke the kiss and softly bit into her lower lip. She startled and groaned, sensations running inside her like lightning.

His lips dropped to her throat, where her pulse jumped. He nuzzled the point and nibbled around it, causing her pulse to beat rapidly. Nicholas released her hands, his fingers sliding up her arms and coming to rest along the sides of her neck. Once more, his lips returned to hers. Katelyn found herself kissing him back with everything she had. She wished time would end, here and now, for she didn't think she would ever know greater happiness.

Nicholas' mouth finally parted from hers. He gazed into her eyes and Katelyn saw need written in them. She realized nothing good could come of this dangerous game. She'd played with fire and now had been burned—because she felt her heart slipping from her grasp, as if she had no power to stop it. She hadn't intended to give her heart to this man but she could stop any further pain from occurring for either of them.

"I don't think we should kiss again," Katelyn told him.

CHAPTER FOURTEEN

NICHOLAS STOOD UTTERLY still, his hands still resting along Kate's slender neck. Though he longed to stroke the satin skin with his thumbs, her words had brought everything to a halt.

Why would she want to cease their kisses?

He knew she'd enjoyed them from her response. As they'd kissed the last two days, he hadn't limited them to a single kiss. He'd allowed each one to melt into the next, allowing them both to become familiar with the taste and feel of one another. Though certainly an innocent, his new wife had taken to the art of kissing. Her skill didn't match his—yet—but she had done a few things that surprised and delighted him. Nicholas knew once he got her into their bedchamber and consummated the relationship, he could look forward to many years of pleasure.

So why, after two enjoyable sessions of kissing, did she wish to put a stop to it?

He looked at her lips, swollen from their love play, and decided it might be fear taking hold of her since she had experienced a wedding night with his father. Nicholas hadn't forced Kate to do anything he thought she might be uncomfortable with but who only knew what his father had done to her? Kate must realize that these heated kisses between them would definitely lead to even more heated caresses. Mayhap the idea of passion unnerved her. Growing up among nuns, who knew little of the outside world and probably had deemed all physical contact between men and women as carnal and base, his bride might be worried about what lay ahead, especially if Cedric Mandeville had used her roughly, as Nicholas suspected.

Demanding to continue their daily kissing could frighten her off for good. Foolishly, he had told Kate it was her choice to make on whether or not they remained wed after a month's time, thinking he would easily persuade her to stay in the marriage. Nicholas already knew she was the only woman for him and yet he couldn't take away the choice he'd promised her. Too many people had disappointed—or even lied to her—in her life. Besides, he had promised never to break his word to her. That meant he must now tread softly and make her feel safe.

"If that's what you wish for, Kate," he said simply, dropping his hands to his sides. He knew his response startled her. Those amazing emerald eyes darkened and went wide with surprise.

"You . . . agree?"

He shrugged. "I merely said that kissing was one way for us to become better acquainted. We still can do other things to ensure we know each other more intimately. Simply spending time together in various activities. Conversation is a wonderful way to come to know another person."

Nervously, she wrung her hands together in front of her. Nicholas could see her trying to formulate a response.

"You would . . . still come to visit . . . even if no kissing was involved?" she finally asked.

"Aye. I come to see *you*, Kate. Our kiss is simply a pleasant addition to everything else."

"I see." She twisted her hands until she realized what she did and quickly crossed her arms. "You don't have to visit me daily, Nicholas."

"I don't have to—but I want to. You are an interesting woman, Kate. I am intrigued by you."

She huffed. "I don't see why. I haven't led an exciting life. In fact, it's been the opposite. Very sheltered."

He smiled wryly. "And yet here I am, captivated by everything you say or do."

"We should head back to the manor house," she said abruptly.

"If you wish."

Nicholas loosened Sunset's reins. Before Kate could protest, he seized her hand and kept it firmly in his as he led them from the woods. Mounting the horse, he leaned down and brought her up in front of him, his fingers splayed against her belly. She grabbed on to the pommel instead of his arm but he didn't remark on that slight change. Instead, he made sure she fit snuggly against him and took off at a brisk pace. Knowing she wasn't familiar with the estate, he took a longer route returning to the manor, savoring the feel of her against him and the smell of vanilla wafting from her skin.

They saw Alfred once they approached their destination and waved to the knight. Nicholas climbed down first and then lifted Katelyn from Sunset's back, releasing her more quickly than he had earlier.

She stroked Sunset's neck and rested her cheek against the horse for a moment, her long, dark lashes sweeping across her pale cheeks as she closed her eyes and savored the moment. Then she kissed the horse's neck and told him farewell.

Nicholas captured her hand and brought it to his lips for a tender kiss. "I will come again tomorrow, Kate."

When she opened her mouth to protest, he shook his head. "I *will* come. Until then." Nicholas kissed her hand a second time and then quickly mounted his horse and rode off.

He had a little more than three weeks to win Kate over. Nicholas had never lost anything important to him.

His wife would be no exception.

NICHOLAS RETURNED EVERY day during the following week, always bringing some small gift with him. The first day, he came with the promised parchment and ink. The next, he brought a satchel full of candles. The third, he brought scented soap. Each day, he found something new that might please Kate in some small way.

And each day, he still insisted upon a kiss.

Not the kind of kisses that they'd shared before. He knew better than to attempt one of those. At the close of each visit, he would award her a brief kiss. On her cheek. Against her brow. On the top of her head or hand. Nicholas wanted for there always to be some type of physical contact between them. He wanted Kate to miss their kisses as much as he did.

Nights had been the worst. He found it hard to fall asleep in the solar, knowing her head had rested against the same pillow for a brief time. He fantasized about what he would do to her in this bed. The ways he would touch her. How he would worship her tall, slender body, which held curves in all of the right places.

Finally, he saved his best ideas for last and would gift her with them on two separate occasions. Nicholas had no difficulty using the weapons he had at his hand and his greatest weapon was one she wouldn't be able to resist.

Bethany.

He and Kate usually spoke about his sister during every visit he made and he understood that Kate had not only taken an interest in Bethany but expressed compassion for her. On Bethany's part, she continually mentioned Kate and how Nicholas would take her to see her new friend.

Today would be that day.

He went to Bethany's bedchamber after breaking his fast and found she and Mary had just finished their simple morning meal.

"Nicholas! You came!" Bethany flung herself at him with her usual joy.

He stroked her hair and then asked, "How would you like to see Katelyn today?"

Her eyes lit up. "I go see Kate-lyn? Now?"

"Now," he confirmed. He looked to Mary. "You, too, Mary. Since it takes an hour to get there, I'll bring you both in a cart."

"Oh, Lord Nicholas, that would be splendid. Wouldn't it, my lady? You'll get to see the countess."

Nicholas stepped closer to Mary. In a quiet voice, he said, "Mayhap, you will stay overnight. We will have to see how Bethany accepts being in a new situation. If she does, I will leave you both and return tomorrow."

"I can't say how she'll react, my lord, but I'll pack a few things for us both all the same."

"What about Kit?" Bethany asked, holding the growing kitten to her chest. "Kit go?"

"Of course, Kit can go with us," Nicholas reassured her. Turning back to the servant, he said, "I'll hitch a horse to a cart and bring it to the keep."

"We'll be waiting for you, my lord," Mary promised. "Thank you. This will be good for Lady Bethany."

"I think so, too," he agreed.

Within a half-hour, they were driving out the gates of Northmere. Bethany sat close to Nicholas, her arm looped through his, turning from side to side as the horse trotted along. Kit sat in her lap, wrapped in a small blanket, fast asleep. Mary sat in the bed of the cart, a small bundle of their things next to her, in case they did stay the night.

Usually, Nicholas came later, in the early afternoon. This time, they arrived before mid-morning. He helped his sister and Mary from the wagon and they approached the door of the manor house.

"Kate-lyn live here?"

"She does," Nicholas said as he rapped on the door.

For now . . .

Dorinda answered his knock. "My lord, you are early today. Lady Katelyn will be surprised." She glanced behind him. "Oh, Lady Bethany. 'Tis good to see you."

Though normally shy, Bethany nodded and made no attempt to hide or bury her face against him. Once again, more progress.

"Come in," Dorinda urged, stepping aside to admit them.

Bethany looked around, studying her new surroundings. "Where Kate-lyn go?"

"The countess is digging in the garden. Shall I take you to her?"

"Nay. Bethany and I will find her. Mary can stay and keep you company. Come along, Bethany. Let's surprise her. Leave Kit here. She can explore the great hall."

His sister handed the kitten to Mary and he led them back out the door and around to the side of the manor. Kate was nowhere in sight so he placed a finger against his lips and took Bethany's hand. They crept around the side of the building and he spied Kate on her hands and knees, digging in the dirt.

Nicholas pulled Bethany back and said softly, "Walk quietly and tap her on the shoulder. I'll stay here."

Bethany took slow, small steps away from him, though she looked over her shoulder several times. Nicholas encouraged her to move forward and she finally reached Kate. As he'd told her, she lightly touched Kate's shoulder. He could hear her gasp of surprise from where he stood.

"Oh! Lady Bethany! You gave me a start." Kate stood.

"I surprise you." Bethany laughed sweetly.

"You certainly did. Come here."

Kate wrapped her arms around the younger girl and held her close. She glanced to Nicholas, her brows arching. He headed toward them, not bothering to keep the grin from his face.

Kate released Bethany but kept an arm about her. "I think you must have had a role in this wonderful surprise, my lord."

"Someone had to drive Bethany here."

"I'm glad you did." A smile lit her face. She looked back to Bethany. "As you can see, I'm working in the garden. It's been sorely neglected. Mayhap you would like to help me?"

Bethany nodded. "I help Kate-lyn." She looked to him and shook her finger. "Not Nicholas. Just me."

"That's quite all right," he told them. "I will sit under the shade of that tree and watch you at work."

The next two hours were pleasant ones for Nicholas could observe Kate without her worrying about him staring at her. She quickly became lost in explaining what she was doing to Bethany and helping the girl dig in the earth and plant seeds before covering them up and smoothing the dirt flat again. He enjoyed hearing both of them laugh and how Kate paid such attention to Bethany. It didn't hurt that as she leaned over the ground, her skirts tightened against her rounded bottom. Between that and focusing on the curve of her breasts, he thought the time spent sitting against the tree trunk some of the most productive he'd engaged in for some time.

Finally, it looked as if their work was about to cease. Nicholas stood and moved toward them, assisting first Bethany and then Kate to their feet.

"I'm afraid I've muddied your hand," Kate apologized to him.

He brushed the back of his fingers against her cheek, removing a smudge of dirt lying against it. The air between them seemed to crackle.

"I so tired," Bethany proclaimed. "I dirty and thirsty."

Kate pulled her hand from his grasp and turned. "We need to wash our hands. Let's go inside. I'll want to change into something else."

"I change, too," Bethany said, skipping ahead of them. "I go get Kit." She vanished around the corner.

"Thank you," Nicholas said as they returned to the manor at a more leisurely pace.

"For what?"

"Bethany adores you. It's obvious. You speak to her as if she is ordinary. As if nothing is wrong with her."

"I don't think there is. Mayhap others should treat her the same."

"If you come to live at the keep, you could lead by example. Think of the progress Bethany has made already."

Kate lowered her eyes, a flush spreading across her porcelain cheeks. She took a long breath and expelled it before raising her eyes to his. "Don't make this about Bethany, Nicholas. I don't want to feel guilty."

"You mean you would feel guilty if you choose to seek an annulment? If you had to leave Bethany behind? Or me?"

Her lips thinned. "I will make my decision without any undue influence or pressure from you, my lord." Her brows arched. "And don't think I don't know what you're doing, bringing all these small gifts every time you come."

Nicholas gave her a crooked smile. "I merely mean to please you, Kate."

"And convince me to stay," she added.

"Is it working?" he asked teasingly. "Nay. Don't answer that."

He took her arm and led her back inside. She and Bethany vanished for a few minutes. Lucy brought him water to wash his own hands and then Nicholas sat in a chair beside the fireplace in the little great hall, Kit purring in his lap.

Kate was very smart to realize his tactics in trying to win her over. It was another reason he needed her as his countess. As his lover. As his wife. His true wife, in every sense of the word. Life with Kate would never be dull.

She returned, wearing a cotehardie of palest yellow, her dark braid a sharp contrast against the material as it hung down her back past her waist. Nicholas longed to undo the thick braid and run his fingers through the mass of raven hair.

"Bethany is hungry after all of our hard work. Would you mind eating a bit early?" Kate asked.

"Nay." He handed the kitten to his sister and stood.

"I've told Lucy that we will eat in the solar."

Kate led them upstairs, where the meal had already been laid out on the table. Bethany insisted upon eating next to Kate so Nicholas took the seat opposite them. They ate a spiced starling, surrounded by onions and peas, and finished the meal with baked apples and cheese.

Bethany yawned. "I so tired. I sleep." She went to the bed. "I sleep here?"

Kate drew the curtains so Bethany and Kit could sit on the bed. She removed Bethany's shoes and helped her slip under the bedclothes. Kit curled up next to his mistress and both fell promptly asleep.

Returning to Nicholas, she said, "We should leave so she's not disturbed by our conversation. Allow the door to remain open. I'll have Mary come up and sit with her so when she awakens, Bethany is not alone in a new place."

They exited the solar. Pausing outside the door, he said, "She's not used to so much activity. I think it was good for her, though."

Kate laughed softly. "The nuns would agree with you. They believed the busier you stayed, the less likely you were to fall into any kind of temptation."

Her words confirmed what Nicholas had thought. "Did they speak against what a man and woman do together? When they become intimate?"

Kate blushed. "They did."

"Is that why you decided we shouldn't kiss anymore?"

She frowned. "Nay. I thought kissing . . . made us . . . too close. That you were becoming more interested in it than in me. Than getting to know me."

He took her wrist and rubbed the pad of his thumb against her palm in slow circles. "I'll admit that I enjoyed our kisses. But I've also appreciated our conversations. Strolling with you. Telling you about Northmere. Hearing about you running away from the convent. Naming your chickens and goats."

"Nicholas . . ." Her voice trailed off.

Continuing to circle her palm, he asked softly, "What, Kate?"

She looked at him with eyes full of yearning. "I wish . . . I wish that . . ." Without finishing her thought, she pulled away from him and hurried away.

Nicholas followed her, his stride long enough to catch up with her before she reached the top of the stairs. He saw Dorinda climbing them.

The servant spotted them and said, "Lady Katelyn, there is some-one here to see you."

Nicholas glanced to the foot of the stairs and fumed when he caught sight of the man making his way toward them.

It was Bryce.

Chapter Fifteen

K ATELYN HEARD NICHOLAS curse softly as she said, "Thank you, Dorinda."

The servant scurried down the stairs.

Nicholas took her arm and drew her several feet away, out of view from Bryce. Quickly, he said, "Do not let him know Bethany is here under any circumstances. She is terrified of him."

Before Katelyn could ask why, Bryce had arrived and stepped toward them. He took her hand and brought it to his lips. Katelyn deliberately withdrew it before he could press a kiss of greeting upon it.

"What? No welcome, Katelyn?" Bryce looked from her to Nicholas and back again.

"I am surprised you are here," she replied coolly.

"And I was surprised to hear you were in the solar with my brother. Shall we retire there and talk—or are you embarrassed for me to see the rumpled bedclothes from your afternoon love play?"

She knew he tried to upset her and would not allow herself to be goaded into anger.

"It's not any of your concern what goes on in my solar," she said curtly.

Bryce held his hands palms up. "Are we not family now? Of course, I have an interest in you. I supposed since you were raised with no family surrounding you that you do not understand how family members share with one another."

"When have we shared anything—other than hatred for one another, Bryce?" Nicholas interjected.

Bryce's mouth turned down. "Brother, I meant no harm. I got along quite well with Katelyn on the journey from Windsor to Northumberland. She's been gone from the castle more than a week. I simply thought to check on her welfare."

"First, you charm me. Then, you wound me. Is that how family members are supposed to act toward one another, Bryce?" she asked.

"I'm delighted to know I charmed you," he replied smoothly. "I've always felt a special connection with you. Despite the fact that you were wedded to my father." Bryce glanced to Nicholas. "I suppose you are charming Katelyn, as well. All the castle's inhabitants know how you ride away to visit her each day, neglecting your duties to the estate."

"I neglect nothing," Nicholas said evenly.

"Especially not Katelyn," Bryce said and chuckled. "I assumed because of your many visits to your new wife, you've reneged on your vow to leave her untouched for a month. I can understand why for she is a tempting morsel. Any man would be besotted with her. Even if she was first sullied by Father. It's too bad you may never know if she's with Father's child—or yours."

Katelyn slapped Bryce hard. His head snapped, the neck making a loud crackling noise. Her palm stung as if she'd dipped it in fire but she would never give him the satisfaction to know how it much it hurt. She thought the pain worth it, seeing the shock in his eyes.

"I did not ask you here, Bryce. I don't ever plan to extend an invitation to you. Nicholas has been nothing but a gentleman toward me and that includes keeping his word. You, on the other hand, have displayed ungallant behavior. Leave. Now," she ordered.

A sudden wail distracted her. Katelyn looked over her shoulder and saw Bethany standing in the solar's doorway. The young woman's eyes were wide with terror as she pointed toward Bryce. Her howl began to die down into a pitiful whimper. Then she stepped back into the solar and slammed the door.

Katelyn whipped around. "What did you do to her to make her so frightened of you?"

Bryce shrugged. "Ask her." He turned and strolled down the stairs.

Katelyn and Nicholas rushed to the solar but couldn't enter. Bethany had locked the door.

"Bethany!" Nicholas cried, pounding against the wood. "Let me in. He's gone. You're safe."

When the door didn't open, he told Katelyn, "I will break it down. Step back."

"Nay," she said softly. "Bethany is already frightened enough. Tearing down a door will only add to her fear."

She knocked on the door, praying that the Virgin would give her the right words to say.

"Bethany, it's Katelyn. Come to the door and listen to me." She waited, hoping the girl did as she asked. She saw Mary had also arrived, looking distraught.

"I am sorry that Bryce woke you from your nap. It's hard to wake and be disoriented and then find someone so scary nearby. I did not invite Bryce to my home. I told him he will never be asked to come. I don't want him here. But I do want you here. I'm happy Nicholas and Mary brought you to see me. Won't you open the door and let me in?"

Katelyn held her breath and finally heard the latch scrape. The door opened a sliver.

"Could I come in?" she asked. "Just me. I am so tired after all that digging that we did." She yawned loudly. "I would love to curl up with you and Kit and rest for a bit. Would you let me do that?"

Bethany's hand appeared along the doorframe. The door opened enough to admit Katelyn. She looked to Nicholas. He nodded.

Entering, she heard the door shut swiftly. Bethany turned, tears streaming down her face.

Katelyn opened her arms and Bethany came to her, allowing Katelyn to wrap her in a close embrace. She let Bethany weep until no more tears came and then led her to the bed. They climbed onto it and Katelyn put an arm about the girl. Bethany rolled into Katelyn, clutching her cotehardie, while Kit jumped up and nestled at Bethany's feet.

They remained that way for a good hour. As Bethany dozed, Katelyn wondered what horrible thing Bryce had done to make his sister terrified to see him.

Finally, Bethany stirred.

"I want Mary," she murmured.

"I'll bring her to you."

Katelyn slipped from the bed and went to the door. Opening it, she saw both Nicholas and Mary waiting patiently.

"She asked for you."

Mary hurried inside the solar and Katelyn closed the door behind her. Suddenly, Nicholas was next to her, wrapping her in warmth and comfort. She leaned into his strength, peace radiating through her as she felt safe in his arms.

"Is she all right?" he asked. When Katelyn nodded, he studied her. "Are you?"

"Aye. Would you tell me what is between them?"

"Come downstairs."

Nicholas didn't rush her. He led her back to the great hall and a chair. Lucy brought her a cup of wine. One sip and warmth flooded Katelyn.

"Bethany was a bright child. Full of curiosity. Ten years younger than I and eight younger than Bryce. He wasn't happy when she arrived. Bryce was always a selfish child and wanted more than his fair share of attention. Mother had despaired of ever having more babes. After so long a time without conceiving, Bethany was a true gift in her eyes."

"Bryce was . . . jealous? Of a newborn?" Katelyn asked, shocked.

"Aye."

She listened as he explained how Bethany had been kicked in the head by Lord Cedric's horse, thanks to Bryce leaving her in the temperamental animal's stall.

"Bethany was a changed child after that. Quiet. Barely speaking. And panic-stricken anytime Bryce came near her." Nicholas paused. "My heart tells me Bryce tried to kill our sister and failed. She's no threat to him now but I wonder sometimes if he would ever try the same with me."

Katelyn gasped. "You believe Bryce would harm you?"

"My brother has always wanted more than was his. He's furious that he's the second-born son and has no claim to the earldom or Northmere. He played what Father said were tricks upon me in our childhood but I think he hoped they would bring me permanent damage. Let's just say that I keep a watchful eye on him."

"You should order him to leave Northmere," she said. "You shouldn't have to sleep with one eye open and worry about if Bryce plots to maim or kill you. I can understand your father allowing him to return to his home once he attained his knighthood but you are the earl now, Nicholas. You must make him leave. For your sake as much as your sister's."

"I have given that consideration. It would allow Bethany to move about more freely. I think part of why she stays confined to her bedchamber so much is so that she doesn't have to run into him. The times she and Mary roam outside the keep are when Bryce is gone."

Katelyn placed her hand on his arm. "You owe it to Bethany to protect her from that monster."

He placed his hand over hers and squeezed it gently. "You have convinced me that I have no other choice. I will return home now and tell Bryce he is no longer welcome at Northmere. I had hoped Bethany might be comfortable enough to stay the night with you. It would be better if she did. I don't know how Bryce will react."

"He seems unstable to me. I'm sure he'll lash out at you. Blame you."

"Or you," Nicholas said. "He might think you, too, are being protective of Bethany and have convinced me that he is a danger to her."

"I don't care," Katelyn said. "Northmere will be better off without the likes of Bryce Mandeville."

NICHOLAS UNHITCHED THE horse from the cart. It would take far too long to drive it back to the castle. Determination filled him to rid himself of his worthless brother before he could change his mind. Too many times in the past he had given Bryce another chance. This day would prove to be his brother's last at Northmere.

He only hoped Bryce wouldn't hold this decision against Katelyn.

Though he'd never liked Bryce, he supposed somewhere, deep inside him, that some love existed for his brother. As the oldest of the Mandeville children, he'd been tasked by his parents to look out for his younger siblings. He had done it all his life but he could no longer excuse Bryce for his words and actions. It was time for him to depart.

Reaching the castle grounds, he took the horse to the stables.

"He's been ridden hard. Give him a good rubdown and an extra measure of oats," he told the stable lad and then went to the training yard where he hoped to find his brother.

Nicholas spotted Bryce sparring with one of the younger soldiers. He'd noticed Bryce always singled out those younger, shorter, and weaker than he was. All to make himself look better. Though he longed to order Bryce from Northmere now, he would not embarrass his brother in front of all of their men. Instead, he would speak to him in the privacy of the solar. That way, no prying eyes or ears would see or hear their conversation. Once Bryce left, Nicholas would not make any announcements. The men could think what they chose.

He called a page over and told the boy to tell his uncle to come see him. The boy ran around the edges of the training yard and made his way toward the raised platform, where Rafe Mandeville stood assessing the men at their exercises. He bent and listened to the boy and nodded before calling over a knight to take his place. Rafe hopped from the platform and slipped from the yard, coming straight to Nicholas.

"You wish to see me?"

"Walk with me, Uncle."

Nicholas moved at a steady pace, keeping silent until they were out of sight from the soldiers. Turning, he said, "I have decided to ask Bryce to leave Northmere."

Rafe's eyes narrowed. "I was afraid it might come to this. Think on it, Nicholas, I beg you."

"I have thought about it, Uncle. Long and hard. It was something Father should have done long ago but couldn't because he favored Bryce so."

"Are you jealous of your brother?" the knight asked.

"Never," Nicholas said firmly. "He is a terrible soldier, though. Lazy. Inefficient. Unwilling to better himself. And he's not been much of a brother to me. Or Bethany."

"Still, banishing him cuts you off from your past," Rafe insisted. "Your father and mother are gone. With Bryce sent away, you only have Bethany. And me, of course."

Nicholas looked Rafe in the eye. "I have my wife."

"Do you?"

"Katelyn will make an excellent countess. She will prove loyal to me. Something Bryce never has been."

"I rather thought she liked your brother. They seemed to get along well while we traveled north from Windsor."

"That's before she knew him," Nicholas snapped. "She even ordered him to stay away from the manor house this afternoon."

Rafe's eyes gleamed with interest. "So, this is Lady Katelyn pressing you to expel Bryce from Northmere. Not you."

"It is my decision, Uncle. No one else's. I am the Earl of Northmere. I alone hold the power to send Bryce away. For good."

"I hope you know what you are doing," Rafe murmured.

"What? Do you think Bryce would retaliate?"

His uncle shrugged. "'Tis hard to say what Bryce might do. He's unpredictable."

"Send him to the solar when you've finished with the men for the day."

Rafe expelled a long breath. "Sometimes, Bryce chooses to end his training earlier than the others."

"Then before he leaves the field, make sure he understands that I wish to speak with him." Nicholas glared at his uncle, daring him to speak again.

Rafe inclined his head. "As you wish, my lord."

The two men parted, going opposite directions. Nicholas returned to the keep and went to the solar to wait. It didn't take long before a knock sounded and Bryce breezed through the doorway.

"You wish to speak to me, Brother?" Bryce plopped down in a chair and poured himself a cup of wine. He downed it in a single swallow and slammed the cup on the table. "I would have thought we'd had enough talk between us for one day." He crossed his ankle over his knee. "Go ahead."

"You are to leave Northmere immediately," Nicholas said, keeping his tone even. "You may take your possessions and your horse. Don't plan on returning."

Bryce's face turned red. "You wouldn't dare!" he exclaimed, leaping to his feet.

Nicholas also stood and stared at him. "There's no daring involved, *Brother*. The Earl of Northmere wishes you to vacate his estate and never come back."

"It's that little slut who's making you do this. Forcing you to exile me from my home. From my flesh and blood."

"Kate has nothing to do with this."

"She has *everything* to do with it," Bryce retorted. "The king's cousin ordered you to dismiss me from sight. She snapped her fingers and my foolish, besotted brother instantly dances to her tune, not thinking of the consequences."

"I am the earl," Nicholas ground out. "*I* resolved to see you banished. You care nothing for your flesh and blood. You loathe me. You don't give a thought to Bethany. You despise Uncle Rafe and Aunt Ellyn. You only care for yourself, Bryce. It's time you grew up and became a man, not a whining boy."

Bryce howled with laughter. For a moment, Nicholas thought his brother had descended into madness. Then he gave Nicholas a sly smile.

"You may think this is the end of things between us, Nicholas. I assure you it's not. Be on guard, Brother, for you never know when I might come for you. Tomorrow. Next year. A score of years from now. I will take everything you value and see you beg on your knees."

Bryce abruptly fled the room without a backward glance.

Nicholas felt as if he'd allowed a mad dog that should be put down to crawl away. He would have to remain wary the rest of his life, knowing that Bryce might come for him at any time. More than that, Bryce had sworn to take what Nicholas valued. Possessions had never meant much to him.

Only one thing could hurt him—and that was losing Kate. Nicholas would give his life to protect her.

No matter what the cost.

CHAPTER SIXTEEN

NICHOLAS WAITED UNTIL he saw the last person enter the great hall and then rose. Before he could call out to address those gathered to break their fast, the room began to quieten and then fell into total silence. The eyes of the people of Northmere were upon him and he could tell they wondered what he would share with them.

"I could speak to you of how well our harvest is going and the winnowing and tying. I am pleased with all of your hard work and will announce a celebration once that work has been completed. I might speak of how well our soldiers continue to train and patrol our lands so that we don't live in fear every minute, worried that Scottish rebels will invade our homes. I could compliment those who live at the castle and express how well they do their jobs. All of that I will save for another time.

"Today, I share with you one thing you must know—and that is my brother, Bryce Mandeville, is never to set foot upon Northmere lands again. The reason I will keep to myself. But know that none of my people are to have anything to do with Bryce or you, too, shall be banished. I ask everyone to be on guard to make sure he never enters again."

He sat and motioned for the servants to bring out their trays. The lingering silence appeared deafening. Gradually, conversation started up. Nicholas ate without speaking to either his aunt or uncle, both seated to his right, but he could feel the waves of disapproval coming from Rafe Mandeville.

Once the meal ended, Nicholas stood and stepped from the dais. He held a hand out to assist Ellyn. His uncle joined them, his eyes glowering in anger.

"Was it necessary to announce to the world that you'd exiled your only brother from Northmere?" Rafe demanded. "Did he need to suffer such humiliation?"

"First, Uncle, Bryce is not present and will never hear about such humiliation. Second, I could have dismissed him from the training yard yesterday and had all the soldiers gossiping about what they overheard. I allowed him to come to the privacy of my solar for our conversation. In it, he threatened me. I don't take kindly to threats. From now on, I want everyone at Northmere to be wary. Bryce is a dangerous enemy—now and always."

"So be it." Rafe stormed away.

Ellyn placed her hand on his arm. "You did the right thing, Nicholas. There has always been something loathsome about Bryce. I don't understand why Cedric never saw it." She squeezed his arm in support. "I know this must be hard on you, though. You have recently lost Favian, who was a true brother to you, and now had to send away your own flesh and blood."

"No need to worry about me. I am fine, Aunt."

Her hand dropped away. "I know you are. A concern I have, though, is Katelyn. She is isolated at the manor house. I would not put it past Bryce to try to hurt you through her."

"That's been taken care of," Nicholas assured her. "After warning the gatekeeper yesterday to never admit Bryce, I sent six more knights to the manor house to protect her."

"Will you tell her of Bryce's threat against you? She might feel safer if she returned to the keep instead of staying where she is."

"I'll inform her that Bryce has left for good but I don't want to worry her unnecessarily. She has my best men surrounding her. I'll allow her to remain where she is for now. It's what she wants."

Nicholas kissed Ellyn's cheek and bid her good day before heading to the stables. He saddled Sunset and had Mary's son also ready a horse. Bethany liked the young man and Nicholas would have him drive Bethany and Mary back to Northmere. He then saddled another horse. His last present to Kate. He would surprise her with it after his sister left.

Waiting for him in the bailey were eight soldiers. He'd spoken to each of them last night. They would ride with him to the manor house and serve as an escort for Bethany as she returned to the castle. From now on, the women in his household would always be accompanied by a full guard, no matter where they traveled. Nicholas could no longer guarantee they could move freely and safely about Northmere.

After an hour's ride, they arrived at Kate's, along the way passing three of the additional men he'd sent yesterday. Henfrey hurried out to greet him.

Handing him the reins, Nicholas told the squire to lead both horses to the rear of the manor house and secure them.

"Not a word to the countess," he warned. "And once you hear the group of soldiers departing with my sister, make yourself scarce."

Henfrey's eyes lit up with excitement. "Is this horse for Lady Katelyn? Oh, she will be most happy, my lord."

He nodded and watched the boy lead the horses away. He turned to the men still on horseback.

"You'll be leaving shortly." Looking to Mary's son, he said, "Hitch your horse to the cart and be ready to depart."

"Aye, my lord."

Nicholas went inside the manor house. Dorinda greeted him and said, "The ladies are in the solar, my lord."

"Let Mary know to prepare to leave for Northmere."

He went to the solar and stood in the open doorway a moment, observing Kate guiding Bethany's hand as she drew on parchment. His sister concentrated on her task, her brow furrowing.

"That's very good, Bethany," Kate praised. "You will have to give this to your brother."

"What am I getting?" he asked and entered the room.

Bethany ran to meet him and took his hand, leading him back to the table.

"I draw for you."

"Is that me?" he asked. "And you? And . . . Kit?"

She nodded. "I draw Katelyn, too. She go here." Bethany pointed to a blank spot.

"You can add me to your drawing the next time you come to visit," Kate said. "I'll keep it in a safe place until you return."

"Good." Bethany whispered into Kate's ear and she nodded. Looking at Nicholas, Bethany said, "I sing for you."

Nicholas felt tears sting his eyes. "That would be lovely."

His sister looked back at Kate hesitantly. "I . . . need help."

"You know the song, Bethany. We practiced it several times."

"Sing a little. With me."

"All right," Kate agreed. "I will start and sing a few lines but then you'll have to finish the rest on your own."

Bethany nodded enthusiastically.

The two began singing. True to her word, Kate's voice began fading until she finally ceased singing and allowed Bethany to complete the song.

When his sister finished, she looked at Nicholas hopefully. "You like it?"

He enveloped her in his arms. "I adored it. You need to sing more often. Every day," he suggested.

"We go home?" she asked.

"Aye. You and Mary are going to drive in the cart and I will stay and visit with Kate for a bit."

Panic filled Bethany's eyes. "Bryce?"

He kissed the top of her head. "I asked Bryce to leave Northmere. I've told everyone that he's not allowed back. That means the gatekeeper will not let him inside the castle walls. You'll be free to go wherever you want and never see him. The farmers and soldiers also know he can't come anymore so you and Mary will be able to walk outside the gates, as well."

"No more Bryce?" Bethany asked, disbelief on her face. "Ever?"

"Ever," Nicholas promised.

"Good. Bryce so mean."

"He is. That's why he can no longer live with us."

His sister hugged him tightly. "Thank you, Nicholas. I go home now." She ran into the corridor. "Mary, no more Bryce!" she hollered with enthusiasm.

"It was a good decision," Kate said.

Nicholas turned to her. "I've needed to make it. I appreciate you spurring me into action." He paused. "I can't thank you enough for what you've done for Bethany. She sang all the time when she was a small child. To hear her voice again is like a miracle. You've worked wonders for her, Kate."

"With Bryce gone, I think you'll see even more progress." She went and scooped a napping Kit from the bed. "Time for you to go home, as well, little fur face."

They went downstairs and Kate returned the kitten to Bethany.

"You come see me, Kate-lyn?" Bethany asked hopefully. "And Kit?"

"You'll need to come back here first and finish your picture."

They stepped through the doorway and Kate stumbled back, bumping into Nicholas. He righted her.

"What are so many men doing here?" she asked.

"I passed one of my patrols as I approached the manor house. I send them out regularly, day and night, to ride the estate and the surrounding roads to the border. I thought they could escort Bethany home so that I could stay a few hours with you."

"There are so many. They startled me."

"I would rather err on the side of too many men than have too few." He decided not to tell her about the extra knights he'd stationed to watch over her for now.

They bid Bethany farewell and Nicholas said, "It's a pleasant day. Would you care to go for a ride?"

He saw conflicted emotions cross Kate's face. They hadn't ridden together since she had expressed a desire for them to refrain from kissing. He knew she would be reluctant to ride next to him, their bodies pressed together, and yet he knew they both derived pleasure from it.

"Why don't we stroll instead?" she suggested.

Taking her hand, he placed it through the crook of his arm. "Let's head to the north today."

Nicholas led her to the side of the manor house and then they turned the corner. Kate froze in her tracks, her fingers tightening on him. He saw Henfrey had disappeared, as requested. Only the two horses stood in sight.

She turned to him, her eyes questioning him, no words coming from her parted lips.

"She's yours," he confirmed.

"Oh, Nicholas." Kate kissed his cheek quickly and lifted her skirts in order to run toward the horses.

He stood and drank in the beauty of the moment as she approached the solid black animal and lifted her hand, palm up, in order to allow the animal to sniff her fingers. Then she stroked it lovingly as she spoke to the creature. Finally, she looped her arms about the horse's neck, a mixture of joy and contentment on her features.

Nicholas ventured toward her. "You like her?"

Kate beamed at him. "I adore her. What's her name?"

"This is Ebony. She's a palfrey, a little over two years of age."

"Her coat is gorgeous."

"It reminds me of your dark hair," he said. "And you will look fine riding her."

"Can we go riding now?" she asked, trying to contain her excitement and failing.

"I thought you wished to walk," he teased.

"Nicholas!"

"Let me assist you."

He helped her into the saddle and loosened the reins. Handing them to her, he did the same for Sunset and mounted the horse.

"Where to?" he asked.

"It doesn't matter," she proclaimed.

They started at a walk in order for Ebony to get used to a new rider. It made conversation easy between them, as Nicholas kept Sunset and Ebony side-by-side. After a quarter of an hour, they increased their speed to a canter. Eventually, Kate told him that she wanted to gallop. Nicholas allowed Sunset his head and the horse took off, pulling ahead of Ebony. Glancing over his shoulder, he saw Kate riding behind him, her cheeks flushed with happiness, her long, thick braid bouncing merrily in the air. He promised himself he would never forget the way she looked in this moment.

As he turned back to face ahead, something below him gave way. Before he could figure out what was wrong, he went sailing over Sunset's head and landed hard on the ground, his horse galloping away.

"Nicholas!"

As he lay on his back, he heard Kate scream his name. A wave of nausea hit him. He struggled to inhale and found he couldn't breathe. His head throbbed unmercifully.

"Nicholas!"

Kate was beside him. He felt her lightly touching him. Heard her sobs.

Then everything faded into darkness.

CHAPTER SEVENTEEN

KATELYN KNELT AT Nicholas' side, trying to squelch the panic racing through her. She touched his face. Gently shook his shoulder, calling his name. She angrily wiped away the tears that would do him no good and rolled him to his side to see if her suspicions were confirmed. Moving her fingers along his head, she found a huge knot in the center of the back of his head. He'd landed hard, with no time to break his fall. That might have actually kept him from snapping a wrist or arm, throwing it out to brace himself. It was his head that had received the worst of the impact.

Once more, she moved her hands along his limbs and believed nothing was broken. Still, he remained unconscious, his pallor gray.

What was she to do?

He was much too heavy to lift onto Sunset's back. The horse had run away at first but now circled around and stood nearby, as if he awaited further instructions. Ebony had joined him.

Katelyn decided she must ride for help. Fortunately, she'd paid attention to where they rode today, thanks to the fact that she'd been atop her own horse. When she'd ridden with Nicholas at her back, she'd had a tendency to concentrate more on the feel of him than where they went.

She brushed away the hair that had fallen across his brow, thinking she'd never seen him so still, as if in death. Pushing that thought aside, she clutched his cotehardie and leaned over until their noses practically touched.

"Don't you dare die on me, Nicholas," she ordered. "I won't allow it. Do you hear me?"

He lay unmoving, causing a sob to escape from her.

Katelyn brushed her lips against his tenderly. "I love you, you foolish man. You cannot die. Do you understand? I will never forgive you if you do so."

She placed her palm against his face and closed her eyes briefly, sending a desperate prayer to the Virgin to save Nicholas' life. Then she kissed him once more and stood.

Going to Sunset, it surprised her that the horse wore no saddle. Only the bridle remained, the reins dangling from it. Katelyn had no time to puzzle over this and said to the animal, "I must ride for help. Stay here, Sunset. Keep watch over him. Please." She stroked the horse once and turned to Ebony. "You, my fine lady, need to get me where I am going as fast as you can."

She thrust herself into the saddle and took off toward the manor house. Though she wanted to look back, she kept herself from doing so. Katelyn was afraid if she saw Nicholas all alone, it might be her last memory of him, lying helpless in the dirt.

Swiftly, she rode across the land, a constant prayer hovering on her lips in time to the beat of the horse's hooves. She spied two more riders and urged Ebony on. As she approached, she recognized them as the knights Nicholas had assigned to patrol the area around her manor.

Both men rode quickly toward her. Pulling up on the reins, she drew in a few calming breaths so she could make herself understood as they reached her.

"Lord Nicholas fell from his horse. He is unconscious. I don't think he has any broken bones but he has a nasty knot that's swelling large on the back of his head."

"Show us the way," Sir Albert said.

Katelyn wheeled Ebony and rode to where she'd left Nicholas. All three riders rushed to him. Albert reached him first.

After assessing his condition, the knight said, "I don't want to lash him facedown to his horse. Bouncing along might aggravate his head wound. I think we should tie him to his horse, sitting up. Gerald and I are too large to ride behind him to keep him upright, though. Do you think you could hold him, my lady?"

"I will do whatever it takes to get him back safely to the manor house," Katelyn told the knight.

"Then let's give it a try," Gerald said. He had Albert help raise Nicholas to his feet and the two men moved him over to a waiting Sunset.

"Where is the saddle?" Albert asked, clearly dumbfounded. "We need it to secure him."

"Sunset galloped off after Lord Nicholas was thrown," she explained. "He returned without it."

"Then we must attach him to your horse, my lady," Albert said.

The knights brought Nicholas to Ebony. Katelyn took Gerald's place, wrapping her arms about Nicholas' waist as Gerald ran to his own horse and opened the satchel attached to it, pulling out a few lengths of rope.

"If we need more, we can get it from Albert."

It took the two men a few minutes and much maneuvering, but they managed to get Nicholas onto Ebony's back. Albert lashed his wrists to the pommel and Gerald fixed rope about his waist and brought it under Ebony's belly and back a few times before wrapping it around the pommel and tying it off.

"Let's get you in place, Lady Katelyn," Albert suggested. "And don't worry—I'll take the reins and we'll walk the horse. You're there to keep Lord Nicholas steady."

Gerald helped her up and Katelyn brought her arms about Nicholas, whose head hung, his chin resting against his chest. It worried her that he still hadn't awakened but she tamped down her fears. She would need to concentrate on the task at hand and keep him fixed in the saddle.

Gerald tied Sunset to the back of his horse as Albert took Ebony's reins. Together, the trio began walking their horses. She tried not to think about what was wrong with Nicholas. Getting him to a bed and sending for a healer was what was important. She leaned her cheek against his broad back and held tightly to him.

After what seemed like hours, she heard shouting and heard men running. Opening her eyes, she saw several soldiers appear. She didn't care where they'd come from. She only wanted them to take care of the man she loved.

Katelyn had buried her feelings until now but she could no longer keep pretending to herself. Nicholas Mandeville, Earl of Northmere, was the most remarkable person of her acquaintance. She relished every moment spent in his company. She loved his intelligence and teasing manner. His kindness and handsome face. The way he cared about his people. Even though she still planned to ask for an annulment from him, she would love this nobleman until her last breath.

"Let go, my lady. We have him," a soldier said gently.

Reluctantly, she withdrew her arms from Nicholas and allowed the man to help her dismount. Daggers were produced and used to slice through the rope binding Nicholas to Ebony. As they handed him down gently, she spotted Henfrey.

"Henfrey!"

He raced toward her.

"Ride as fast as you can to Northmere. Bring back the castle's healer. Tell no one what has happened. Do you understand?"

"Aye, my lady," Henfrey said.

"Take Ebony," she commanded. "There's no time for you to saddle your horse."

The squire climbed onto Ebony's back and took off as if the Devil Himself chased after him.

Katelyn followed the men into the manor house and instructed them to take Nicholas to the solar. They placed him on the bed. She ushered them back downstairs and gathered every soldier in sight.

"You are not to speak of what has happened," she said solemnly. "We do not want word getting out to the Scots, especially when we don't know the extent of the earl's injuries. Keep to your duties. Patrol as scheduled. I've sent for the healer and will tell you what I know once she has examined Lord Nicholas."

They nodded their approval and separated, going back to their posts and mounting their horses.

"Sir Albert, since Henfrey is gone for a few hours, will you remain inside the manor?"

"Of course, my lady."

Katelyn saw Dorinda and Lucy awaited her and asked them to bring clean towels and boiled water to the solar. She returned upstairs and went to the bed. Nicholas still looked pale. She decided to remove his clothing and see if he had any wounds she could tend to. First, she took off his boots, struggling for some minutes. Then she slipped off his pants, followed by his cotehardie. She had to pull him to a sitting position to ease it over his head and then gently lay him back down.

Some bruises had begun to discolor his skin but she saw nothing that needed her immediate attention. She couldn't help but stare at his naked form for a moment. Though her experience started and ended with Cedric on their wedding night in seeing a man unclothed, she doubted many lived up to this kind of perfection. Nicholas' arms and legs were sculpted in muscle. His broad chest was covered in a fine matting of light golden hair that tapered below his waist. His manhood nestled in a bunch of dark curls.

Though she longed to run her hands along every inch of him, Katelyn did not want to violate his privacy any more than she had. Fortunately, the men who'd brought him upstairs had thought to pull the bedclothes back before placing him on the bed. She covered him with them and sat in a chair that she pulled close to the bed. Katelyn slipped her hand under the covers and found Nicholas' hand. She brought it out and held it in her lap.

"Please don't die," she whispered.

Dorinda and Lucy appeared with buckets of the boiled water and towels. They wanted to stay but she told them she would rather they go. Katelyn tilted his head to the side and bathed around the huge lump that had swollen to the size of her fist. It frightened her to see it so large and wondered if it would take his life. The longer he remained unconscious, the more her anxiety grew. She left him on his side, hoping that might bring some relief to him, not lying directly on the bump. Taking his hand again, she stared at his beautiful face.

And prayed.

"My lady?"

Katelyn dragged her eyes from Nicholas and saw a birdlike woman entering the solar. She was the size of a large child, with deep green eyes and hair as white as snow. Her face was unlined. She could have been between two and four score. Katelyn didn't care. All she needed to know was if this woman could bring Nicholas back to her.

She released his hand and stood. "I am Katelyn Mandeville. Are you the Northmere healer?"

"Aye. Young Henfrey summoned me. We slipped from the castle unseen, using the sally port. The squire told me you told him to tell no one we came here." She nodded in approval. "I am Elewys. It's best that the Scots not get wind of the earl's accident." She paused. "If it is an accident."

Katelyn frowned. "I hadn't thought about the cause. One minute we were galloping. The next, Lord Nicholas flew from the saddle."

Elewys' lips thinned. "The earl has been an expert rider from the time his father put him in the saddle. He rode as soon as he could walk. There has to be a reason he fell." She glanced to the bed. "Tell me everything."

Quickly, Katelyn related how she'd checked him for broken bones immediately after his fall and found none. That she'd undressed him and seen nothing but bruises on his body.

"What's given me concern is the large knot on the back of his head. His head took the brunt of the fall when he hit the ground. The swelling has continued to grow. He's not regained consciousness since then."

The older woman took her time examining Nicholas. Katelyn stood nearby with watchful eyes, ready to do anything the healer asked of her.

Finally, Elewys stepped back, her lips pursed. "Head wounds can be complicated," she began. "The earl might wake up and have no knowledge of what occurred, either during the incident or even the few days before."

"He wouldn't remember Sunset bolting and tossing him?" Katelyn asked.

"Aye. Or he could awaken and merely have a bad headache." Elewys frowned. "Sometimes, though, it can be worse."

"How much worse?" she asked, a lump forming in her throat.

"I have seen severe head wounds kill a man," the healer said. "Or when the injured person comes to, they are not the same as they were before."

"What do you mean?" Katelyn's heart began pounding fiercely.

"An outgoing man may suddenly be quite shy." She paused. "A once happy man might grow . . . sullen. Or angry."

"Would the person return to as he was after time passed?" she asked hopefully.

Elewys shook her head sadly. "Usually not. We won't know until Lord Nicholas awakens how this blow will impact him. And those around him."

Katelyn blinked back tears. "I love him," she blurted out.

The healer touched her arm lightly. "That is good. You will be able to help him recover from whatever ails him." She paused. "And help him learn what truly happened."

She thought a moment. "Sunset ran off after he threw Nicholas. When the horse returned, he no longer wore a saddle."

"Find the saddle—and you'll discover the truth."

"Is there anything I can do to help you?"

"Nay, my lady. I plan to mix some salve to slather on his bruises to promote quick healing. I'll fashion a poultice with herbs such as lavender and rose to place on the swelling. When he awakens, we'll know if he has a headache or nausea and deal with those things."

"I'll let you care for him then," Katelyn said. "For now, I need to find his missing saddle. Excuse me."

She left the solar and returned downstairs to where Sir Albert still stood guard, even though Henfrey had returned. She sent the squire upstairs to assist the healer if needed.

"My lady, how is the earl?" the knight asked anxiously when she came to stand next to him.

"Still fast asleep. Elewys is tending to him. I need your help, though."

"Anything. I am at you service."

"Elewys tells me Lord Nicholas is an excellent rider. That's certainly what I've seen. I want you and Sir Gerald to ride back to where the accident occurred and locate the earl's saddle. Sunset galloped off and came back without it. It's imperative to locate and examine this saddle."

Albert's eyes lit with understanding. "You think someone tampered with it."

"I do. But I need proof. Speak to no one about this."

"I'll go now. And send another knight inside to stand watch. We have plenty to choose from."

She remembered seeing more soldiers about than usual. "Did the earl send more men to the manor house?"

The knight nodded in confirmation. "He felt it wise after dismissing his brother from Northmere."

"I see. Bring me the saddle the minute you return, Sir Albert."

Katelyn returned upstairs. She and Henfrey watched how Elewys made the poultice so they could do the same and then helped apply the salve to the bruises that covered Nicholas' body. The healer explained how to brew ginger root and chamomile in steeped water and have Nicholas drink it once he awakened in order to treat any nausea or headaches that might occur.

"There's not much else I can do for him, my lady," Elewys said. "I have showed you all you need to care for him and will leave with you the herbs we discussed. If you truly want to keep what happened to the earl a secret for now, I should return to the castle."

"Will anyone have missed you?" Katelyn asked anxiously.

"I often leave to search for herbs and flowers. I have my satchel with me. When I return with it, that is where others will think I have been."

"Henfrey can take you back to Northmere now." She thought a moment. "Will you give me a few minutes? I want to send a missive to Sir Rafe."

Katelyn went to the table and put aside the drawing that Bethany had been working on and took out a fresh parchment. Dipping her quill into the ink she penned a few lines to Rafe Mandeville.

Sir Rafe –

I have foolishly turned my ankle while Nicholas and I walked this afternoon. He insists on staying with me a few days to keep me company while I mend. He allowed me to write to you because I have not practiced my letters since I left the convent and do not want to lose this skill. You are to take care of Northmere for him. Give my best to Lady Ellyn.

Lady Katelyn Mandeville

"Bring me Lord Nicholas' signet ring, Henfrey," Katelyn directed as she rolled the parchment and tilted a candle to its edge. After the wax dripped on the paper, she gave Henfrey the candle and pressed Nicholas' ring into the warm wax, marking it as officially from him. She only hoped Rafe didn't question her words or the reason why Nicholas would be absent from Northmere.

"Drop Elewys off near the castle walls and ride alone to the keep. Give this to Sir Rafe."

"Am I to wait for a reply?"

"If he chooses to respond." Quickly, Katelyn explained the excuse she had given the knight in case he quizzed Henfrey. "If he asks when Lord Nicholas will return, play ignorant."

"Whatever you wish, my lady." The squire looked to Elewys. "I'll be waiting for you downstairs."

Once he left, Katelyn drew the old woman into an embrace. "Thank you for caring for Nicholas."

Elewys smiled. "Thank you for loving him, my lady. He's a good man and has been a lonely one. You will make him a fine wife."

Katelyn refrained from telling the healer why she could never be Nicholas' wife and merely said, "Take care."

The healer left the solar and Katelyn returned to her bedside vigil, looking for any small sign that Nicholas might awaken. She didn't know how much time had passed when a knock sounded on the solar's door.

Quickly, she got to her feet to admit the visitor, hoping it was Sir Albert. Opening the door, she was relieved it was the knight and ushered him and Sir Gerald in. Henfrey followed behind them. Between them they carried Sunset's saddle and hoisted it onto the table as the squire shut the door.

Albert's face told her what she needed to know before he even spoke. "You were right, Lady Katelyn. Someone meddled with the girth."

CHAPTER EIGHTEEN

"**S**HOW ME," KATELYN demanded, anger at an unknown person who'd set out to harm Nicholas building inside her.

"Here." Sir Gerald lifted a piece and pointed to a spot. "Someone sliced through the girth. Not all the way. Lord Nicholas would have to have ridden a while before the stress on the damaged leather gave way."

She sat on the bench and took the girth in her hands, studying it carefully.

"Lord Nicholas is very particular with his horse," Henfrey said. "He usually saddles it himself. Occasionally, he lets me do it for him. Since I was at the manor house, he would have done so himself."

"He would have noticed it at once," Sir Albert added.

"Which means someone meddled with it after he arrived here," Katelyn said. "Since Nicholas and I usually stroll outside instead of riding, the girth would have broken apart once he was on his way back to Northmere."

"Aye," Sir Gerald agreed. "Lord Nicholas would have been alone and vulnerable to attack if thrown from Sunset. 'Tis possible the Scots would have captured him and held him for ransom."

"They do that?"

"Aye, my lady," Sir Albert replied. "It's a common tactic and helps to fill their coffers in times of need. The Earl of Northmere would have been a valuable prize to them."

Katelyn turned to Henfrey. "Did you care for Sunset when the earl arrived?"

The boy nodded. "Lord Nicholas instructed me to take Sunset and Ebony behind the manor house so Ebony would be out of sight. He wanted to surprise you with the palfrey. He asked for me to return to the soldiers gathered in front, those who were intended to escort Lady Bethany back to the castle."

"That left Sunset unattended for a few minutes then," she said.

Henfrey nodded, his eyes filling with tears. "I should have stayed with the horses," he whispered, guilt obvious on his face.

Katelyn put a hand on the boy's shoulder. "You did exactly what the earl told you to do, Henfrey. No one would have expected for the Scots to be so close and cause such mischief."

But she wondered if this was truly the work of Scottish rebels. Only yesterday, Nicholas had exiled his brother from ever returning to his home. She leaned toward believing that somehow Bryce might be involved but held her tongue.

"I'll make sure the soldiers on duty are alerted that a few Scots slipped across the border without sharing any specifics," Sir Gerald said.

When he started to lift the saddle, Katelyn stopped him. "Nay. Leave it here. Lord Nicholas will want to see it."

The three excused themselves and exited the solar. She returned to her vigil at Nicholas' side. Lucy brought broth and bread for the nobleman in case he awoke and begged her to eat something, as well.

Katelyn waved the servant away. "I'll eat when I'm hungry. Go to bed, Lucy. I know it grows late."

After Lucy left, Katelyn yawned and decided to put out the candles so she could try and get some rest herself. Taking a seat in the chair again, she held fast to Nicholas' hand and soon fell asleep, a prayer for his swift recovery on her lips.

NICHOLAS FROWNED AS the image of a laughing Kate riding Ebony began to dissipate. His eyelids fluttered a few times and he discovered himself in total darkness. Before he could think where he might be, a wave of nausea rolled through him. He swallowed the bile and then realized his head pounded something fierce. Reaching a hand to his head, he touched material wrapped around it, smelling the herbs from a poultice. Underneath it he felt a bulge that was quite tender and decided that was the cause of his headache.

Lowering his hand, he caught the scent of vanilla in the air and realized Kate held his other hand. He tried to sit up but the throbbing grew worse so he stilled.

"Nicholas?"

"Aye, Kate. Is that you?"

He heard a choked sound and then Kate wrapped both of her hands around his. She pressed fervent kisses to his knuckles, which suddenly grew wet with her tears. He slipped his free hand atop hers.

"What's wrong, sweetheart?"

"I thought . . . I thought you might never wake up."

He frowned. "How long have I . . . where *am* I?"

"You are in the solar at the manor house," she told him. "Do you remember what happened?"

Nicholas tried to remember the last thing he'd done. "We were riding." He smiled, her image coming to him again. "You seemed so happy on Ebony's back."

"I was," she said softly.

"Then . . . I don't know. Something gave way. I felt—or heard it—

and then I was falling."

"Your head slammed against the ground."

"That's where the knot comes from," he mused.

"Does it hurt much?"

"My head does ache."

He sensed that she stood and was about to move away and gripped her hands to keep her from leaving.

"I have something to help you," she explained. "Elewys left some herbs I can use to alleviate any headaches or nausea you might experience."

"Elewys? She was here?"

"Aye. I had Henfrey bring her. No one knows, though. I didn't want word to leak that you had been injured. Henfrey returned Elewys to Northmere after she'd been here a few hours."

"So, it is the same day?"

"It's night now. The dead of night." She tried to pull away again. "Let me fetch the herbs."

"Nay. Stay with me, Kate. Please."

"But your head—"

"It doesn't ache much," he lied. "It's a hard one, you know. Mother always teased that it was as sturdy as a stone wall. I was always falling and tearing about when I was young."

"Are you hungry?"

"I am. For you."

Nicholas sensed the air grow heavy between them.

"Would you come lie beside me?"

Kate didn't say anything.

"Please? It would comfort me."

"All right."

He released his grip on her hands and felt her weight come down on the mattress. She nestled against him, her cheek against his beating heart. His arms went about her. He pushed the pulsating pain away so he could enjoy the feel of her. One warm palm rested against his bare chest and he realized that he was naked.

If only Kate were.

Gradually, she relaxed against him. In the darkness, he was more aware of the scent of vanilla rising from her skin. Her soft breaths. The feel of her smooth cotehardie. Having Kate in his arms made him feel complete. Nicholas only hoped she believed the same.

It startled him when he suddenly understood why this felt so right. His heart finally told his head what he'd known all along.

He loved Kate. Loved her. *Loved her.*

She was still so skittish that he knew he could never say the words aloud to her. There was a time for words—and a time when actions spoke in place of words.

He kissed the top of her head, her hair silky against his lips.

"Thank you," he said.

She raised her face. "For what?"

"For taking such good care of me."

Without asking, he brought his mouth down, brushing his lips against hers. It seemed a lifetime since he'd kissed her. Slowly, he teased her lips open and leisurely began exploring. His tongue ran along her straight teeth and slid along the roof of her mouth. She giggled and he grew bolder, stroking her tongue and then capturing it between his teeth. Soon, Kate joined in his games and kissed him with a matched fervor.

His hand moved to the back of her neck, holding her steady as the onslaught of kisses grew more heated. Then he broke the kiss and feathered light ones along her jaw. His teeth grazed the side of her neck and Kate moaned softly. Emboldened by her reaction, his lips trailed lower, moving to the valley between her breasts. One hand cupped her breast and she trembled.

"Nicholas . . . I thought you weren't going to kiss me anymore," she murmured.

Through her gown, he rolled her nipple between his fingers and heard her gasp.

"You can tell me to stop," he said, praying fervently that she wouldn't as he pushed aside her cotehardie and licked the upper curve of her breast.

"Oh!"

"Does that mean stop?"

"Nay," she gasped.

Nicholas continued, his tongue finding her nipple and teasing it. Kate trembled beneath him.

"What are you doing?"

He heard curiosity in her question and decided that this was one thing his father hadn't done. Cedric Mandeville had been a selfish man and Nicholas could easily believe him to be a selfish lover. He doubted his father had done anything for Kate's pleasure. Only his own.

Breaking the contact, he lifted his head, wishing he could see her eyes. Instead, only the pitch black of the dark night surrounded them.

"I am doing what I can to pleasure you. Kissing is but one way we can know pleasure."

"And what about consummation?" she asked anxiously. "You said you were going to wait a month."

He laughed. "There are many things we can do that fall between kissing and completing the marriage act. I would like to show you a few. None will get you with child. They will only bring you satisfaction." He paused. "Are you interested?"

"Aye." The word was so soft, he barely heard it.

Nicholas went back to lavishing attention on her breast, enjoying her squirms and sighs before moving to the other one. His hands stroked her curves, running along her sides from her breasts to below her hips and back again. He kissed his way down to her belly, holding her hips steady. Though he longed to go lower and taste her, he knew not to press her too quickly. Instead, he returned to her mouth and kissed her deeply as his fingers reached under her cotehardie and glided along her smooth thighs. He found the nest of curls and pushed a finger inside her.

Kate jumped. "Oh, Nicholas! What are doing?"

He slowly stroked her. "Making you happy, I hope."

"Are you supposed to *do* this?" she asked, uncertainty in her voice.

It angered him that his father had not even done this for her, which meant Cedric hadn't prepared her on their wedding night. No wonder Kate seemed so frightened of what their passion would lead to. Her groom had mounted her and thrust inside her, spilling her virgin blood in a harsh manner.

Nicholas would make it up to her, a thousand times over.

"A husband and wife can do whatever they want when they are together. Nothing is wrong. Only what makes each other happy and fulfilled is what is right."

He continued to stroke her as he spoke and then added a second finger.

"Nicholas!"

He covered her mouth with his again, his kisses as deep as his fingers as he teased her along. Sensing she came close to fulfillment, he found the sweet nub and began fondling it. Kate's nails dug into his bare shoulders as her body began shuddering. She moved against his hand and he sped up his strokes.

Suddenly, she cried out and pushed against him, over and over.

"Ride it, Kate," he urged. "Ride it."

She did as told, clinging to him, tightening around his fingers, whimpering. A violent tremor shook her. Slowly, she stilled and he kissed her lovingly.

"What did you do to me?" she asked, wonder in her voice.

Nicholas wanted to say that he'd loved her but knew he couldn't. Instead, he gave her a swift, hard kiss. "I brought you joy, my lady."

Kate giggled. "That you did, my lord."

He nestled her against him again. "I am tired, Kate. I must sleep."
When she tried to move away, he tightened his arms about her.
"Stay."

"That sounds like a command," she murmured against his chest.

"It was. Your liege lord—and husband—orders you to keep still."

"Aye, my lord."

Nicholas listened as her breathing evened out and her limbs relaxed. With each breath he inhaled the faint scent of vanilla, which
seemed to calm him. He didn't fall asleep, though. He supposed he'd
already had too much of it.

As he lay next to Kate, he thought about Sunset throwing him. It
was unlike the horse to be temperamental. Something had occurred.
When morning came, he would discover what.

He must have dozed eventually. He awoke as Kate began to stir.
She burrowed against his neck a moment and then stretched. Soon,
every day would be like this one. He would wake with Kate in his
arms. The difference would be that he would make love to her after
she did. And again in the afternoon. Once more before they fell asleep.
Nicholas could even believe he would wake her during the night for
love play.

Bryce had been right about one thing—he was besotted with his
wife.

"Mmm."

He felt her push back the bedclothes and slip from the bed before
she pulled them over him again.

"Where are you going?" he asked.

"You must be famished. I had bread and broth here for you when
you awoke. Let me light a few candles and I will bring it to you. How
is your head?"

"A dull ache. Nothing more." The pounding had begun again as
his stomach growled noisily. "I suppose I am hungry."

Nicholas heard her padding across the floor. He closed his eyes and stretched his arms over his head, feeling lazy. Mayhap he could claim to need another day of rest and keep Kate to himself all day long in this bed. He sensed her coming toward him and rolled to his side, propping his head up with a hand. That helped relieve some of the pressure in his head.

Opening his eyes, he said, "I hope you'll join me in breaking my fast."

The mattress moved with her weight but he couldn't see her.

"I thought you were going to light a candle, Kate."

She didn't speak. He sensed heat near him, as if she held a raised candle nearby.

"Kate?" He tried to hold his panic at bay.

"Nicholas. Look at me," she instructed.

"I am . . . but I don't see you."

He reached a hand out and touched her wrist. His fingers went up her hand and he found she held a candlestick.

But he couldn't see it. He couldn't see her.

He was blind.

CHAPTER NINETEEN

NICHOLAS SUCKED IN air as if he couldn't breathe. The pounding in his head magnified. He wanted to scream in frustration.

Kate's palm touched his face. "I am here, Nicholas."

It was as if her hand scorched his face. He fell back against the pillows and winced, the knot throbbing painfully as he landed on it. Quickly, he rolled to his side, trying to calm himself—and failing.

"This could be temporary," she said. "I know you are frightened but the blindness may not last. The tumble you took was nasty. You need to give your head time to heal."

He flung all his fury at her. "And what if it *does* last? How am I to be the Earl of Northmere? How can I care for my people? How could I lead men into battle?"

"Worrying about it won't help," she pointed out calmly. "You need to concentrate on getting well. Are you feeling ill? Does your head ache?"

"Both," he growled, wishing she would leave him alone.

"Elewys thought you would experience both. I will go to the kitchens and boil some water to steep the herbs she left. There's ginger to combat your nausea and chamomile to sooth your aching head. I'll also prepare a new poultice to apply to the swelling."

Nicholas sensed her move back a few feet. Already, his hearing seemed more acute with his sight gone.

"I'll return soon with fresh broth and bread. You'll need to keep up your strength."

He listened as her steps receded and then slammed his fists against the mattress, feeling as helpless as a newborn. Being the earl of the largest estate in Northumberland brought a great many responsibilities. Nicholas couldn't begin to imagine how he could fulfill them in his current state. And if the Scots discovered how vulnerable he was, they would invade swiftly since his estate was the first one on the English side of the border. He would be useless in any attack that occurred. He would let down not only his own people but his king and country.

Tears began to fall. He couldn't recall a time when he'd ever cried. Not when his Mother passed. Not when Favian died in his arms. Not any time he'd been injured on the battlefield. Nicholas realized, though, why the tears came now. Though the blindness could be a temporary side effect from his fall, he had to prepare as if this would be his permanent state. That meant he knew exactly what he must do.

Seek an annulment from Kate.

Nicholas wouldn't burden her with marriage to half a man. He loved her enough to let her go. That meant pushing her away. Proving he didn't want her. Not letting her guess how much he truly needed her, now more than before.

He steeled himself, waiting for her return. He would remain polite but distant. He feared he would compose himself and then fall apart the minute she returned. Drawing from a deep well of courage inside him, Nicholas told himself he did what was best for her.

Because he loved her.

He heard her steps first. Then caught her scent and the smell of bread and meat. Heard the tray being set down. Pushing himself up, he braced his back against the pillows.

"I want you to drink first," she said. "Lift your hands. I'll place the bowl in them."

He did as she asked and could almost see the bowl being placed in front of him. She pressed it against his hands and he wrapped his fingers firmly around it. Tilting it to his lips, he drank greedily, realizing how thirsty he was. When he finished, she told him she had another one for him to drink and he did the same.

"Those contained the herbs to help relieve your pain and ease your belly," Kate said as she removed the bowl from his hands. "I'm going to unwrap the cloth from your head now and replace the poultice with a fresh one."

Nicholas remained still, so aware of Kate's nearness. He fought the urge to capture her face and bring her mouth to his. He pushed the thought aside. Kissing her was a luxury he would never partake in again. Nay, not a luxury. A necessity he must learn to live without.

She completed ministering to him and eased him back into the pillows again.

"You need to keep up your strength. I'm going to set a tray in front of you now." She did and said, "Warm broth is in a bowl in the center of the tray. To its left is half a loaf of freshly-baked bread. Above the bowl rests a leg and thigh of roasted chicken. Directly to the right of that is a cup of cool ale."

His Kate knew him well. He would never want her to feed him like some invalid. Telling him the location of each item on the tray would allow him some small bit of independence.

"Thank you. You may go now."

"You don't wish me to stay?" she asked.

"I'd rather eat alone," he replied evenly.

Nicholas was so attuned to her that he felt the hurt roll from her.

"I see. I'll come back in an hour and retrieve the tray then."

He had much to think on and asked, "Kate, did anyone find something wrong with Sunset's saddle?"

"Aye. Someone deliberately cut through part of the girth," she revealed, causing him to grow cold inside. "The saddle is lying on the table across the room. I knew you would want to inspect it."

He would—only with his fingers now instead of his eyes.

"We should send word to Northmere—"

"I've already done so. I told your uncle that I'd injured my ankle and that you were staying with me as I recovered to cheer me up."

"I see you've thought of everything." Nicholas couldn't help but admire Kate's intelligence. Though he longed to praise her for her quick thinking, he remained silent.

"I'll leave you to break your fast," she finally said and left.

Nicholas knew he'd wounded her but he needed to prepare them both for the time they would part for good. He couldn't count on his sight returning. For now, he needed to guard her heart—as well as his own.

KATELYN RESOLVED TO stay strong as she entered the solar. After Nicholas had discovered he was blind yesterday, he had been curt to her and asked to be left alone. She'd wandered about the manor feeling lost, knowing she couldn't tell a soul what was truly wrong with him. Dorinda, Lucy, and Henfrey obviously knew something was amiss since she only went in to take Nicholas more steeped herbs before quickly retreating. Fortunately, they didn't ask any questions.

Now, she approached the bed where the man she loved lay. In sleep, he looked younger than when he was awake, worrying about everything he should be doing.

And couldn't.

She longed to send for Elewys again but her gut told her the healer would tell her it would take time until they knew for certain if

Nicholas would regain his sight or if it would be lost forever.

Katelyn cleared her throat and watched him stir. He opened his eyes and stared out in her direction. She could tell that nothing had changed. It was hard holding on to hope but she did so fiercely, once more imploring the Virgin to intercede on Nicholas' behalf and grant a return of his sight.

"Good morning," she said as he pushed himself to a sitting position. "How are you feeling today?"

"The nausea is gone," he informed her. "The pain in my head is subsiding."

"That's good news," she said, not too brightly, for she was afraid that would set off his temper again. He'd lost it twice yesterday. Katelyn knew he wasn't berating her but merely finding it hard to cope with the circumstances he found himself in.

"I'll save the ginger then and only give you the other herbs. Hopefully, the pain will continue to recede as the day progresses. May I look at the knot on your head?"

Nicholas nodded. She unwound the cloth that held the poultice into place and then lifted both away. Taking a candle that was burning on the bedside table, she lifted it and inspected his head. Gently, she moved her fingers along it, pleased with what she saw and felt.

"The swelling has diminished. I think I can leave the poultice off."

"Good."

Lifting one of the bowls she'd brought, she said, "Please drink this. If the hurt lessens even more, this may be the last time you do so."

Nicholas took the bowl and downed the contents. He pushed the bowl in her direction and she took it from him.

"I'm placing the tray in your lap again. Everything has been placed at the same spot as yesterday." She hesitated. "Do you need anything else?"

His fingers sought the bread and tore some from the loaf. "Tell me about my saddle again."

As he chewed, Katelyn explained how Sunset had galloped away after the incident and returned without a saddle on his back.

"Once I suspected foul play, I sent Sir Albert and Sir Gerald to search for it. They brought the saddle back and showed me where the girth had been tampered with. I had them leave it so you could see for yourself."

She winced the moment the words came from her mouth, knowing how insensitive they were.

Nicholas merely grunted and continued to eat.

When he remained silent, she rose. "I will excuse myself. I'll be back later to see if you need anything."

Katelyn exited the solar, her heart heavy. If Nicholas did not regain his sight, she didn't know how it would affect him. He was such a strong, capable man, use to leading others by example. It would be very difficult for him to fulfill all of his responsibilities as Earl of Northmere if the blindness proved to be permanent. She halted as the realization hit her.

Nicholas needed her, now more than ever. Though she might not be the best choice of a wife for him, Katelyn understood that it would be important to remain by his side. If she asked for the annulment now, he would always think she rejected him because he was blind. It was important to stand by him, no matter what. *She* could be his eyes. Ride the estate. Visit with his people. Share with him what should be done. She could function as a true partner to him.

In that moment, Katelyn knew she must do whatever it took to remain in her marriage.

Returning downstairs, she went to sit by the fire. She became lost in thought, thinking of what her life would be like as the Countess of Northmere. It would be important to put aside any fear or hesitations she might possess. She needed to be strong—not only for herself—but for her husband and their people.

That meant they needed to consummate their marriage. Soon. It would be hard enough once word leaked out that Nicholas was blind. Her status as the king's cousin, married to the Earl of Northmere, would be more important than ever before. The Scots, as well as the nobles of the north, must understand how strongly the king supported Northmere and Northumberland, wedding his own cousin to Nicholas.

A hand touched her shoulder. Katelyn glanced up to see Rafe Mandeville standing before her. She masked her surprise.

"I would have thought you would still be abed. Or at least sitting with that ankle propped up," the knight said.

"My ankle is much better now, thank you, my lord."

"Where is Nicholas then?" he demanded. "He doesn't need to dance attendance upon you any longer. There are things he must take care of at the castle."

"He is upstairs, resting in the solar," Katelyn began. "He is ill."

"Ill?" Rafe snorted. "Nicholas is never ill. He's suffered a few wounds in battle that made him take to his bed but that's never been for long. I'll see that he attends to business as he ought to."

Rafe strode away. Katelyn leaped to her feet and dashed after the knight as he hurried across the great hall and up the stairs. The nobleman reached the solar and entered without bothering to knock.

She saw Nicholas sitting up in the bed. He'd dressed since she'd left this morning and had placed his tray on the floor.

"What is this about, Nicholas? I can't remember a day in your life when you've been sick."

"I had a fall from Sunset, Uncle," Nicholas replied smoothly, looking in the direction of where Rafe's voice came from. He touched his fingers to the back of his head. "I've got a nasty bump."

Rafe leaned over and inspected the swollen spot. He stepped back and studied Nicholas. Katelyn saw Nicholas continued to look steadily at his uncle. She hoped Rafe wouldn't guess what Nicholas obviously wanted to hide.

"You should have come back to Northmere after it happened," the knight grumbled. "Elewys could have tended to you."

"Nicholas experienced dizziness and nausea, my lord," Katelyn explained. "It would have been impossible for him to ride back to the castle in that condition. Placing him in a cart would have been too jarring. We thought it best he remain at the manor house for the time being."

"We?" Rafe asked. "When does a woman help make decisions for the Earl of Northmere?"

"When she's my wife," Nicholas said firmly.

His words renewed Katelyn's hope that he still wanted them to remain wed. He'd been so distant and hurtful the past two days. She hoped he meant what he said and didn't put on a show of unity for his uncle when none truly existed.

"A wife is to do as she's told," Rafe bluntly insisted. "Not decide anything."

"Katelyn is as intelligent as any man of my acquaintance. I trust her opinions."

Rafe grunted. "You seem fine to me. Get out of that bed. That is, if you can tear yourself away from your pretty wife." He turned to leave. "What's that?"

"That is Sunset's saddle," she said, following Rafe's gaze and letting Nicholas know what his uncle spoke of. As Rafe moved toward the table, she added, "Someone wished to do Nicholas harm."

The nobleman bent and ran his hands along the leather until he reached the girth. "This didn't happen without help." He started back toward the bed. "How on earth did the Scots manage to tinker with your saddle?"

Katelyn saw an odd look cross the knight's face. He paused and stepped to the side and then, lightning fast, threw a glove at Nicholas, who stared at the spot where Rafe had stood moments ago.

It smacked Nicholas in the face. His hands flew up instinctively to protect himself as the glove dropped to his lap.

Rafe raced to the bed and bent, his face so close that his nose almost touched his nephew's nose. Nicholas shoved his uncle away.

"You're blind," Rafe said, stating the obvious. "By the Christ, what happened?"

"The fall," Nicholas said dully. "I awoke to blinding pain and pressure in my head. Somehow, my sight has been affected."

"We're hoping as his pain lessens and the pressure eases that his vision will return," Katelyn quickly added.

"How are you supposed to lead, Nicholas?" Rafe demanded.

"Give him time," Katelyn urged.

"The Scots will use this to their advantage," the knight said in a dismissive tone.

"Then don't tell them about it!" snapped Nicholas.

"How are we to keep it a secret, Nephew? You can't stay hidden away in this manor house forever."

"Tell those at Northmere that the Scots have attempted a new raid across the border," Katelyn suggested. "Say they attempted to attack the manor house. Nicholas often leads the parties guarding the border. Make it known that he does so now. He could be gone a week or more without anyone questioning his absence. No one need suspect a thing."

"Meanwhile, he'll lie in his bed, feeling sorry for himself?" Rafe asked. Then he smirked at her. "Or I suppose you can entertain him, my lady. Of course, you'll have to take his cock in hand and guide it into you. He certainly can't see to do it himself."

Nicholas threw back the bedclothes and jumped from the bed. Unfortunately, he'd forgotten he'd set the tray beside it. He tripped, falling hard, face down.

Katelyn gasped and hurried toward him, helping him rise to his feet. Blood dripped from his nose as he stared angrily, his head turning, trying to locate his uncle.

Rafe sneered at them. "I'll keep your little secret for a week, Nephew. No more. After that, I'll expect you to return home.

"And then you'll renounce your title—and name me the new earl."

Chapter Twenty

N ICHOLAS' BLOOD CURDLED at his uncle's words.

Before he could say anything, Kate's fingers fell from his arm and she said, "Get out. Now."

In those three words, Nicholas heard both courage and resolve. Kate didn't raise her voice to Rafe. She didn't cry or cajole or beg. She told the knight what to do—and waited for him to respond, certain that he would follow her command. Tension hung heavy in the air, as if it could have physically been sliced through with a sword. Nicholas listened, every muscle in his body frozen, and heard his uncle's footsteps begin.

And then recede.

A subtle change occurred near him, letting him know Kate must be following Rafe. Her steps paused and then he heard the door pushed closed. She came back to him and took his arm.

"I'm leading you to a chair. It's about fifteen paces away."

They walked slowly. It was the first time he'd moved across the room since he'd awoken with no sight. His heart raced as if he were about to ride into battle. Fear of the darkness surrounding him threatened to swallow him whole with each step he took—yet he refused to give in to it. The person he trusted most had hold of him. She would keep him safe. Kate brought them to a halt and Nicholas reached out, finding the arm of the chair and lowering himself into it. Her skirts swished subtly, her body heat moving away from him. She returned and set something down nearby.

"I'm going to wash the blood away."

He liked that she always told him what she was doing and where things were located. In the world of darkness he now inhabited, it allowed him to paint a picture in his mind. Knowing what she did now, he listened and heard the cloth dipped into water and wrung out. Felt her wiping under his nose and around his lower face.

"Some of the blood dripped onto your cotehardie. You'll need to remove it so I can try to wash it out."

"Later," he said. "I have more important things to worry about."

She sat in a chair next to him. "Can Rafe force you to relinquish your title?"

"Nay. But he can make things difficult for me. He is Northmere's captain of the guard and the eldest member of the Mandeville family. He has the respect of our many soldiers for he is a skilled one himself, proven many times over. They would listen to him—and his words could poison them against me. Normally, I couldn't have foreseen any circumstance where Rafe might speak out against me.

"My blindness changes everything."

Nicholas thought for a moment and then added, "Custom dictates that a liege lord offers his protection to his people. They, in return, give him their labor and loyalty. If the people of Northmere believe I cannot provide a safe haven for them, especially since we are so perilously close to the border, I might witness a gradual shift in their allegiance. My uncle could stir up enough doubt to make them question their fidelity to me and clamor for me to be replaced."

"Why would you name him earl, though?" Kate asked. "I cannot understand that. If, for any reason, you did decide to step down, wouldn't Bryce succeed you? If anything happened to you, your brother would be next in line to succeed."

"Legally, that would be true. I fear that Rafe would not only incite my people but he would be bold enough to take his case and petition the king. Edward alone has the authority to strip me of the earldom and award it to whomever he chooses. It happens rarely but it's not unheard of."

Her fingers entwined with his, bringing Nicholas not only warmth but the knowledge that she still believed in him, despite his impairment.

"Then that is where I can step in. I may not know my cousin well but I am his cousin. I would have his ear more than Rafe ever could. The fact that Landon is my brother and has served Edward loyally for so many years would sway the king in whatever I might ask of him." Kate squeezed his hand. "Have faith, Nicholas. We can stop Rafe. Together."

Her words ripped his heart in two. If she had spoken to him this way before the incident, he would have been jubilant, knowing she finally committed to him and their marriage.

Nicholas withdrew his hand from hers. "Circumstances have changed, Kate. I cannot allow you to be attached to me anymore. Any battles to be fought with Rafe will be ones I must fight on my own."

"What are you saying?" Her tone was sharp.

"I no longer think being wedded to one another is the wisest course of action. I will be the one to seek an annulment."

"I won't let you!" she cried.

"It doesn't matter," he said sadly. "As a man, I have more legal standing than you. I made known in front of witnesses my vow to leave you untouched until a month has passed."

"But you didn't," she insisted. "You *have* touched me intimately. We are wed, Nicholas."

"We have never consummated our marriage, Kate."

"I pledged before God and others to be yours. I will keep that vow," she insisted.

Knowing it would hurt her, he grit his teeth and then said, "If I have to commit you to a nunnery, I will. It's my choice, Kate. And I choose to free you from me."

Her shocked silence blanketed him. Nicholas sat still, waiting for her to speak.

Finally, she said, "You would send me back to a convent. Knowing what my life was like among the nuns. All to free yourself from me."

Nicholas drove the final nail into the coffin. "I would—unless you agree to an annulment."

Kate cradled his face and pressed a sweet kiss to his lips. It took everything he had not to respond. She pushed her fingers into his hair, combing them through it as her tongue swept slowly back and forth, insisting he open his mouth to her. He remained firm and resolved not to react.

Even if it killed him.

Her fingers and tongue ceased moving. She withdrew.

"You need me," she said firmly. "Whether you know it or not. Blind or with sight. You need me—as much as I need you." Her voice broke on that last word and then she choked out, "I love you, Nicholas. Now and forever. Please, don't send me away."

He stared straight ahead, not blinking, not acknowledging the precious words she'd spoken, keeping secret that he returned her love.

Her lips brushed against his brow. "Farewell," she whispered.

The door opened and closed.

Nicholas sat in the chair.

And wept.

KATELYN FLED TO the chamber across the hall from the solar. She allowed herself to weep for a few minutes and then angrily brushed the tears away. Tears would not solve her current dilemma.

How could one man prove to be so stubborn?

At first, he had pursued her, trying to convince her they should remain in their marriage. Now, when he needed her the most, he pushed her away. Threatening to send her to a convent let her know how serious he was about wanting an annulment.

Yet, she knew of the bond between them. It had grown slowly, through kisses and conversation. The love in her heart for Nicholas Mandeville was all too real. Whether he returned her love or not, she refused to give him up.

Katelyn spent hours thinking about what to do and finally decided on a course of action.

The remainder of the day she tried to stay busy. As usual, she brought meals to Nicholas but didn't bother to engage him in conversation. She didn't trust that she could keep from weeping. Others would have to wait upon him come tomorrow. Though no one in the household knew yet of his blindness, they would soon.

Once she was gone.

She sought out young Henfrey and asked if he would accompany her on a stroll. He eagerly accepted.

"How is Lord Nicholas? You know I could be helping you care for him, my lady."

"I know. Thank you for your kind offer. I have something else to ask of you, though."

Henfrey smiled. "I am your humble servant, Lady Katelyn."

"It could be dangerous," she said.

The boy's eyes lit up. "Then you most certainly will need my protection. What am I to do?"

"I need you to accompany me to Ravenwood early tomorrow morning."

"Ravenwood?" The squire frowned. "You have the need to see

Lady Catherine?" He thought a moment. "I could always deliver a missive to her for you. That would be much simpler."

"Nay. I must speak to her in person on a matter of grave importance."

Katelyn had determined that she must travel to Windsor and speak to King Edward in person on Nicholas' behalf, both to ensure he kept his title and that she would remain as his wife. If she requested knights from Northmere to accompany her on the long journey, she believed that Rafe would prevent that from happening since he might also want to visit with the king, as Nicholas suspected would occur. If she could explain the severity of the situation to Catherine Savill, Katelyn believed her friend would immediately provide soldiers to escort Katelyn south to her cousin.

And Rafe Mandeville would never know where she'd gone.

"We would need to leave before daybreak tomorrow. Are you willing to guide me to Ravenwood? 'Twould just be the two of us." She paused. "And no one can know about our short trip. In fact, you will probably return to the manor house while I remain with Lady Catherine."

Though the young man looked uncertain, he nodded. "I will be ready, my lady, as will Ebony."

"Good." She hugged him. As she drew away, she had to hide a smile as she saw his cheeks flame.

They returned to the manor house and she went to check on Nicholas a final time before bed.

She kept all emotion from her voice as she asked, "How is your head?" These were the first words she'd spoken to him since he cruelly tried to toss her from his life this morning.

He gazed out warily in her direction and said, "The headache is all but gone. Even the pressure seems to be relenting."

"Good. I've brought you some cold ale."

Knowing she might break if she touched him, Katelyn pushed the cup against his chest. He raised both hands and wrapped them around the vessel and she released her grip.

"It's a new brew that Lucy is proud of."

Nicholas sipped it. "It's very good." He took another large swallow.

"Enjoy it. I bid you a good night, my lord," she said formally, hating that none of their usual teasing went on.

Then Katelyn returned to her bedchamber and waited. In the dead of night, she rose and removed her clothing, leaving it neatly folded across the bed she hadn't slept in. Naked, she opened the door and crept across the hall to the solar.

Meeting in person with the king was only part of her plan. The other half involved making sure she was a full-fledged wife to her husband before she left for Windsor Castle.

Faint light came from the small fire still burning inside the solar. Taking her time, she moved slowly across the room. The only sound was the even breathing that came from the bed. She reached it and, as expected, he hadn't drawn the curtains. Why would he? It didn't matter if any light came in. He would never see it.

She hoped he'd drunk all of the ale. In it, she'd mixed some of the herbs that Elewys said would help Nicholas sleep and reduce his pain. She wanted him as sleepy as imaginable for what she would now attempt. Idly, Katelyn wondered if it were possible to seduce one's own husband.

She would soon find out.

Lifting the bedclothes, she slid in and let them fall over her. The first thing she noticed was the tremendous heat Nicholas seemed to generate. At first, she'd thought he had a fever when she'd sent for the Northmere healer but soon learned that was his natural state. She inched toward him, grateful he slept on his back in the center of the bed.

Boldly, she threw a leg over both of his as she snuggled against him, her bare breasts pressed into his side. Her fingers began to lightly play with the fine matting of hair on his chest. He sighed and his arm came about her, drawing her even closer. Katelyn feathered light kisses along his chest and then brazenly repeated what he had done to her.

She licked his nipple.

A gasp came from him. He shifted and another arm came around her, so that she lay entrapped against his chest. She returned to her task, circling her tongue around the nipple and then tweaking it with her teeth. Another gasp and then a low moan sounded. Nicholas' hand slid down her body and firmly cupped her buttock, kneading it. She could feel his manhood growing against her. Tamping down her fear, she toyed with his other nipple, rolling it between her fingertips, the same as he had done to her. She licked her way along his chest, up to his throat, and then captured his lower lip in her teeth. Katelyn bit into it gently and Nicholas growled.

Suddenly, they shifted in the bed and she lay beneath him. She remained silent, not wanting him to hear her voice, hoping that he might think this a dream. His mouth plundered hers as his hands freely roamed her naked body, each stroke lighting the passion she felt, sending her higher and higher. Katelyn played with his hair and then raked her nails across his back, marking him as hers.

His kiss became more urgent. More demanding. More possessive. The fire he stirred now consumed her, her body radiating as much heat as his. She matched him, kiss for kiss, as her hands stroked him feverishly.

Then the moment she'd worried about arrived. She felt his hand leave her and wriggle between their bodies as he sought to guide his cock into her. The tip pressed against her womanly core, which throbbed unmercifully, wanting him desperately. Katelyn tried to relax and failed. She squeezed her eyes closed.

Without warning, Nicholas rammed into her. She cried out against his mouth, the pain blinding for a moment.

"Kate?" His voice was hoarse as he stilled.

The hurt subsided and she whispered, "It's a dream, Nicholas. Love me."

Nicholas began moving in and out of her with slow, delicious strokes. She didn't know if he was totally aware of what he did but it didn't matter. Her maidenhead had been breached. She was his.

And she would never let him go.

His tempo increased and Katelyn found herself clinging to him, calling his name, as he reached a peak and shuddered violently before collapsing atop her. For a moment, she thought his great weight might crush her. She pushed against him and managed to roll him to his side. Her thoughts of slipping from the bed, though, were not to be. Nicholas held her to him fiercely, burying his face in her hair.

"Is it truly you, Kate?" His words slurred and she knew he'd remained half-asleep through the encounter.

"I'm here," she said softly.

Her words seemed to comfort him and set his mind at ease. He relaxed against her, his grasp loosening a bit as his breathing evened out. Soft snores began. Katelyn smiled and brushed his cheek with the back of her hand. She would save words of love for another time. Now, it was enough that he had made their union legal and binding. Annulment would no longer be a possibility.

Easing from his arms, she climbed from the bed and drew the bedclothes over him again, wishing she could see his beautiful face one last time before she left on her mission. She left the solar and returned to her bedchamber. Only then did she notice the stickiness between her legs. Taking the candle she'd left burning from the table, she saw his seed mixed with a small amount of blood against her thighs and remembered how Landon had told her about the spilling of a virgin's blood. Nicholas might be groggy now but come morning, he would discover what had happened.

Katelyn cleaned herself and then dressed. She paused a moment and splayed her fingers across her belly. Even now, Nicholas' babe might grow within her.

Using the candle, she made her way downstairs and packed some bread for her and Henfrey to eat as they rode to Ravenwood. She crept past a sleeping Sir Albert, whom she'd also given a large tankard of ale spiked with the sleeping herbs. He was slumped near the door. Opening it, she stepped outside and looked about. A soldier stood guard twenty paces away but he faced away from the manor house. She kept to the shadows and tiptoed carefully, running her hand along the wall of the manor as a guide.

Reaching the corner, she turned it and continued, doing the same again until she reached the back of the house. In the shadows, she made out two horses.

"Lady Katelyn?" a voice whispered.

"I'm here, Henfrey," she reassured him as he approached.

"Dawn will be here soon," he said, "though I smell rain in the air."

"Help me into the saddle. We'll walk our horses until we are a good distance from the manor."

"Are you sure—"

"I am. And I will go with or without you."

"Then I am with you," he said resolutely. "Two men are to our right but they are engaged in conversation. We'll head directly away from the manor and then curve around to stay out of their sight."

They walked their horses until the manor house was a good distance away and then Katelyn motioned to Henfrey to pick up the pace. As light began to creep above the horizon and thunder echoed in the skies, they broke into a canter. Once they could see better, she would have them gallop.

A whizzing noise pierced the air and Henfrey grunted. He fell from his horse. Katelyn pulled up on her reins and threw herself to the ground. She ran to where he lay and saw an arrow protruded from his shoulder.

"Henfrey!"

His pain-filled eyes met hers. "Run."

Katelyn jumped to her feet and lifted her skirts, hoping she could reach Ebony in time to escape. As she ran, she heard horses galloping toward her. She managed to get her foot into the stirrup as two horses were upon her. Before Katelyn could cry out, one of the riders leaned down and scooped her up, tossing her face down in front of him. She couldn't catch her breath to scream as she bumped along.

They rode for a few minutes as the heavens opened and rain came pouring down. Then the horse below her came to a halt. Hands gripped her waist, bringing her to the ground and spinning her about. A red-bearded man grinned as she gasped for air.

"Bind the lass, Alec. Quickly," the stranger said. "Our waiting has finally paid off."

Chapter Twenty-One

NICHOLAS AWOKE AND stretched lazily, a feeling of satisfaction blanketing him. His tongue felt thick, as if he'd imbibed too much strong drink the night before. At least the constant pressure no longer held in head in a vise. No pounding remained. He almost felt like his old self.

He'd dreamed of Kate. Not just dreamed of her—but dreamed he'd finally had her. His fingers remembered stroking the smooth, rounded buttocks and silky hair. He licked his lips and almost tasted her. He inhaled deeply.

Vanilla.

The scent seemed to surround him. He turned his face toward the pillow and smelled it. Pressed his fingers to his nose and took a deep breath.

She *had* been here. It hadn't been a dream.

Nicholas remembered thrusting into her, over and over.

"Nay!" he cried aloud.

Throwing back the bedclothes, he jumped from the bed and froze. Light came through the small slit in the wall.

Light!

He stumbled, reaching out to the table next to the bed to locate a candle. His fingers grasped one and he forced himself to tread slowly toward the fireplace, where he could see embers smoldering. Pushing the wick into them, the candle lit and flickered. Nicholas held it up, entranced by the fire's beauty.

"I can see," he said reverently, knowing he would never take his sight for granted again.

He held a hand out in front of him, counting all five fingers. Turning, he looked about the solar and saw furniture. Nicholas fell to his knees and offered a prayer of Thanksgiving to the Virgin. No longer would he be helpless. Dependent on others.

Had his joining with Kate turned the tide?

Oh, she was a wicked one, sliding into his bed in the wee hours and coupling with him. For a moment, disappointment flooded him as only bits and pieces came to him. It was if their love play had occurred in a fog. He could only remember parts of it. Nicholas had wanted their first time together to be special. He'd wanted to gaze into her eyes as he entered her, their fingers entwined, and see how she reacted.

He told himself it didn't matter. There would be no annulment. He had no reason for one now that he was whole again. And Kate had told him that she loved him. He would make it up to her. Something told him he'd coupled with her quickly and selfishly last night. The next time, he would take hours to explore her body. He would bring her to the edge of madness over and over before letting her fall into the abyss. Their love play would last all night and into the next morning.

Why wait?

Right now, he needed her. She slept across the hall. He could creep into her bed and surprise her as she had done to him.

Nicholas put the candle down and went to the solar's door. He peered out. Seeing no one, he hurried across the hall and quickly opened her bedchamber door and closed it.

Kate wasn't there.

Though it was early, she must have already gone downstairs. He would dress. Find her. And bring her back for a morning they never would forget.

Eagerly, he rushed back to the solar. Where had he put his clothes? He hadn't ventured far from the bed when he'd undressed. Then he remembered folding them up and placing them under one of the pillows. Nicholas pushed a knee against the bed and as he reached for his pants, he stopped. Quickly, he grabbed for the candle and held it above the bedclothes.

Blood.

He frowned. Had Kate's courses been flowing?

Then he recalled when he'd entered her. He hadn't fully comprehended at the time, in whatever haze lingered over him, but everything became crystal clear to him now.

Kate came to him as a virgin. *This* was her blood spilled last night from their time together.

That meant her marriage to his father had never been consummated. It made no sense. Someone, Rafe most likely, would have checked the next morning. Had his father been embarrassed at his inability to couple with Kate and cut himself, smearing blood upon the sheets?

Wait. His father had died sometime during the night. Had Kate been responsible for his death?

Nay, it couldn't be. Nicholas put himself in her place. Cedric Mandeville had been old. Mayhap, he couldn't perform his husbandly duty. His heart had given out. Kate, young and far from home, would have been in limbo, wed to the earl and yet not truly his widow. Nicholas believed she had pretended the wedding night occurred as it should have, placing blood against the sheets.

Why then had she not told him? Especially when he let it be known that he waited a month to ensure she was not with child by her first husband.

He would find her and demand the truth.

Nicholas dressed hurriedly and made his way downstairs. He heard noises coming from the kitchen and assumed Lucy and possibly Dorinda were already at work. The great hall was empty. Had Kate gone outside? She'd shared with him her fondness for chickens. Mayhap she gathered eggs.

He went to the door to leave and found Albert pushing himself to his feet. The knight brought his hands to his head and rubbed it, frowning. It was unlike the knight to fall asleep on duty. Nicholas had known the man far too long and trusted him implicitly. Then he recalled how he had felt when he'd awakened and knew in his heart that Kate was somehow responsible. Again, why? It wasn't as if Albert would have kept them from their love play. Why drug the knight?

"Have you seen Lady Katelyn?" he demanded.

"Nay, my lord. How are you feeling?"

"Grumpy," he replied and flung the door open.

A soldier stood guard outside the manor. He, too, had not seen Kate. Nicholas ventured to the rear of the manor house and looked at the group of horses standing there. Immediately, he spied Ebony was missing.

Where had Kate gone? And why?

He doubted she ventured to Northmere. Not after what Rafe had said yesterday. Neither he nor Kate would trust the knight again. If not Northmere, where?

Ravenwood.

Kate and Catherine had enjoyed one another's company immensely. If Kate found herself in trouble, Nicholas suspected she would turn to Catherine Savill. Guilt filled him as he remembered how he'd spoken to her yesterday. He'd threatened to remove her from Northmere and return her to a nunnery if she didn't agree to an annulment. The idea must have repelled her—and frightened her.

Mayhap Kate sought Catherine's protection from him.

Yet, she'd come to him last night. Given her virginity, despite his harsh words. Women had always been somewhat of a mystery to Nicholas. Kate's actions only confirmed how little he knew about them, even his own wife.

Sunset stood munching hay. Dawn had broken but storm clouds hovered above. The horse nickered when he saw his master and Nicholas remembered that he had no saddle. It didn't matter. He would ride bareback. He quickly put on Sunset's bridle and mounted the horse as Gerald rode up from his rounds with two other soldiers.

"My lord. 'Tis good to see you up and about."

"Ride with me, Gerald," Nicholas commanded and wheeled Sunset. He glanced around and saw fresh tracks leading away from the group of hobbled horses and decided to follow them, thinking they might belong to Ebony. Nicholas pointed to them so the knight knew the direction to follow. It puzzled him that two horses had followed this path, making him more determined to get to the bottom of this situation.

Gerald fell in next to him and the two men rode in silence. The tracks led away from the manor house and then arced around and moved in a direct line toward Ravenwood. After some minutes, the threat of rain became a reality. They rode in a downpour, soon losing the tracks. Nicholas followed what his gut told him and kept to the notion that Kate traveled to Ravenwood.

"Up ahead, my lord," Gerald said, pointing to the right.

Nicholas saw two horses in the distance as buckets of rain fell and spurred Sunset on. They reached the pair and saw a rider lying on the ground. As he dismounted, Nicholas recognized Henfrey, an arrow embedded in his shoulder. He'd been shot from behind.

Nicholas quickly inspected the wound and lifted his squire to a sitting position. "What happened?"

Henfrey grimaced, coming to. "I was escorting Lady Katelyn to

Ravenwood when we were attacked."

"Who attacked? How many?" He tried to quell his panic. He needed to squeeze every bit of information that he could from Henfrey.

"I don't know, my lord. I was hit from behind and knocked from the saddle. I could hear other horses approach. Two. Mayhap three. I told Lady Katelyn to run." His voice broke. I'm sorry. They must have taken her."

"Up you go." He brought the boy to a standing position. "Can you ride?"

Henfrey nodded, though he looked unsteady on his feet.

"Return to Northmere and have Elewys take care of you."

"Aye, my lord."

Nicholas assisted Henfrey into his saddle. "I'm tying Ebony to your horse. Take your time. The arrow should remain in place. I've seen men hit in a similar manner before. It will bleed very little until it's removed." He paused. "Henfrey, did Lady Katelyn explain why you were headed toward Ravenwood?"

"Only that she had to speak to Lady Catherine in person on a matter of grave importance. I offered to take a missive but she refused. The countess insisted no one know where she went."

He patted Henfrey's thigh. "Then we should keep her secret. Mention this to no one."

"Even if we didn't reach Ravenwood?"

"I'm sure Lady Katelyn had her reasons. Say nothing other than you were returning to Northmere and a stray arrow struck you."

"Aye, my lord."

Nicholas attached Ebony to the boy's horse and motioned him to ride off. Turning to Gerald, he said, "The rain is too hard to see which direction Lady Katelyn might have been taken but I'm betting 'tis north."

"You think the Scots have her."

"I do. Few highwaymen roam these parts, knowing how frequently Northmere soldiers patrol the roads. It has to be Scots who've taken her."

He tried to tamp down the panic that raced through him. If Kate immediately told her captors who she was, he foresaw no problems. As the Countess of Northmere and cousin to King Edward, she would be treated quite well by them. Then he realized that only a handful of people had witnessed their marriage. No one beyond his uncle, aunt, and Bryce had been present. If Kate claimed to be Nicholas Mandeville's wife, she might not be believed. Still, her family connection to the king should keep her safe.

Unless she refused to tell her kidnappers who she truly was.

That thought chilled him to the bone. If they thought Kate an ordinary woman, they would use her.

Badly.

Would she understand the severity of the situation? She had such little experience in the outside world, having been caged in the convent most of her life. The thought of her being savaged by her kidnappers terrified him.

"Return to the manor house, Gerald. Leave one man to guard it and the two servants. Lead the rest to the border's edge, where we last crossed in the spring. I'm returning to Northmere for my weapons and more soldiers."

"As you wish." Nicholas saw the grave look in Gerald's eyes. The knight added, "We'll get her back, my lord."

"We have to."

Nicholas took off in the rain toward Northmere, a fervent prayer on his lips.

ESCAPE WOULD PROVE impossible if she allowed herself to be bound with the rope the man Alec pulled out.

"Gag her, too," the stout kidnapper added.

"What need is there to restrain me?" she boldly asked. "We are in the middle of nowhere. I have no one to cry out to for help. If I managed to get away, I wouldn't make it but a few feet. My skirts are sodden and too heavy to run in. You would easily catch me. I see no point." She crossed her arms in front of her, daring them to contradict her.

"The lass does have a point, Muir." Alec gave her an admiring glance. "She'll be easier to handle if she has use of her limbs. Binding her makes her harder to maneuver, even more so in this downpour."

"Verra well," Muir said, his brogue thick.

The red-bearded one caught her elbows, lowering his face to within inches of hers, his sour breath giving her pause. "Take care, lass. Do nothing foolish. Especially if ye favor yer head attached to yer neck."

Katelyn stood her ground, staring back at him, though his words chilled her and his touch repelled her. She wondered if they knew exactly who she was. They seemed to. She recalled one of them saying that their waiting had paid off. That meant she had been who they wanted and could only assume it was ransom they sought, as Albert had explained to her.

Desperate men could act recklessly. She would give them no reason to harm her. At least they'd taken her suggestion and left her free from restraints. She would now look for any opportunity to escape their custody.

Alec swung back into his saddle. Katelyn threw off Muir's hold on her and went to the other man, who seemed more sympathetic toward her. Alec lifted her into the saddle in front of him and pulled her tightly against him.

"Behave, lass," he said in her ear. "No harm'll come to you if you do."

Katelyn didn't acknowledge his words.

Muir mounted and they took off again. Though the tail end of summer, the air was chilly, especially with the hard rain added in. She watched carefully where they rode, glad they hadn't blindfolded her, hoping she would soon be able to retrace the same path in the opposite direction. As the rain began to let up, Katelyn saw a city in the distance to the right of them. It must be Berwick-upon-Tweed, which stood east of Northmere and was situated a mere two and a half miles from the border.

They continued to ride north and passed a few scattered cottages. Twice, she saw men working outside but refrained from crying out for help. It would be useless. They were in Scotland now and strangers would not venture to help an English captive. She would only be able to depend upon herself. They rode through a small village and then later a larger one. Again, Katelyn saw a few other people and noticed they averted their eyes as the two horses passed.

Once they reached the outskirts of the second village, they veered to the west. Minutes later, they arrived at a structure similar in size to her manor house. She assumed it to be their destination as the horses slowed. The riders guided their mounts to a small building and handed them off to a young man. Muir took her roughly by the arm and marched her to the house.

Entering, she counted four men sitting about a fire. The gawked at her as if she were a three-headed dragon.

"Get him," Muir ordered.

"He's upstairs. Take her there," one said, his eyes raking over her.

"Move," Muir said, dragging her up a staircase as Alec followed closely behind.

They went down a dimly lit corridor and stopped in front of a door. Muir rapped twice and Katelyn heard a deep voice bid, "Come."

Her captor opened the door and pulled her through. Katelyn glanced about and saw most of the room was in darkness. The only light came from the fireplace, where a man sat. He beckoned them over. As they reached him, she saw he was about two score and stout, with a dark beard and eyes that bored into her.

"She's not bound?" he asked.

"I saw no need," Katelyn quickly responded. "I am but a woman. They are men and twice my size. What Scotsman would bother to help me if I called out for help or tried to escape?"

"You've a quick tongue, Lady Katelyn," the man observed. He glanced at his men. "Leave."

Waiting until they left, he said, "Have a seat," and indicated one near him.

"I'd rather stand. How should I address you?"

"I am Errol Cummins, Laird of Dunbar. You won't need to address me. I'll speak for the both of us or give you permission to speak."

Katelyn wanted to fire off a scathing remark but remembered she was at the mercy of this man and kept silent.

Cummins nodded approvingly at her restraint. "Sit, my lady. 'Tis no request." Once more, he motioned to the chair and she took it, perching on the edge.

"Do you know why you're here?"

"I assume you want to hold me for ransom."

"Aye." He studied her a moment. "I'd heard you were comely and now I know you're clever, too. A lethal combination in a woman."

"Only for men who cannot handle it."

Cummins smiled broadly. "You are here so that I may gain gold, my lady. The king should pay well for the return of his cousin."

Katelyn decided to take a chance. "King Edward is far from Scotland, Laird. It would take a few weeks to send a messenger to Windsor—and that is if the king is in residence there. He might have gone to London. Or any of his other palaces. It could take some time to track him down. Even more to wait to be seen. You can't imagine the number of courtiers who beg for his time every day. Then, he would need to decide if he even wanted to pay."

"Why wouldn't he?" Cummins asked, leaning forward.

She shrugged. "I'm not saying my cousin wouldn't. He did send me north to wed." She smiled sweetly. "In order to show Scotland how he stood strongly against them and with the north of England." She paused and then sweetened the pot. "There are others who would pay—and much more quickly—for my return. You could have your gold in a day or so instead of months, while I could once more be sitting in front of a nice English fire, this misadventure behind me."

"You mean the Mandevilles," he said. "You think they would pay for your return."

"Aye. My husband will."

"You have no husband," Cummins pointed out. "He's dead. Nay, the Mandevilles won't want to part with gold for a woman wed only a few hours into their family. You may have taken their name, Lady Katelyn, but you are not one of them. They don't welcome outsiders easily."

"You're mistaken," she said coolly. "My husband is not dead. He's very much alive. And unless you return me soon, he will probably burn down half of Scotland in order to find me."

"Who is this husband?" insisted Cummins.

"Lord Nicholas Mandeville. The Earl of Northmere," she said proudly. Her hands went to her belly. "I might even be carrying his child as we speak. Nicholas will want me back. I suggest you arrange a trade—and soon."

"You were right," the laird said, looking across the room as he spoke.

"I told you," a voice said as a man stepped from the shadows.

It was Bryce Mandeville.

CHAPTER TWENTY-TWO

"**B** RYCE?" KATELYN SHOOK with anger as he approached her. "How could you betray Nicholas—and your family? To be in league with your sworn enemies? 'Tis not merely disloyal. 'Tis treason."

He sneered at her. "Don't speak to me about betrayal, Katelyn. Nicholas is the one who abandoned *me*. My brother threw me off his lands and ordered me never to return to my own home. Why would I show any loyalty toward him? Besides, I've always hated him. As the elder son, he got everything. My father always wished I could be the one to inherit Northmere for we were much alike."

Bryce reached out and grabbed her braid, coiling it around his fist, forcing her close to him. "Besides, with the trap we'll lay for him, I'll soon have my fondest wish."

Realization slammed into her. "You plan to lure Nicholas by using me as bait."

"You are wise beyond your years, my lady. Not only will Errol receive the gold he so desperately needs but I will lay claim to Northmere—and you."

"Me?" The thought appalled her.

He chuckled. "Just think. You will be Countess of Northmere thrice over."

"I would never wed you. Not under any circumstances!" Katelyn shouted and raked her nails across his face.

Bryce howled and cradled his cheek with his free hand, blood seeping between his fingers as he glared daggers at her. Then he slapped her. Katelyn's head snapped as stars shot across her vision and her face flamed in pain.

"The lady has a point, Bryce," Errol Cummins interjected. "After you murder her husband?" The laird shrugged. "I doubt she'd feel any obligation to marry you."

"She'll do what I say." He yanked hard, winding her braid around his hand again until her scalp burned.

"I'm not sure she will," the Scotsman said. "Lady Katelyn's a spirited one. Mayhap I should take her off your hands. Then you'd be free to wed another woman of your choosing. One more docile."

Cummins rose and came toward them. "Release her. Lady Katelyn is a guest in my home. I won't see her mistreated."

Reluctantly, Bryce untangled his hand from her hair as her host looked to her. "I lost my wife in childbirth recently. All she gave me in five years were three useless girls. You look like you'd bear fine sons, my lady. I would be honored to become your husband." He chuckled. "Wouldn't King Edward be surprised to find me in the royal family, wedded to his cousin?"

"That wasn't our bargain," Bryce hissed. "She is mine!"

Katelyn wanted to shrink from his anger but stood her ground. "I will never be yours."

He gave her a sly smile. "Oh, you will be. We got along well at Windsor and the entire way to Northumberland. 'Twas only after you met Nicholas that I lost your favor. With him dead and gone, you'll see that I'll make you a good husband. For now, though, I'll do as Nicholas swore and was obviously too weak to accomplish. I'll not touch you for a month to make sure your womb is empty."

She looked at him defiantly. "And what if I do carry his babe?"

"If your courses don't come, I suppose I could beat you severely enough to cause you to lose it," he mused. "That might damage you, though, and I certainly want to get sons off you. Nay, I'll wait and allow you to give birth to his brat—and then kill it."

Katelyn gasped. "What wickedness lies within you? You deserve to rot in the fires of Hell."

"Surely, you understand that even with Nicholas dead, any babe of his would have a claim to the earldom over me. I've waited too long to get what I deserve. I cannot chance that."

She narrowed her eyes. "You will never have a chance with me, Bryce Mandeville." Katelyn spit in his face.

Bryce struck her with his fist. The blow sent her to the floor.

"Enough!" cried Cummins.

The laird latched on to her elbow and brought her to her feet. "Stay here, Mandeville," he ordered as he led Katelyn from the room and across the hall.

They entered a small bedchamber and he closed the door.

"This will be your new home for the foreseeable future," he said. "Two men will always be posted outside, as much for your protection as to make sure you don't flee." He gave her a sympathetic look. "I apologize on Mandeville's behalf. Don't worry about him. I'll make sure he doesn't mistreat you again."

"You still plan to partner with him and draw Nicholas out so that Bryce can kill his brother?" Katelyn shook her head. "You seemed to be wiser than that. If Bryce would betray his own flesh and blood, what's to say he won't do the same to you?"

For a moment, she caught a flicker of doubt in the Scotsman's eyes. He recovered quickly and said, "I'm sure you are tired, my lady. I will leave you to rest."

The laird exited the room and she heard his voice boom, assuming he called for a pair of men to come and guard her door.

She'd bragged to the two men that Nicholas would be willing to pay for her but didn't know if he truly would. He'd already told her he would seek an annulment. Why would he part with a goodly sum of gold when he planned to dismiss her from his life? As it was, only she knew why he would never ride to deliver the ransom, much less come to rescue her. A sightless knight would be no match against these bloodthirsty men. He would be a fool if he allowed his enemies to see that he was now blind—and Nicholas was no fool.

Katelyn was on her own. Once more, she'd become a pawn in a political game that seemed to have no end. She curled up on the bed and wept.

NICHOLAS SPIED HIS squire and slowed Sunset as he reached him.

"Are you holding up?" he asked Henfrey.

"I'm fine, my lord. Where I landed on my head almost hurts worse than my shoulder."

He gave the boy a nod and allowed Sunset his head, galloping the rest of the way to Northmere. Waving to the gatekeeper, the gates opened before he reached them and Nicholas sailed through. The rain had slowed to a drizzle as he rode the horse to the stables.

"He's been ridden hard in the storm so take special care of him," Nicholas advised the stable hand that took the reins.

"Aye, my lord. 'Tis good to have you back."

Leaving the stables, he made his way to the keep, passing the deserted training field. He supposed Rafe had given the men a brief rest from their exercises because of the heavy rains. Nicholas looked forward to seeing the surprised look on his uncle's face when he confronted the man.

"My lord!" a woman's voice called out as he crossed the inner bailey. He saw Elewys hurrying toward him.

"I am happy to see you in robust health," the healer said.

"Thanks, in part, to you."

"I did what I could in the brief time I was there. I left you in good hands, though. Lady Katelyn is a most capable woman."

"That she is," he agreed. "My squire will be arriving soon with an arrow protruding from his shoulder. Please attend to him quickly."

"I will, my lord."

Nicholas continued on his way and entered the keep. Ellyn descended the stairs. The minute she caught sight of him, she froze, her hands flying to her mouth. Then she rushed down the stairs.

"Nicholas, are you truly well?" She lowered her voice. "You can see me?"

"So Uncle told you."

"Aye. He refused to allow me to go to you." She placed a hand on his forearm. "Rafe told me about his plans. I am glad to see you will keep him from acting upon them."

"I've always been fond of you, Aunt Ellyn."

She gave him a sweet smile. "And I've looked upon you as the son I never had." Her eyes showed her sadness at being a barren woman.

"Your husband will be leaving Northmere in the near future. You may go with him or choose to remain behind. I offer you my protection if Northmere is your choice."

Ellyn's eyes widened. "Rafe would never allow me to stay though it would be my fondest desire. I would be happy looking after the children you and Katelyn have."

Nicholas placed his hands on her thin shoulders and pressed a kiss to her brow. "Kate and I would both like that. Especially with Mother gone, it would be nice for them to have a grandmother around."

Tears filled her eyes. "I know Rafe has betrayed you in a most horrible way, Nicholas. He deserves whatever punishment you mete out. If you truly don't mind having me stay, I would be forever grateful."

"Consider it done. Where is Rafe now?"

She swallowed and lowered her eyes. "In . . . the solar. He's already made it his own."

Nicholas fought the rage that raced through him at how presumptuous Rafe Mandeville proved to be. "Thank you. Make yourself scarce, Ellyn. Rafe will soon be gone."

He headed up the stairs, seething, but knowing he needed to control his temper as he dealt with his uncle a final time. Though part of him wanted to leave the experienced older man in charge of Northmere while he led a contingent of soldiers in search of Kate, the recent betrayal ran too deep for Nicholas to contemplate that. From the many capable knights in his barracks, he would select one to become his new captain of the guard.

Not bothering to knock, Nicholas entered the solar and found his uncle at the table, papers strewn across it. Shock caused his face to lose all color and he dropped the quill in his hand.

"Nicholas?" Rafe sprang to his feet, uncertainty in his eyes.

"Aye, Uncle. The Earl of Northmere. The man whose ears heard you betray him in the worst way possible and whose eyes now see you have taken over my solar as your own." He lifted one of the pieces of parchment and glanced at it briefly. "It seems you've also decided to take on my business, as well."

Rafe stepped away from the table. "Nephew, you must understand that I—"

"I understand that you are no longer fit to serve as my captain of the guard, much less a servant whom I would allow to polish my boots. I expected your allegiance, Uncle. Your fidelity. To me. To our family. To the people of Northmere. You are the last man, next to Bryce, that I would ever trust."

Fear flashed in the older man's eyes. "You . . . you would not dare to discard me as you did your brother," he said, his voice trembling.

"There's no daring involved. Your treachery sealed your fate. The minute you threatened me—and Kate—you became dead to me. Get your things and leave."

"I will not!" his uncle spat out. "I was a knight who'd already killed dozens of England's enemies on the battlefield before you were even born. This is my home as much as it is yours. You can't merely wave me away with a flick of your wrist, Nicholas. I have years of experience that you cannot replace. Northmere's proximity to the border is reason alone to keep me as captain of your guard. I refuse to let your head be turned by that woman—"

"Enough!" Nicholas felt rage ripple through his body. "*I* am Earl of Northmere. Not you. I make the decisions for my land and my people. Not you. You've proven yourself untrustworthy, devoted only to yourself. After your betrayal, I could never rely on you to support me or do what is best for the people of Northmere. You are a snake, Uncle. A deadly viper whose poison I'll abide no more. You should be glad I'm letting you leave with your life." He paused. "And as for Kate? You aren't fit to even say her name. She has more loyalty to me and Northmere in her smallest finger than you do in your entire body. Kate is the woman I love. The one I trust. You are nothing. Get out—now—before I change my mind and have you strung up and disemboweled."

Rafe's shoulders slumped. Within seconds, he went from a proud, powerful knight to a broken man. Nicholas had no sympathy for him, though. Rafe had brought this upon himself.

His uncle rallied and issued a final challenge to him. "What if your blindness returns? What will you do then?"

"It was a result of my fall. My head no longer aches and the pressure that had been a constant is gone. I can tell you this, Uncle. I would rather command Northmere with Kate by my side than have you guide me. She may be a woman but she has the heart and courage of a man. And she loves me. Now, leave my sight before I have a mind to run my sword through you."

Rafe accepted his fate and silently left the solar.

Nicholas doffed his wet clothes and dressed quickly in new ones. Without Henfrey to aid him in putting on his armor, it would take more time than he wanted to spend. He decided to go to the barracks and speak to his men directly. He would name his new captain and select the soldiers who would accompany him to Scotland and then have one of them help him don his armor.

As he came down the stairs, he found Rafe lingering there.

"Where is my wife?" his uncle demanded.

"Aunt Ellyn will not be accompanying you. I wish her to stay at Northmere."

The knight's face flushed dark red in anger. "Nay, Nicholas. She's my property, to do with as I see fit."

"Ellyn is under my protection, Uncle. You will vacate Northmere without her. You haven't been a husband to her in many years. Consider yourself a free man and no longer responsible for her."

"This doesn't sound like you, Nicholas. I think your new wife has been influencing you in all the wrong ways. I have a mind to ride to the manor house and—"

"She's not there!" shouted Nicholas, his temper finally exploding. "The Scots have taken her."

Rafe grew still. A worried look crossed his face. "What are you planning, Nicholas?"

He ground out, "I plan to fetch her and teach those bloody Scots a lesson they'll never forget."

The nobleman took a step toward him. "You can't do that," he insisted.

Nicholas glared at his uncle. "I've told you that I'm the earl, not you. The decision to act is mine alone. The Scots have gone too far, taking my wife. I will rain fire and brimstone down upon them for their cowardly act. Once I'm done, they'll never even think to act against me again for decades to come."

"You will not," Rafe said evenly. "You can't, Nicholas. You're thinking with your heart and not your head. Love has made you forget the delicate balance between our two countries."

"Scotland is England's enemy, Uncle. And now they've made it personal by taking Kate hostage. No one can stop me from retrieving my wife from their slimy grip."

Rafe held up a hand. "Nicholas, think a moment. Put aside your quarrel with me. Remember that the king has made peace with them. If you cross the border with an army of soldiers and cause mayhem— all for one woman—you will start another war between our nations. I beg you, Nephew. Don't do this. You will infuriate the king. Upset the balance. Anger the northern nobles.

"You might even lose your own head for such foolishness."

"I would gladly lose my life to save Kate's," he insisted.

"Think, Nephew," Rafe insisted. "Calm down. Be rational for a moment. If you bring war down upon us, it won't be merely you and Katelyn involved. It will be your soldiers. The people of Northmere. All of the nobles in the north and their soldiers and people. The peace now is a delicate one. What you suggest will plunge the north—nay, all of England—back into war."

The words pierced Nicholas' soul. Rafe was right. The fragile peace between England and Scotland would be ruined if he led his men in search of Katelyn. It would take burning villages and the deaths of too many to count before he might locate where his wife had been taken. In the meantime, it would give the Scots an excuse to set aside the peace treaty as the two nations plummeted back into war.

As much as he wished it, he could not go after Kate.

Nicholas had never felt so helpless in his life.

CHAPTER TWENTY-THREE

"**M**Y LADY. WAKE up," a voice insisted as someone gently shook her shoulder.

Katelyn forced her eyes open. Her head pounded something awful and she shivered with cold. She'd fallen asleep in her wet clothing and it now weighed her down into the mattress.

A large, warm hand pressed against her brow, causing her to shudder. "'Tis a fever you have."

She glanced up and saw the voice belonged to Alec, the kidnapper who was but a few years older than she was.

"I'll be back."

Closing her eyes again, her body trembled violently as chills rippled through her. She needed to remove her soaked cotehardie and smock but had no strength to do so. She lay still until Alec returned and fought to open her eyes once more.

Errol Cummins now accompanied Alec. The laird hovered over her, touching her forehead with the back of his hand.

"You're right. She's got a fever. We should send for a healer. She's too valuable a hostage. I can't afford to have her die on us."

Katelyn glared up at him, her head throbbing. "I don't intend to die, Laird. I plan on returning to my husband and giving him a good dozen children."

The Scotsman's lips twitched in amusement. "Still fiery, even in the grips of fever."

"You might recall that my mother was a healer," Alec said. "I learned enough from her to care for Lady Katelyn."

"What needs to be done?" the older man demanded.

"First, she's chilled to the bone. She'll need to be moved so she can be close to a fire though I doubt you'll want her downstairs will all the men."

Katelyn remembered the group she'd seen on their arrival and wanted nothing to do with them.

"Nay. Even sick, a woman this beautiful would be too much temptation to dangle before them. Take her to my chamber instead."

"I can set up a pallet for her near the fire. I still keep a few herbs on hand and will steep some in hot water."

"Go make your preparations then. I'll stay with the lass until you return."

Alec left the room. Katelyn's teeth began to chatter. Cummins took one of her hands in his large ones and rubbed it between them, trying to warm her, and then repeated his action with her other hand.

Even through the fog of her fever, she knew this might be her last chance to plead her case to the laird and said, "I hope you considered what I mentioned before. I understand that you must ransom me but please—let it be an honorable transaction. Let me return to Nicholas. Do not harm him."

The Scotsman kept silent so Katelyn pressed on. "If you assist in killing the most powerful nobleman in all of Northumberland, you'll have to live with the consequences. Is it worth plunging into a war again with England?"

Cummins looked down on her, lines of worry creasing his brow.

"I don't know what kind of bargain you struck with Bryce but his word is worthless. Cut your ties with him before he makes a fool of you in front of your men. Send a missive to Nicholas at Northmere. Get me home to my husband and be happy with the gold you'll earn from him."

The laird studied her a long moment. "You love him? Lord Nicholas?"

Katelyn's eyes welled with tears. "I do. Very much. Did you love your wife?"

He shook his head. "My father arranged the marriage. In the five years we were wed, we spoke little. I knew nothing of her, even though she bore me three bonny lasses."

Katelyn took his wrist, her fingers tightening around it. "I am sorry. I hope one day you will find a woman you can love and receive her love in return."

Cummins grunted, the look on his face telling her he had no belief in love. Her fingers fell away. She'd used the last of her strength. Her eyes closed again.

A shuffling noise awoke her and someone said, "I'm ready to move her." Strong arms lifted her, carrying her from the bedchamber and across the hall. Alec placed her in a chair and held her steady when she began to sway.

"I'll leave you to care for her," Cummins said. "Remember how valuable she is, Alec. I'm counting on you to make her well again." He exited the room.

"My lady, I want you to drink this."

Alec lifted a wooden bowl to her lips. She was too tired to raise her hands to hold it herself so he held it for her. Bit by bit, she drank the fragrant brew in small sips until she emptied the bowl.

"Very good. Now, we need to remove your clothes."

"Nay," Katelyn protested feebly. No man had ever seen her unclothed, not even Nicholas, due to his blindness.

"Don't worry. I won't hurt you," he promised. "In fact, I won't even notice. I don't . . . feel that way. About women."

Gradually, he worked off her clothes and wrapped her in a soft blanket before lifting her from the chair and lowering her to a thick pallet on the floor. A fire crackled next to her. She desperately yearned for its warmth. Alec covered her with another blanket as she turned her face toward the flames.

"Go to sleep, my lady. I'll be here when you awaken."

KATELYN GRADUALLY OPENED her eyes and the room came into focus.

"Ah, you're awake," Alec said from the chair next to the bed she now lay in. He leaned toward her and felt her brow. "Cool to the touch. Your fever has broken. How is your head? You complained about it mightily."

She licked dry, cracked lips. "Better. It no longer aches."

He helped her to sit up, pillows propped behind her, and reached for a bowl sitting on the table. "Here, let's get some broth in you. It will warm your belly."

It took her some minutes but she finished everything in the bowl.

"How long have I been ill?" she asked. "My limbs feel as if I haven't used them for a long time."

"Four days."

Katelyn frowned. "I remember you making me drink something several times. I seemed to fall asleep each time I did so."

"Some of the herbs I gave you were to reduce your fever and quell the pain in your head. Others did help you to sleep. Mother always said sleep was nature's way to help someone recover from fever or an injury."

"You said your mother was a healer?"

"Aye. And English."

She smiled weakly. "That explains why your brogue isn't nearly as thick as the others. I can understand you much better than them."

A shadow crossed his face. "It's what keeps me from being a true Scot," he said bitterly.

"Merely because your mother was English?"

"There's enmity between all Englishmen and Scots."

"Then how did your mother marry your father?"

"She was caught up in one of the border raids," he explained. "Usually, those are to gain livestock. Occasionally, a woman or child is brought back. No good usually comes of it. But Father was taken with her and insisted upon wedding her. It made him an outcast among his own people and left her with no one but him. And me."

"I'm sorry," Katelyn said. "It seems so unfair. Are you still close to them?"

"Father died the year I turned nine. Mother passed the following year. Errol took me in after that. As laird, 'tis his duty to look after his people." He sighed. "It made no difference. People judge me because of my mother's blood."

"You're a grown man," she said. "I'm surprised after so many years, you would still be considered an outsider in the land of your birth."

Alec shrugged. "'Tis the way of the Scots. They're an untrusting lot to begin with."

"You're alone then? No friends at all?" she asked gently.

"Nay."

She hesitated a moment and then ventured, "You said before that you didn't feel that way. About me." She paused. "About women. Is that the true reason why you're not accepted?"

He blew out a long breath. "I didn't think you'd recall that. You seemed delirious to me by that point." His eyes filled with pain. "Please, don't mention what I said to the others. If they knew that . . ." His voice trailed off.

Katelyn was unsure of what he meant. "I don't understand. Please, tell me. I want to help you. You've been kind to me."

Alec shook his head. "I'm not like other men. You're wed. You've kissed your husband. Lain with him."

She nodded, thinking how she missed her daily dose of kisses from Nicholas.

"I have no desire to do that with a woman. I wish I could do it with a man."

She tried to mask her surprise. "I didn't know that was possible."

He snorted. "Neither did I. I always felt different. Not like others. I couldn't understand why. Finally, after my father died, I admitted it to my mother." He raked a hand through his unruly hair. "She told me her brother was that way. That she'd caught him kissing another boy when they were young. He begged her not to tell anyone. She didn't. Not even on the day he wed a girl from their village. Two days later, Mother was taken and never saw her family again."

Katelyn took his hand and squeezed it. "You must feel very alone, Alec."

"Alone. And ashamed," he admitted.

"It is who you are, Alec. I'm not saying it's something to flaunt in front of others. Obviously, they would not understand."

"They would kill me if they knew," he muttered.

Katelyn said soothingly, "Still, it is how you feel. Mayhap, you'll find another man who feels the same as you do." She released his hand, her heart aching for this handsome young man and the terrible secret he lived with.

He changed the subject. "I'm sure you'll be needing a bath to wash away the fever sweat. It'll make you feel whole again, being clean."

Glancing down, Katelyn saw she wore a man's shirt.

Alec must have noticed her puzzlement and said, "'Tis an old one of the laird's. I dried your clothes by the fire but it was easier to have you in one of Errol's night shirts as I bathed your limbs, trying to bring your fever down."

He stood. "I'll go downstairs and warm water for your bath."

"Could you bring me something to eat? I'm very hungry."

"I can do that." He paused. "My lady, I beg you to keep our conversation between us."

"Of course, Alec. I would not see you harmed in any way. Especially since you have cared so well for me during my illness."

He left and she closed her eyes again. She'd never really been ill before and found that their simple conversation had worn her out.

The next thing she knew, she heard water sloshing and watched as Alec poured buckets into a wooden tub in the far corner of the room.

Seeing she was awake, he said, "We'll get you clean first and then feed you."

"I don't know if I have the stamina to walk across the room, much less bathe myself."

Alec emptied a final bucket into the tub. "That's why I'm here to help, my lady."

"Please. Call me Katelyn. I haven't been a lady for very long. It still sounds odd to my ears."

He helped her from the bed and let her lean heavily on him as he led her to the tub, lifting the laird's night shirt from her. Offering her his hand, she stepped shakily into the bath, feeling awkward at first being naked in front of him. He seemed to think nothing of it and took over when she couldn't lift a hand. Alec washed her hair and then lathered her entire body with a sweet-smelling soap that had a hint of mint in it before rinsing the suds away. He pulled her to her feet and wrapped her in a bath sheet before bringing her to sit in front of the fire.

"Let me comb your hair before it gets tangled."

Katelyn's limbs felt heavy and she relaxed as he worked a comb through her locks and then fanned her hair about her.

"Stay here by the fire so your hair can dry. I'll find a clean night shirt for you. No sense in putting your own clothes back on until you're up and about."

She chuckled. "I'm so weak I couldn't go anywhere."

"I'll be back with food shortly," he promised.

She closed her eyes and basked in the warmth of the fire against her back, wondering how lonely Alec must have been his entire life. First, his family had been isolated from others merely because of his mother's place of birth. Then, he'd lost both parents and come to live with the laird as a young boy. Last, he held no feelings toward women. She'd noticed he scrubbed her efficiently with no lewd looks. It musts be incredibly difficult to hide his feelings from the world, never having a friend to share anything with. The fact that he'd told her, a total stranger, revealed just how solitary an existence he led.

Alec returned, bringing broth with bits of chicken floating in it and fresh bread. Katelyn insisted on feeding herself, knowing she needed to build her strength again.

Because she needed to escape.

As she ate, she asked, "Has the laird sent a missive regarding his ransom request?" wanting to know what had occurred while she'd been so ill.

"Nay. He wanted to make sure you wouldn't expire before he did. He and Bryce have argued about it several times. Bryce wants to send word to the English king and Lord Nicholas, trying to squeeze monies from them both. Errol favors ransoming you to your family at Northmere since it wouldn't take months to receive payment."

Katelyn liked that Alec confided in her. Mayhap, he might be persuaded to help her when she attempted to flee.

"Shouldn't the laird have the final say? 'Twas his men who took me and his house I stay in."

Alec nodded. "He's said as much to Bryce."

Suddenly, the door flew open. Errol Cummins entered the solar, with Bryce Mandeville close behind him.

"You're looking much better, Lady Katelyn," the Scotsman commented. "I've looked in on you each day and today is the first one I see a marked improvement."

"I don't remember much about the previous days. But I know without Alec tending to my health, I would not have recovered it."

Bryce appraised her, a lascivious look on his face. Katelyn realized she was still wrapped in the bath sheet and had nothing on beneath it. She tightened it about her.

"Have her courses come?" he asked Alec.

"Nay," the younger man said, a blush staining his cheeks.

"Let me know when they occur," Bryce said and left the room.

Cummins closed the door and came to face her. "I have thought long and hard about what you said, my lady."

Katelyn's heart skipped a beat. "About trusting Bryce?"

The laird nodded. "I've come to believe that the pact between us is one-sided and that Mandeville would probably not live up to his end of it."

"Thank you, Laird. You are showing great wisdom."

"He's not to know," Cummins shared. "I will send a missive to your husband in two days' time. You should be blooming with good health by then and able to travel once more."

"Will you give Nicholas a place to meet and exchange me for the ransom?" she asked. "Even better, will you ask him to stay away and allow his knights to perform the trade? That way, Nicholas would not even be present and kept from danger."

"Nay, I will insist he come to handle the transaction—but instead of my men setting upon him as Bryce expects, I plan to hand his traitorous brother over to the earl."

CHAPTER TWENTY-FOUR

NICHOLAS SAT NUMBLY as the priest droned on during morning mass. Almost a week had passed since Kate had been taken. No word of ransom had been sent. At this point, he believed the kidnappers had bypassed him and taken their demands straight to the king, thinking they could claim more from the royal treasury than from a northern nobleman.

Only a handful of men knew she was missing. Once Nicholas had seen Rafe Mandeville through the gates of Northmere, he'd ridden to the rendezvous point where Gerald and the other soldiers awaited him. He briefly explained to the men why they could not go after Kate and begged them to maintain silence regarding her disappearance. He didn't want anything to endanger her wellbeing.

The days had passed as if he lived underwater, moving languidly, everything a blur. The one good thing had been naming Gerald as his new captain of the guard. Nicholas had met with all of his soldiers at one time, explaining that his uncle was being replaced. Gerald had proved a popular choice, already having the men's respect for his fighting skills and even temper. Nicholas had watched the knight carefully as he led the training exercises in the yard and knew his decision had been a sound one.

His thoughts returned to Kate. She would most likely feel abandoned by him and utterly alone in captivity. If the ransom demand did go to the king, it might be months before she would be released. First, the messenger would have to ride to the south and discover which of the palaces the royal court occupied and then gain an audience with the king, both of which could take some time. Then the monarch would need to decide whether or not he would meet the kidnappers' price or if he would insist upon negotiating with them. Though Edward was known as a fair king, Nicholas had heard talk of how mercurial he could be. If the missive caught him at the wrong time, the king might wash his hands of Kate altogether.

If not and Edward was willing to pay, it would still take time to gather the gold and journey with it back to Scotland. All the while, Nicholas would hang in limbo, having no idea where Kate was. That threatened to destroy him.

Moreover, Edward might place the blame for Kate's kidnapping at Nicholas' door. He could easily require the Mandevilles to reimburse the royal treasury for whatever price was paid for Kate's return. Even then, Edward could instruct for his soldiers to bring Kate back to the royal court instead of returning her to Northmere. Kate would tell her cousin that her husband demanded an annulment. Edward would see to it. Because of that, Nicholas might never even lay eyes on her again. The thought of losing her forever haunted him day and night.

And what if, by chance, she had conceived a child when they'd lain together? The Scots would most likely demand ransom for the babe, as well. To imagine Kate alone, giving birth, thinking he no longer cared for her . . .

Movement started up around him and Nicholas realized mass had ended. He followed the group of people leaving the chapel, shuffling along, dreading another day lived in uncertainty.

"My lord!" Henfrey pushed his way through the crowd, holding up a scroll attached to a rock.

Hope flickered inside him. This might finally be the ransom request. Nicholas made his way to the squire and Henfrey placed the scroll in his hands. The two of them moved away from the crowd.

"It was found just before mass began. A guard on the wall walk saw a rider approach and sling it over the wall. By the time he alerted those on guard below, the rider had disappeared." Henfrey swallowed. "Do you think—"

"It has to be," Nicholas said fervently.

Too many people surrounded him. He needed privacy. Nicholas hurried to the keep and retreated to his solar. Taking a seat, he broke the seal, which bore no identification, and unrolled the parchment. Nestled within the larger scroll was a smaller one. He opened it first.

Nicholas –

I am not allowed to tell you where I am or who took me but I am unharmed. The only thing I will say to you is that I love you. Now and always.

Kate

Tears of relief fell onto the parchment, blurring a few of the words. He wiped his eyes with his sleeve and then brought the parchment to his lips, reverently kissing where Kate had penned her name. Rolling the message up, he slipped it inside his gypon, next to his heart. It would remain there until he had Kate back.

And then he would never let her go.

Turning his attention to the larger scroll, it read as he expected. The missive told him how much the kidnappers wanted for her return and the place to assemble tomorrow morning at dawn in order to make the exchange. It even limited the number of men he could bring with him. Steely resolve filled Nicholas.

By this time tomorrow, Kate would be his once again.

He hurried to the great hall, where the morning meal was in progress. Heading to the dais, he stood to address his people. A hush fell over the room as soldiers, servants, and workers noticed him standing there and awaited his words.

"Good people of Northmere, I come to you today because I need your help," he began. "My wife, Lady Katelyn Mandeville, has been taken hostage by the Scots."

A buzz filled the room, not only at the news that Katelyn had been kidnapped—but that she was his wife. Nicholas let it die down before he continued.

"I wed Lady Katelyn almost a month ago. She is intelligent, kind, and capable and will make a wonderful countess for Northmere." He paused, fighting the emotions that threatened to overcome him. "Moreover, I love her. With all my heart."

Again, the hall erupted as those present took in the announcement.

"I have a received a ransom demand from the Scots and will meet with them tomorrow at dawn so that I may bring my wife home. I will ask for a small group of soldiers to accompany me. When we return, I want the keep to be sparkling and a feast to await us to celebrate my beloved's return and our marriage."

Immediately, soldiers sprang to their feet, eager to volunteer their services. Nicholas went to the tables where they ate and handpicked twenty of his best knights.

He said to Gerald, "You will be left in charge of the castle. Be wary. I may be walking into a trap and the Scots might attack while I am away. Keep everyone within the castle walls after we leave for their protection."

"Aye, I will not let you down." The knight placed a hand on Nicholas' shoulder. "You'll get the lady back, my lord."

"I have to. Or die trying," he replied.

Nicholas took the score of men who would accompany him on his mission to the solar. He read the missive to them and then opened for discussion the route they would take to the border and the formation in which they would ride.

"Wear your armor and take your weapons as if we go into battle," he cautioned. "I know not how many Scots will greet us. Though the rules of engagement regarding handing over a hostage are clear, I cannot the trusts the Scots to be as honorable as Englishmen. We must be prepared for an ambush at any point—on the way to the border, at it, or once we return to Northmere."

"What time will we leave?" Albert asked.

"Sunrise is a few minutes past seven but I want to be there at least three hours early. The missive directed me to only bring half a dozen men along and you can see I want many more present. Six of you will stay with me while the others fan out and remain hidden from our enemies."

Nicholas told them the time to meet at the stables in order to embark upon their mission and then dismissed them.

Albert remained behind as the others filed from the room. "Do you think your saddle being tampered with is connected with Lady Katelyn's kidnapping?"

Nicholas steepled his fingers. "I don't know. I might have been their original target. I was riding alone back and forth between the manor house daily. If someone spied upon me, they would know that. If I hadn't taken Kate riding that day, the girth would have torn apart while I was on my way back to the castle." He shrugged. "We may never have an answer."

"'Tis fortunate the Scots did not try and ransom her back to the king. As his cousin, she is a valuable hostage."

He nodded. "They must be desperate in their need of quick payment." Nicholas rose. "Take care tomorrow, Albert."

"I will, my lord." He smiled. "'Twill be nice to have Lady Katelyn home where she belongs."

"I agree."

KATELYN PACED THE small bedchamber she'd been confined to, feeling like a caged animal. Late last night, Errol Cummins had her pen a short note to Nicholas and told her she would soon be going home. She assumed he'd sent a man out during the night to ride to Northumberland and deliver not only her brief message but his ransom demand. Nicholas would have received it this morning, most likely at first light.

She assumed the laird would give Nicholas a day to access the gold and believed today would be her last day spent in Scotland as a hostage—and pawn.

The more she paced, the more nervous she grew. Cummins had sworn her to secrecy and told her he planned to hand over an unsuspecting Bryce.

What if he lied to her?

The canny laird might only be telling Katelyn what she wanted to hear to keep her quiet and obedient. If she believed that Nicholas would not be killed, she wouldn't call out any warning to him. Would the Scotsman try and trick her?

She couldn't take that chance. She must find a way out of here and back to the border before the exchange was to occur. Her thoughts turned to Alec again.

Would the half-Englishman be willing to help her?

A light rap sounded on the door. She hoped it would be Alec bringing her something to eat. The door opened and he entered, closing it behind him. He brought over a tray and set it down.

"How are you feeling, Katelyn? You appear well again."

That was a good sign. He called her by name, as she had asked. She didn't have long but she needed to build trust with him.

"I'm feeling much better, thanks to your care, Alec." She glanced at the tray. "Would you stay with me while I eat? I'm as starved for conversation as I am food."

"All right," he agreed and sat.

As she pulled meat from the chicken thigh he'd brought, Katelyn said, "Tell me more about your mother."

Alec's eyes softened. "She was a bonny lass. Full of sweetness and light, despite how the clan treated her."

"What did you do with her?"

He shrugged. "A little of everything. I helped her with all of the chores when I was young. Hanging the washing outside to dry. Bringing the rug out to beat the dust from it. She loved to sing while we worked and would teach me a new ditty with every chore."

"Can you sing me one now?"

He laughed. "I haven't thought about them in a long time."

"Try," she urged.

Alec closed his eyes and began singing softly. He had a sweet, rich voice that comforted her. When he finished the song, he opened his eyes.

"By the Christ, it's been a long time since I sang." He wiped away a tear. "Remembering that song brings back a piece of her to me."

"You should sing more often. You've a wonderful voice."

He snorted. "Singing's for the weak, the laird would say. Fighting's what counts. I'll be keeping my songs to myself." Alec paused. "But I do thank you, Katelyn, for bringing back some nice memories."

Abruptly, he stood. "I'd best be getting back."

Knowing time ran out, Katelyn also came to her feet. She grabbed his wrist and his eyes widened.

"Alec, I'm asking you to help me escape. Before tomorrow. I can't trust either the laird or Bryce and I won't see the husband I love murdered before my eyes."

He began shaking his head furiously. "I cannot help you, my lady. 'Twould mean a death sentence for me."

Alec tried to pull away but Katelyn clutched him more tightly.

"Listen!" she commanded.

He froze, uncertain what to do.

"You and I are more alike than you realize," she began. "I told you I hadn't been a lady for long. My father committed treason against the Crown. Because of that, I was placed in a convent when I was five years of age. I grew up among strangers, as alone and frightened as you. I was beaten each time I tried to escape. Starved for breaking absurd rules. Left on my own since I had no calling to God and did not seek to join their religious order."

Sympathy grew in his eyes.

"At least you had a mother and father that you can remember. Mine were taken from me. My father, executed as a traitor. I had no friends or family. No one I could depend upon." She paused. "Then my brother found me after years of searching. I was taken to the royal court and found out I was cousin to King Edward. A week later, I was sent north to wed, a pawn in a political game between England and Scotland. My marriage was to make a statement to the Scots and keep the north firmly united.

"My husband died on our wedding night. I was forced yet again to wed. This time to a man who became my friend first, then my lover. Nicholas has offered me a future I never dreamed could be mine. And I will not see that future taken away from us by his conniving brother, Bryce, or your laird."

"I wouldn't know where to start—"

"You might not. But I do," Katelyn said. "If you help me, you can come to live in England. The land of your mother's people."

Alec rolled his eyes. "As if they would trust me any more than the Scots."

"I offer you a place at Northmere," Katelyn continued. "Doing whatever you would like." She gave him an encouraging smile. "And you would have a friend in me, Alec, where you have none here. My friendship would count for a great deal since I am the Countess of

Northmere. Nicholas, too, would be a powerful ally and eternally grateful to you for returning me to him.

"So, what say you? Will you help me escape?"

Alec grinned. "All right, Katelyn. Let's put our heads together and decide how to get you home to the man you love."

CHAPTER TWENTY-FIVE

KATELYN'S SCALP BEGAN prickling. Goosebumps rose along her arm. She heard footsteps in the hallway and men's voices outside her bedchamber and knew the visitor she'd expected had finally arrived.

The door opened and a confident Bryce Mandeville entered.

"Come to gloat?" she asked, remaining seated in the only chair available.

He gave her a smug smile. "I can see you've recovered fully from your illness." He bent and studied her face. "Too bad the bruises haven't totally faded."

"You shouldn't have struck me."

"You should learn to hold your tongue." He stood upright again. "You will. As my wife, you will speak only when you have my permission."

Glaring at him, she said, "I have always spoken my mind and will continue to do so. You'll have to cut out my tongue if you don't wish to hear my voice."

His eyes gleamed. "Don't tempt me."

Katelyn lowered her eyes. She longed to shout at him that she would never be under his thumb and soon he would be held account-able by Nicholas for conspiring with the Scots and arranging for her kidnapping. Since she couldn't, she decided not to look at him.

Bryce placed a finger under her chin and lifted it. "I like the fire in you, Katelyn, but I also know it must be controlled." His palm moved to cradle her face. Softly, he said, "Give me time. I will make you forgot all about Nicholas."

"Never!" she hissed, turning away in disgust.

"By mid-morning tomorrow, you and I will be back at Northmere. Nicholas will be dead. I will claim the earldom and the estate. We can wed—and then bed."

She looked at him with narrowed eyes. "Nicholas is superior to you in every way. *Especially* his skills in bed."

He raised his hand to strike her again and then lowered it. "Oh, you do try to provoke me, Katelyn. Marriage to you will be such a challenge."

"The challenge will be trying to get me to repeat the vows," she retorted.

"I'll manage to find a way," Bryce promised.

"Spoken by the man who said he would murder my babe? I have nothing to lose, Bryce, and will always remain a thorn in your side. You might as well kill me when you try to kill Nicholas. If you can."

He lifted her braid and she flinched, angry that she did so. Toying with it, he said, "I have always wanted what my brother had. Soon, I will have his title. His land. And his wife. Nay, Katelyn, I would never do away with you. I want you too much. I need to leave my mark upon you. Make you forget everything about Nicholas. I'm certain that you'll come around."

"And if I don't?" she challenged.

The look he gave her caused her to shudder.

"Then I will keep you from our children," he said. "I'll get you with child, over and over, and they'll be taken from you the moment you give birth. Others will suckle them. Bathe them. Walk with them and teach them to speak. All while you remain locked away, never seeing your precious babes."

"You are a monster," Katelyn said, her tone deadly.

He beamed at her. "Then I'll be your monster. I'll tie you to the bed and take you as many times as I wish. No one will dare come to your aid for I'll be the Earl of Northmere, the most powerful nobleman in the north of England."

She snatched her braid from his fingers. "Go. I can't stand the sight of you, knowing what you'll do to Nicholas. And me."

His low chuckle chilled her more than any winter's day ever had. "Pleasant dreams tonight, Katelyn. We'll be up early in order to meet Nicholas at dawn."

Bryce left. Katelyn found herself shaking uncontrollably. She whispered another fervent prayer to the Virgin, begging the Holy Mother to pave the way for her escape and protect Nicholas, no matter what happened.

Several hours later, Alec arrived with her evening meal.

"I cannot stay long. The herbs have been added to the ale the men will consume," he assured her. "The laird has ordered everyone to bed down after eating since we'll need to rise in the wee hours in order to ride to the border for the arranged meeting. The men should fall asleep quickly."

"And stay asleep," she added. "I remember the herbs I ingested kept me asleep for long amounts of time. Even when I awoke, I felt groggy."

"I'll bring you something dark to wear. Pants and a shirt. It'll be easier for you to ride that way."

"Will I have my own horse?"

"I thought to saddle Muir's horse for you but I think it will be safer if we ride together. We'll have to go slowly. Even with a lantern, it'll be hard to see the road." He paused. "You're sure you're wanting to do this?"

Determination filled her. "I'm leaving Scotland tonight. Nothing can keep me from Nicholas."

"Then I am your most humble escort. And friend."

Katelyn embraced Alec. "I know how risky this is." She kissed his cheek. "Thank you. For everything."

He blushed. "Mayhap, I'll find I like being an Englishman better than a Scotsman. Who knows? I might even seek out my mother's family. Eat up. I'll be back when the deed is done."

She wasn't hungry but knew it was wise to eat something and forced down a few bites. She finally pushed away the tray.

And waited.

Good as his word, Alec slipped into the room with new clothing for her. Katelyn had already removed her cotehardie and smock and wrapped herself in a blanket to stay warm. She didn't want to waste precious time undressing. He handed her the pants and she wriggled into them.

"Here's a length of rope to tie them about your waist."

She secured the pants and eased the shirt over her head. Both pieces were dark and made of rough wool. She would take a few hours of itching wool against her skin over a lifetime of wearing silks as Bryce Mandeville's wife.

Handing her a baselard, he said, "Slip this into your boot. You might have need of it."

Holding the dagger in her hand gave her pause. She had never touched a weapon before. The cold steel glinted in the light. If using it guaranteed her return to Northmere, she wouldn't hesitate. She only wished she could cut out Bryce's heart with it.

If he had one.

"Take the blanket," he suggested. "You can drape it across your lap or put it about you if you're cold."

Alec opened the door and Katelyn saw a single guard next to it, slumped to the ground. Quickly, they moved along the hall and down the stairs. She heard loud snores and saw several men sleeping on the ground near the fire. Alec eased the door open and led her to where the horses were stabled. He lit a lantern and she held it so that he could see to saddle his horse. Giving her a boost, he helped her into the saddle and handed her the lantern before mounting behind her as she settled the blanket across her lap.

"Where are the other horses?" she asked, realizing they were missing.

"I released them from their stalls and shooed them away before I came for you. I thought that wiser than trying to bind each man with rope and chance that one might awaken while I did so."

Katelyn rewarded him with a grateful smile. "You not only have courage but are a quick thinker. It must be the English coming out in you, Alec," she teased.

"I've one bit of bad news before we take off," he said. "Bryce never returned to the house after he left this afternoon. I don't know where he is or if arranged to meet the laird's men somewhere along the way."

Katelyn fought the rising panic, knowing Bryce could be anywhere, and said, "It doesn't matter. Let's be off."

"Hold the lantern steady. If you tire, I'll take it."

Alec led them away from the house at a walk. Once they reached the road, he guided his horse into a trot. She wished they could ride faster but knew it was safer to keep the horse at a slow, steady pace to avoid any hazards in the road. Gripping the lantern in one hand and the pommel in the other, she kept her eyes on the path ahead—and prayed no one would prevent them from reaching the border.

Especially Bryce.

They reached the nearby village and continued down its main street. Suddenly, Alec swore under his breath and wheeled the horse into a narrow alley.

"Hide the light," he hissed as he grabbed the lantern from her.

Katelyn lifted the blanket and held it wide, blocking the lantern's light. She glanced over her shoulder and, moments later, saw a rider pass. Though in silhouette, his familiar profile caused her heart to skip a beat. She whipped her head around and held the blanket in shaking hands, holding her breath.

"You can lower it," Alec said in her ear.

She released the blanket, settling it back across her lap. "What was Bryce doing here?"

"I should have realized when he vanished that he'd come to the village to see the widow he's bragged about coupling with so many times."

"He'll reach the laird's manor within minutes," she said anxiously. "He'll try to rouse the men to come after us."

"Even if he can—and I doubt he'll be able to—they won't be able to chase us down without their horses. I'll pick up our pace but we can't afford to have the horse stumble into a rut and break his leg."

Katelyn knew if that occurred, they would be in the middle of nowhere, vulnerable to attack. Bryce would find them easily. Without a doubt, he would kill Alec.

Who knew what he might do to her?

Alec turned the horse and led them back to the street. They soon left the village behind. She took the lantern from him, holding it high and watching the road for any obstacles, forcing herself to push aside thoughts of Bryce. Sometime later, they came across the second, smaller village that she remembered in their flight from England.

After they passed through it, she allowed herself to hope. Bryce would have wasted time trying to stir the men once he arrived at the manor house. More time would have been squandered in discovering that no horses stood in the stables. By the time he set out to give chase, they had a decent space between them. Bryce would also have to be wary as he rode after them for the darkness would affect him as much as it did them.

Still, she remained alert as they continued on.

"We're about a quarter of an hour from the border," Alec said loudly.

Katelyn nodded in understanding. She switched the lantern to her left hand since the right one tired.

For no reason, her arms broke out in gooseflesh. She locked her hand around Alec's forearm and said over her shoulder, "Bryce is coming."

He slowed the horse and turned it to face north. "I don't see a thing, Katelyn."

Her gut lurched. "There!" she cried.

A tiny speck of light appeared on the horizon.

"I know it's him. Hurry!" she urged.

Alec kicked the horse, which broke out into a gallop. Katelyn realized at once they were going too fast.

"I can't see!" she yelled. "Slow down."

As he pulled up on the reins, the horse stumbled. The lantern's light fell on a dead carcass of some animal lying in the road and then sailed from her hand and hit the ground. As the light extinguished, she fought to stay in the saddle, gripping the pommel tightly. Alec's arm remained around her waist as he battled to keep his own balance and get the horse under control.

"Hold on," Alec ordered once the horse halted. He swung from the saddle. "I want to see if anything's wrong with the animal."

After a moment, he said, "I think he's all right."

Katelyn glanced back and saw the beacon of light approaching quickly. "Do something!" she cried.

Alec drew his sword. "Keep going. I'll fight him off as best I can."

"I can't leave you."

He clasped her calf in his hand. "Katelyn, you must. If only one of us makes it to England, it should be you. Go."

Releasing her leg, he slapped the horse's flank and the beast cantered away. She looked over her shoulder and saw that Bryce was almost upon Alec. Her friend stood ready, both hands around his sword's hilt, as Bryce galloped nearer and unsheathed his own sword.

Katelyn yanked on the reins, bringing the horse to a halt. She couldn't abandon the one person who had been so kind to her. She wouldn't have made it this far without him. Whirling around, she urged the horse forward as Bryce threw his lantern at Alec, hitting him the head. The young man staggered back, bringing a hand to his forehead as Bryce pulled up next to him. Without hesitation, he rammed his sword into Alec.

A scream filled the air.

Bryce's booted foot then shoved Alec back. His sword came free as the young man fell to the ground just as Katelyn reached them. Bryce had already jumped from the saddle and lifted his sword to finish Alec off.

"Don't you dare," she warned. Leaning down, she removed the blade Alec had given her from her boot and gripped it in her hand.

Bryce walked cockily toward her. "Foiled again, Katelyn," he boasted.

As he reached her, she brought her hand up with as much force as she could muster, striking him in the throat. She buried the dagger to the hilt in his soft flesh.

Bryce's hands flew to his throat as he made an odd gurgling sound. Then he crumpled to the ground and lay silent.

Katelyn leaped from her horse and hurried to Alec. She fell to her knees and pressed her fingers to where the sword had entered him.

"He struck just below your shoulder, Alec," she said.

"It still hurts like Holy Hell," her friend muttered.

"Lie still," she ordered and ripped away his shirt. Tearing it into strips, she wound them about his upper chest to stanch the bleeding. Then she ripped the bottom portion of her own shirt and tied it around him to keep the strips more secure.

"We're close to home. You're going to make it. You will live." Raising him to a seated position, she added, "I need to get you atop your horse."

"I don't see how."

"You will do as I say, Alec. I'm not losing you. You mean too much to me. You were willing to die for me moments ago. The least you can do is offer to live for me now."

He chuckled. "Aye, my lady. Anything for the king's cousin."

It took a few tries but she managed to get him to his feet. By sheer willpower, Katelyn situated him in the saddle, her strength now almost exhausted. She climbed in front of him and then lifted the blanket draped in front of her and wrapped it around his back. Bringing it forward, she tied it as tightly as she could around the pommel.

"We're bound together now, Alec. Lean on me. Wrap your arms about my waist. Put your head on my shoulder. We're going home."

She nudged the horse and kept him to a trot, heading southward, counting in her head as she used to do when waiting to hear the bells chime at the convent every quarter-hour. Alec had said they were fifteen minutes away. She hoped he was right.

Katelyn watched carefully as they rode, knowing they couldn't afford another mishap. She doubted she could get Alec back in the saddle if he fell. Already, he leaned heavily upon her. They had to reach help before he bled to death.

A group of horses stood in the distance ahead. She wanted to wave her arms about but couldn't chance disturbing Alec. She rode toward them steadily, praying they would help.

Suddenly, one of the riders separated from the pack and came swiftly toward her.

It was Nicholas.

Chapter Twenty-Six

N ICHOLAS GAZED OUT across the horizon again, seeing no activity. Dawn would arrive soon. Already, faint pink streaks glowed in the distance as a new day tried to break through the skies. Restlessness filled him. He prayed the Scots would keep their word and bring Kate to him. Each soldier that accompanied him had two sacks of gold tied to his saddle. Nicholas would have given all the gold in England to have her back.

"My lord. A rider approaches," Sir Albert said.

A lone horse appeared on the horizon, moving toward them. Mayhap, it was a scout of the laird that had taken Kate, one that would inform him of her arrival shortly. He watched with suspicion, his mistrust of all Scots running deep through him. Living so close to the border had taught him to always be on guard.

As the rider drew near, something struck him as familiar. Nicholas pushed forward, cantering to meet this individual. His pulse began to race and he urged Sunset into a gallop, even as he heard his men calling out to him, trying to catch up. A sweet rush of relief swept through him.

Kate was the rider.

She brought her horse to a halt, relief and joy on her face. He pulled up next to her, his hands falling from the reins as they reached out to cradle her face.

"Kate," he uttered, his voice hoarse.

"Nicholas." Tears welled in her eyes as her hands touched his face.

The world stopped for a moment as they gazed longingly at one another then his knights thundered up. Nicholas finally saw the man slumped against her.

"Who's this?" he asked.

"This is Alec. He's been wounded. We must get him to Elewys quickly."

"A miserable Scot?" one of his soldiers said. "Let the bastard die."

Nicholas watched fire spark in Kate's eyes as she glared at the man. "Alec's mother was English and it's the best part of him. He risked everything to help me escape. *Everything!* And then he faced down Bryce and was wounded, trying to defend me. As your countess, I demand you take him to Northmere and do whatever it takes to save his life. Do you understand?"

"Aye, my lady," the knight said contritely. He dismounted and came to her. "I'll take him."

"We don't have time," she said impatiently. "We're but two miles from Northmere. Lead the way, sir!"

As the man remounted his horse, Nicholas said, "What you said. About Bryce." A sick feeling grew within him.

"Bryce was in league with the Scots. He was behind my abduction."

Her words twisted like a knife in his belly.

"Where is he now?"

"A few miles north of where we stand."

"I'll kill him!" roared Nicholas.

The Scotsman spoke for the first time. "No need to, my lord." He gave Nicholas a crooked grin. "Lady Katelyn already took care of that."

Before he could reply, the horses began to move. Nicholas kept Sunset next to Kate as the sun rose and they made their way back to Northmere. Albert rode ahead to alert the gatekeeper and summon the healer. They quickly passed through the open gates, which closed behind them. Kate led their group straight to the keep. Nicholas used his sword to slash through the wool blanket that she'd used to keep her rescuer anchored in the saddle with her. He stepped back and two of his men removed the man Nicholas now thought of as a hero and carried him up the stairs.

Elewys appeared, carrying a basket. She linked arms with Kate.

"Tell me about the wound," the healer said as they hurried inside the keep.

Nicholas followed them upstairs. His men placed the Scot in a bedchamber and left. He watched as the two women began to attend to the wounded man and knew his presence wasn't required. He retreated to the solar and found that Henfrey awaited him.

"Let me help remove your armor, my lord," the squire offered.

Nicholas allowed the boy to strip him of the bulky armor. When finished, Henfrey placed it in a corner of the room.

"I am happy you returned with Lady Katelyn, my lord. She's been most kind to me."

Nicholas only nodded and fell into a chair as numbness consumed him. His brother had allied himself to the Scots. He had Kate abducted by their enemy. Nicholas sat lost in thought, wondering what had turned Bryce so against him.

Suddenly, a hand rested on his shoulder. He glanced up and saw his wife, looking disheveled and bruised—and thought her the loveliest sight he'd ever seen. His hands captured her waist and pulled her into his lap. He kissed her hungrily, as if he would never get enough of her.

Breathless, she finally lifted her lips from his and gave him a brilliant smile.

"You can see again."

"Aye. And all I ever want to see is you, my love."

Nicholas stood and carried her to the bed. Their bed. He set her down gently.

"This time, I want to see every inch of you. Hear every sigh you make. And by the Christ, I'll remember every moment."

The corners of her mouth turned up. "Then what are you waiting for?"

He needed no further invitation. He removed his boots and peeled away his clothing then his fingers sought the ragged ends of the shirt she wore and lifted it from her. Perfect, round globes of temptation greeted him. Nicholas fastened his mouth to one breast and kneaded the other. A gasp sounded. Then a sigh. Finally, low moans came from Kate as he lavished attention on each breast.

Nicholas worked his way back up her throat and pressed gentle kisses along her jaw and up to her ear. She shivered as his tongue circled it and then darted in and out. Her hands stroked his bare chest, lighting a fire inside him. His lips trailed to her mouth and he kissed her deeply. His hand slid down her body and cupped her, rubbing seductively. Kate's hips rose, her breasts pressing against him.

He broke the kiss and untied the rope holding up her pants before sliding them down milky white thighs. He stopped to remove her boots and then slipped the pants from her altogether.

Gazing in admiration, he told her, "You are the most beautiful woman in the world."

Her fingers teased his nipples. "And you are the most beautiful man ever born." She leaned up and licked one of his nipples playfully, causing him to shudder. "And you are mine. All mine, Nicholas Mandeville."

He smiled. "And you are mine, sweet Kate. I am ready to feast upon you."

Nicholas kissed his way from her belly to her core. He parted her folds and thrust his tongue deeply inside her. Her startled, satisfied cry was music to his ears as he tasted her essence and brought her to her peak. Kate writhed beneath him, calling his name over and over, as her hips bucked wildly. She squealed with delight as she came, her fingers tightening in his hair.

"Oh. Oh. Oh," she repeated in wonder.

Quickly, he slipped his cock inside her and slowly pulled away. He continued, gradually entering her and withdrawing until she begged him for more. He sped up his pace and then found himself thrusting frenziedly, clutching her buttocks, wild feelings of joy zipping through him. They both climaxed at the same time, his shout as one of victory.

Falling against her, he nuzzled her neck and then rolled to his side. He brought her close. Her cheek rested against his chest. His hands lightly skimmed the satin skin of her back.

"I love you," he said. "I regret not telling you before. I wanted to but was afraid the intensity of my feelings would frighten you away. You seemed so determined to annul our union."

"Did you push me away and demand an annulment because of your blindness?"

"Aye. I didn't think it fair. You deserved a whole man, not part of one."

Kate stroked his cheek. "I loved *you*, Nicholas. Sight or no sight."

"Then why did you press for an annulment?"

Her hand fell away. "I'm not like other women you've known. I didn't feel worthy to be your countess, much less your wife. I have no experience in being a lady."

He kissed her softly. "Being unlike other noblewomen is your greatest strength, sweetheart. I value you as you are, Kate. Your previous experiences have made you the woman I need. You are the one I want by my side, until the end of time."

Need for her grew in him and he made love to her again. Slowly. Sweetly. Savoring each taste and touch.

Once more, she lay nestled within his arms. Everything felt right as she absently stroked his arm. Love for this woman radiated from him—and yet he still wished for answers from her.

"Can you share what happened to you this past week?" he asked. "Or is it too painful to talk about?"

Kate snuggled closer to him. "Now that I'm safely back with you, I will gladly tell you everything."

She explained why she wanted to ride to Ravenwood and how she and Henfrey had been attacked. Nicholas was touched that Kate would have journeyed all the way to the king to protect her husband.

"I loved you. Even if I hadn't, I would never have wanted to see you cheated out of your title and estate by your uncle."

"Rafe is gone now. I could not trust him ever again after his declaration against me, especially when I needed him most."

"You made the right decision. I'm only sad to know Ellyn suffered because of her husband's actions."

"Nay, Ellyn stayed," he informed her. Grinning, he said, "She wanted to make sure she was around to help care for our babes."

"Oh, really?" Kate playfully nipped his throat. "Who knows? We may already be on our way to producing the first one. Of many."

"You have exhausted me, Wife," Nicholas said. "I need time to recover before I can pleasure you again."

"Mayhap you should lie still and let me pleasure you instead."

Her fingers clasped his cock and tugged on it.

"Later," he told her, looking forward to their love play but growing serious. "We still have two things we must discuss. Tell me first about Bryce."

She grew silent.

"Tell me, Kate. You don't need to hide anything from me. I should know the truth."

"Bryce made some kind of agreement with Errol Cummins, Laird of Dunbar. I don't know exactly what was involved or what the Scots would gain from their bargain." Her hand grasped his. "All I know is that once the gold was exchanged this morning, an attack would have occurred. The laird's men were to kill you and any soldiers that accompanied you."

"And with me being dead, Bryce would become the new Earl of Northmere." His fingers entwined with hers. "My guess is he wanted you as his wife."

He sensed her nodding against him.

"Bryce told me he'd always been jealous that you were the heir. He said he was the most like Lord Cedric and that your father would have wanted him to have the title. He was willing to resort to murder to see he gained it," she said quietly.

Nicholas' gut told him Bryce had said much more to Kate but he knew the essence of what had occurred.

"Will you search for and claim his body?" she asked.

"Nay. Let the wild animals of Scotland have at it." He ran his fingers through her raven locks. "Are you sorry you killed him?"

Kate looked up at him with large eyes. "Will you think I'm a bloodthirsty heathen if I tell you no?"

Nicholas smiled. "If you are, at least you're my bloodthirsty heathen." He gave her a reassuring kiss. "We need never mention his name. His wickedness will not touch our lives ever again. And though I have you back now, my love, and Bryce is dead, the Scots still need to pay for taking you."

"I don't think that's wise, Nicholas. I truly believe we have nothing to fear from them at the moment."

"Why do you say that?" he asked, stroking her hair, loving its silky texture as he glided his fingers through it.

"Though Bryce thought the plan was to eliminate you, I'd spoken several times to Cummins, trying to drive a wedge between him and Bryce. Your brother had already proved himself untrustworthy to you and so I tried to convince Cummins he would also renege on any deal the two of them had struck. I believe Cummins had changed his mind and would have turned Bryce over to you—along with me—to ease the problems between the Scots and English. Besides, the laird treated me with kindness during my time in his household."

Kate touched her hand to his face. "Please, Nicholas. Do nothing. I'm safely back at Northmere. No other action is necessary."

He kissed her brow. "I will do as you ask. That's how great my trust is in you." Relief washed through him, knowing he wouldn't need to seek retribution and that the peace might hold for a while longer.

He paused and then asked, "I do have something to ask you, though. Nothing to do with the Scots. Would you tell me why you kept secret the fact you were still a virgin?"

"I was afraid," she said softly. "When your father tried to bed me, he couldn't. Then he died and I feared what might happen to me. I pretended he had made me a true wife. Then once Rafe wed me to you, I was terrified to be caught in the lie."

He stroked her hair. "You could have told me the truth."

"But I didn't know you," Kate reminded him. "You were this large, powerful knight. A stranger. A man who was unhappy to find himself wed to me. Angry, in fact. And once I did come to know you—even love you—I was ashamed to have created the lie in the first place."

Nicholas kissed her tenderly. "It matters not. You did what you had to do in order to protect yourself. We are strangers no longer, Kate. We are a true husband and wife."

They lay contentedly for some minutes and then she asked, "Nicholas? Will you make a place for Alec at Northmere? He has led a most unhappy life. The Scots never trusted him because of his English mother. He is my friend."

"Alec has a lifetime of my goodwill," he assured Kate. "He is the man who restored my beloved wife to me."

"Am I your beloved?" she asked, uncertainty in her voice.

"You are the dearest person in my life, Kate Mandeville. If everything went away and I was only left with you as my wife, I would still be the richest man in all of England."

Nicholas kissed her deeply, hoping his kiss showed Kate everything she needed to know.

EPILOGUE

KATELYN AWOKE WITH the feeling of nausea again. This was three days in a row. Catherine had told her signs that would indicate she was with child. Besides the roiling in her belly, her courses had ceased. Even her breasts were tender to the touch and felt fuller than usual. She thought Nicholas would have noticed their increase in size with as much attention as he paid to them.

She turned her head and took in the wonderful man stretched out beside her. Her husband. Her lover. Her friend. Her everything.

His eyes slowly opened and his hand went to cup her cheek. Before she knew it, they were entangled together, loving one another fully in a dance she would never tire of.

Nicholas gave her a final, swift kiss and rose from the bed.

"Stay and rest, sweetheart. You look exhausted."

"I'm sure it has nothing to do with you waking me in the middle of the night," she teased.

He grinned. "At least it was only once. Unlike the night before."

Dressing quickly, he told her he would have a tray sent up for her and left the bedchamber. Katelyn snuggled back into the pillow, breathing in his scent. She would tell him about the babe later today.

After she dozed another hour, she rose, her belly still queasy. She dressed and found a tray awaiting her in the solar. She did her best to break her fast, taking in small bites of bread and a few sips of ale. It seemed to calm the churning. Since she felt better, she went downstairs and saw a stranger handing a parchment to Ellyn.

"I'll be sure she gets it. Thank you."

"What's that?" Katelyn asked.

"You've a missive from Ravenwood," Ellyn replied as she handed over the scroll. "I do envy you for knowing how to read," she said wistfully.

"I'd be happy to teach you. I taught the oblates at the nunnery to read and write."

The older woman looked gratefully at her. "I would appreciate it, my dear."

Something brushed Katelyn's skirts and she saw Kit run by. Bethany appeared and scooped up her growing cat.

"I help Kate-lyn make candles?" she asked hopefully.

In the time Katelyn had returned to live in the keep, Bethany had been her shadow. The young woman had given up hiding in her chamber since Bryce no longer hovered about, waiting to antagonize her. Katelyn had taught Bethany a few simple stitches and they had worked in the castle's garden together. What Bethany enjoyed most, though, was making candles.

"I was going to ask you to help me with the candles," Ellyn told her niece. "Would you like to do that? We can surprise Katelyn with how many you can make."

Bethany beamed. "We do that, Aunt. Bye, Kate-lyn."

After they left, Katelyn opened the missive, eager to hear Catherine's news.

Dearest Katelyn –

I have given birth to a boy and cannot wait for you and Nicholas to meet him. I've named him Favian, after his father. He has a lusty cry and is the picture of good health.

Please come as soon as you can to share in my joy.

Your sister in friendship,
Catherine

Katelyn held the scroll to her, overcome with emotion. By Catherine birthing a male, she would be allowed to stay at Ravenwood and raise its heir. Katelyn placed a hand against her belly. If she carried a boy, mayhap the two could foster together and become close friends, as their fathers had. And if, by chance, 'twas a girl? What a wonderful way to unite the Mandeville and Savill families by betrothing the pair.

The front door opened and Nicholas entered. The warm smile that lit his face when he caught sight of her let Katelyn know how very loved she was.

"I saw a rider from Ravenwood departing. Did he bring news from Catherine?"

"Aye. She's given birth to a son and wishes us to visit her as soon as possible."

"If you have no other plans, we could go now," he suggested.

"That would be lovely," she replied. "Let me tell Ellyn where we'll be."

"I'll gather a few men and have our horses saddled."

Nicholas departed and Katelyn shared the good news with Ellyn, telling her they would be gone most of the day.

"Give Catherine my best," the noblewoman said. She smiled. "Soon, you will share in this kind of blessing."

Katelyn excused herself quickly, afraid if she lingered she would blurt out to Ellyn about the coming babe. It was important to her that Nicholas be the first to know. Making her way to the stables, she saw six soldiers already in the saddle. Ever since her abduction, Nicholas insisted a guard go with Katelyn wherever she went, even if it was only to the neighboring estate. It pleased her that Alec was one of the men chosen to accompany them. Nicholas had given him the option of becoming a soldier or learning a skill, such as blacksmithing. Alec jumped at the chance to live in the barracks and fight to protect the Mandeville name and people.

He now gave her a smile and nodded his head. Surprisingly, he had been accepted quickly into the ranks of Northmere's men. She suspected Nicholas had something to do with that, though he told her it was Alec himself who'd won the others over. His fighting skills were sharp and all recognized that Alec had been the man who'd rescued their countess and helped foil the plot to murder Nicholas. Regardless, she was happy Alec was now a vital part of Northmere.

Nicholas helped her mount Ebony and their party moved at a brisk pace to Ravenwood. Once they arrived, the estate's steward met them and had a servant escort them upstairs.

Catherine sat in a chair by the fire, little Favian asleep in her arms. Tears of happiness stung Katelyn's eyes as she looked upon the pair.

"I'm so happy you could come," Catherine said. "Would you like to hold him?"

Katelyn bent and lifted the babe, bringing him close. She rocked back and forth as she studied his perfect face. His eyes opened sleepily and a hand flew up, wiggling the tiniest fingers she'd ever seen. She offered him one of hers and he clasped it.

"He's a strong one," she said. "And so very handsome."

Nicholas came and stood next to her, looking at the babe over her shoulder. "I can see a bit of Favian in him. About his eyes and chin."

They talked for an hour and then food arrived. While they ate, Catherine nursed her babe and then put him down to sleep.

"He is everything I dreamed he would be," she said. "I only wish Favian were here to see his namesake."

Nicholas put his hand over hers. "He is here in spirit, Catherine. He watches over both of you."

After another hour, Catherine's eyes began to droop. Katelyn nudged her husband and signaled him that it was time depart.

"We must be off, Catherine."

"I hope you will come again soon," she said and covered a yawn.

"Bring Bethany next time."

"We will," Nicholas assured her.

They went arm-in-arm down the stairs and returned to their horses, arriving home minutes before the sun set.

"Why don't we take our evening meal in privacy tonight?" Katelyn suggested as Nicholas helped her from Ebony's back.

"I like that idea. I will see you shortly."

Katelyn went and told Cook they would dine in the solar and then she went to wash and change after their long ride. Once again, her hands went to her belly, thinking of the miracle that grew inside her.

A servant arrived with their meal as Nicholas washed up. By the time he finished, Katelyn had wine poured for them.

She offered him a cup and he held it up. "A toast," he declared. "To us and all of the blessings we have."

Katelyn touched her cup to his. "And to our future blessings," she added.

They drank and set their cups down. Nicholas wrapped his arms around her.

"Have I told you how happy I am to be your husband?" he asked. He kissed the tip of her nose.

"You may think you are happy now but more happiness is to come," she replied, her smile widening.

He stared at her a moment and then understanding dawned in his eyes. "Kate? Do you . . . is it what I think . . . are you . . . ."

"I am with child," she confirmed. "Your child. Our child."

"We're going to have a babe," he whispered in wonder. Then his hands spanned her waist and he swung her around with glee. "We've going to have a babe!" he shouted.

Finally, he set her back on the ground, joy filling his face. "You have made me the happiest of men, my love." Nicholas kissed her tenderly. "Do you know how much I love you, Kate Mandeville?"

Katelyn did.

THE END

About the Author

Alexa Aston's historical romances use history as a backdrop to place her characters in extraordinary circumstances, where their intense desire for one another grows into the treasured gift of love. She is the author of Medieval and Regency romances, including *The Knights of Honor* series.

A native Texan, Alexa lives with her husband in a Dallas suburb, where she eats her fair share of dark chocolate and plots out stories while she walks every morning. She enjoys reading, watching movies, and can't get enough of *The Crown* and *Game of Thrones*.

Made in the USA
Coppell, TX
09 November 2021